BONDED TO THE GODS
BOOK THREE

R.A. RAINE

SING ME HOME

BONDED TO THE GODS BOOK 3

R.A RAINE

ISBN

Ebook: 978-1-7643224-1-6

Discreet Paperback: 978-1-7643224-2-3

Illustrated Paperback: 978-1-7643224-3-0

Hardback: 978-1-7643224-4-7

Credits:

Discreet Cover by Miblart

Illustrated covers by Alli at Artsiidaisy

Edited by Brittany at BLD Editing

Map by Karina at Shepengual

Dove and Fury illustration by Mary Begletsova

Group illustration by Kidana

Headers and page breaks by Etheric Tales

To my readers.

*May your cups overflow, your flowers always bloom, and your
stories be everything you desire.*

For the last time, welcome back, friends

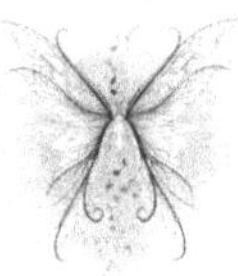

—to the world of Maia. If you're new to the Forgotten Lands, please start with books one and two in the *Bonded to the Gods* Trilogy, *Sing Me Awake* and *Sing Me Free*. And if it's been a while since you've read the first two books in the trilogy, here's a short, spoiler-filled synopsis.

Our story began with Dove, a human servant who was set on saving the Kingdom of Haven from a tyrannical king. Along the way, she fell into the arms of Gideon, the warden wolf shifter, Rivern, the fae prince, and Fury, the fallen God —whom God-bonded.

Sing Me Free saw Rivern and Dove coming together after Dove and Gideon were sent on a mission to the Silver Sands to retrieve ancestral God-created offspring from each of the three peoples created by the Gods, Oona, Osear and Oriel, which would ultimately help in freeing Fury—the God Orion—from his island prison.

It was on this journey that Rivern denounced his betrothal to Moyrie and sealed the bond with Dove.

Securing a deal with the silvers, Moyrie agreed to support Dove, Rivern and Gideon in finding the last heir from the void, where they find out a species called the mers live.

After falling into the mers' clutches, Moyrie and Dove are on the brink of being eaten alive by a kraken—until they find out he's one of Fury's beasts, and the creature agrees to help the pair reunite with Dove's protectors. Meanwhile, Gideon and Rivern are being held captive by a horde of mer women, who need strong men for breeding.

With the kraken—Ken—now on their side, Dove and Moyrie escape, finding Gideon and Rivern, making another deal with the mers in exchange for their freedom: capable breeding men in the form of silvers in exchange for their release and freeing Fury from his island. Dove and Gideon also come together, realising they have been dancing around the fact that they are more than damsel and bodyguard; they are mates.

With misunderstandings set aside, the silvers and the mers are now on board with helping Dove, and they all set out to Fury's island, where they meet Saff's baby, Oro for the first time. Fury also admits his true motivation of love for Dove, and for the first time, she lets herself feel the love she has been harbouring for the God.

With their world finally looking up, Dove, her protectors, Moyrie and the mer queen begin the ritual to free Fury, only to find out it doesn't work, and Dove's blood was the key to the fallen God's escape this whole time.

Finally free, Fury is set on revenge, but first, he must kill the king of Haven to satisfy his deal with Dove. When Dove, Fury, Rivern and Gideon head back to Haven to get rid of the king and save the kingdom, the other Gods kidnap Dove and take her back to their new land. In a rage, Fury orders Saff to set fire to the king and his son.

That is where *Sing Me Home* starts…

On the next page, you will find a short glossary of terms to help you acclimatise to the world of Maia.

Over the next couple of pages, you will discover a map of the Forgotten Lands and a new destination found on the planet of Maia, as well as an author's note.

Finally, this is book three in the *Bonded to the Gods* trilogy. As such, this story ends with multiple epilogues and a happily ever after for the main characters!

Thank you for returning for one last time, travellers.

GLOSSARY

Throughout this story, I wanted to move past the words we use for time and show how the people of the Forgotten Lands rely heavily on the movement of their planet, the suns and the moon to witness this. I have kept to our everyday definitions for the bigger accumulations of time.

Movement: Seconds/minutes

Turns: Days

Rotations: Years

Cycle: Referencing a period of time

Rhythm: Time

Note: The word time is still used throughout the story for functionality.

Below are other terms used throughout the book that hold new meanings in this world.

Primary: Big sun

Secondary: Small sun

Bonded: Two people who are fated together by the Gods

Intimate: An animal with wings that chooses a fae to cohabitate with. A best friend who brings Oona's children closer to the stars and the Gods

Godlin: Small golden servant creatures created by Oona to serve her

Knot: The rounded base of a werewolf shifter's penis

Knotting: The intimate act of love between a werewolf shifter and their partner when their knot enters their partner's body

God/Goddess: Name for higher power deities with the ability to create life forms and manipulate energy

Forgotten Lands Gods

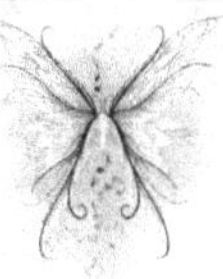

Orion (Fury) - God of the beasts
Oona - Goddess of the fae
Osear - God of the silvers
Oriel - Goddess of the mers

SILVER SANDS
KINGDOM
OF SEAR
THE VOID
THE FORGOTTEN LA

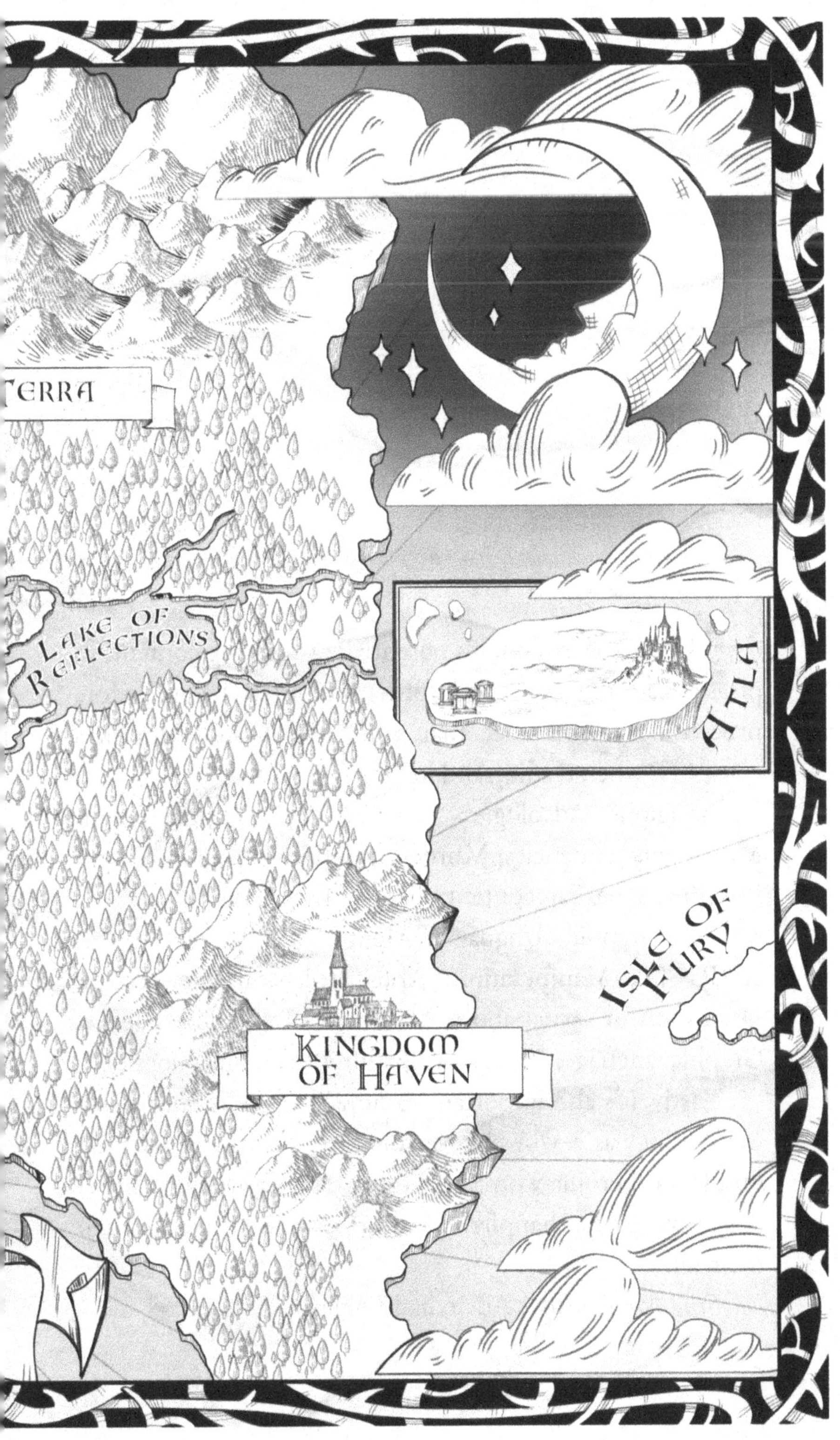

TERRA
LAKE OF REFLECTIONS
ATLA
ISLE OF FURY
KINGDOM OF HAVEN

AUTHOR NOTE:

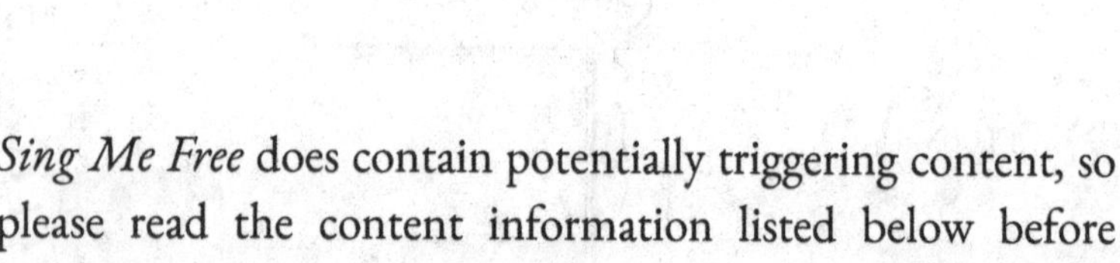

Sing Me Free does contain potentially triggering content, so please read the content information listed below before proceeding. Remember that your health and happiness come first when reading and in life.

Religious ideologies; Kidnapping; Imprisonment; Murderous tendencies; Murder; Mentions of blood; Death; Descriptive sexual content; FM, MFM and FMMM sex scenes; Graphic language; Mental health rep. (anxiety/PTSD); Manipulation; Abuse (physical and verbal); Discussion of sexual abuse; Memories of childhood abuse; Graphic language; Pregnancy; Birthing scene (in epilogue).

Lastly, it's also important to note that the *Bonded to the Gods* trilogy is a why-choose romance. For this story, that means our heroine won't have to choose between love interests to receive her happily ever after because she gets to keep them all.

Sing Me Free uses Australian English.

I've heard it in the chillest land -
And on the strangest Sea -
Yet - never - in Extremity,
It asked a crumb - of me.

Hope is the thing with feathers
Emily Dickinson

THE CREATION AND DESTRUCTION OF ATLA

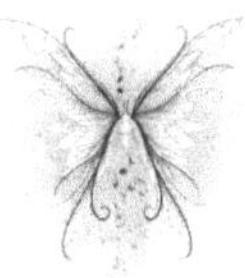

When the three Gods fell, they did without remorse.

The land they chose was already inhabited, filled with the humans they sought to destroy. Until they realised how easily manipulated they were. How they could click their fingers, and people would bow to their will.

So, regardless of what the humans wanted, the Gods took over, causing unrest until all people were under their rule. The Gods possessed much power in their corporeal forms, and the humans found themselves unmatched in force and depravity.

Now, Oona, Osear and Oriel—the three Gods of Atla—rule for their own pleasure, unaware of the snake in their midst. The one they call a monster. The one they made in their God brother's likeness. The one who has had enough of conforming to the will of others. The one who will soon understand his true potential, as willed by the fates.

And the one who will help a once-broken bird burn it all to the ground with the help of her protectors.

ONE

OONA

It's pathetic. These humans are all the same. I don't see it. What drew Orion to this female on the floor? She doesn't have a curve on her. Osear, Oriel and I tower over the woman, her body lying limp before us, barely moving.

It wasn't hard to find the thread I placed for the fae and how it joined with her. Upon snatching her from Orion, I snapped that bothersome inconvenience, which was enough to knock her out. Limp, mousy brown hair spills out over my once-clean golden marble floors.

The godlins race around the dirty human, trying to clean up the mess she has made. My pure gold servants reach up to the height of my knees, big enough to take care of my castle with none of the needs of onerous humans—and they are my favourite colour, of course.

I made the godlins on a whim when I found it aggravating to look upon humans for extended periods of time, especially after watching over them for millennia. Unless they were pleasuring my body, I didn't want them near me.

"What of Orion's bond?" Oriel murmurs next to me.

"Together, our power far outweighs whatever Orion has placed on the girl." Closing my eyes, I search for the last of the threads to be pulled. Unlike the beautifully delicate golden threads that wove my fae to the human, Fury's connection is gritty and tainted, thick black threads locking every organ, every muscle. There's nothing within her he has not touched with his bonding magic.

I'll see about that.

"Rip out all the darkness you can find. If we work together, we should get her stripped within moments." I hold my hands out on either side of me—an invisible invitation for Osear and Oriel to take hold and pool the zapping power running through all of us.

Once we join hands, the nonexistent breeze of the foyer within the castle entryway ruffles our hair. The fabric of my thin white dress flutters around my voluptuous body.

With my eyes closed, I get to work pulling, tearing and severing anything that connects the bag of flesh and bones before us to the God who abandoned us to his beasts, to this world.

Long-suffering moans and screams fall from the lips of the human being internally dissected. Opening my eyes at the last thread, I see her body prone in the air, arms and legs falling down by her sides. One last black thread hovers over her heart.

I saved the best part for last.

She looks pathetic on the precipice of death, her skin alabaster grey. Yet, her breath still comes short and sharp. That she's hanging on surprises me, but when we cut this last line to Orion, she'll be gone from this world—and gone to him.

My lips pull up high at the sides. *Death has never looked so good.*

I send a zapping shock towards her heart. It breaks the thick, inky thread, the frayed edges rolling in on themselves. Smoke billows from her barely breathing form, and she drops to the harsh marble floor with a deafening thud.

"It is done." Burnt honeycomb fills my nostrils, and I tense, noticing the slight rise and fall of the human's chest. *She still draws breath.* Anger rises in my stomach, hitting the back of my throat in acidic rage.

"She should be dead," Osear and Oriel speak the words I am thinking. I pull my hands from theirs in unrestrained ire. Strong, steadily measured steps come our way. I know who it is without having to look beyond the infuriating human still breathing on the floor.

Why won't you fucking die? I don't need space to mull over this annoyance in my expansive foyer; she is going to become Wrath's problem now. I have no patience for humans who won't do the one thing they are designed to do: *die.*

Two

Rivern

She stands before me, my Goddess, soothing the throbbing pain radiating over every inch of my body. The sight is a balm to my soul. A dusting of freckles over her nose, moss-coloured eyes. The curves at the corners of her lips that smile upon me make me want to melt into the spot where she's found me—my nothing.

"Dove," I whisper her name, and she holds out her delicate hand to clasp mine. My palm moulds to hers like they were always meant to be.

"I found you," she answers. The darkness around us is vast until I take a moment to tear my stare away from hers and notice it's not just darkness, but starlight we stand beneath.

Like a man starving for his first drink of water, I pull her into me and smell, taking raking lungfuls of breath until vanilla, honey and rose are buried deep in my nostrils. Her fingers dig into my back, and we savour this finite embrace.

"You are my everything," I say it in my head, knowing she will hear.

"I miss you—" She's torn away before I can grip her tighter, not that it will make a difference.

"I miss you so godsdamned much..." I groan up at the winking lights, my hands falling limp at my sides.

THREE

SAFF

The room glints in a sparkling array of rubies, sapphires and magenta. Oro darts from geode to sharp-pointed quartz, his wings slapping against the edges, making me flinch internally.

I've waited centuries for this moment, for my son to know something of his father, where he would've grown up. Now, because of the Gods, that dream has been dashed. And now the Gods have *her*.

Oro is too young for us to travel. He does not know his strength or have the muscle definition within his wings. Currently, they flap haphazardly at his sides. If he were still tightly tucked away in his egg, I would have flown after them, breathing fiery hell upon the deserters of the Forgotten Lands.

Instead, my heart breaks for losing a friend—the first true friend I have ever claimed.

Dragons are mostly solitary creatures, except if we mate.

I never expected to find a soul that spoke to mine in such a quiet and unassuming way.

Billowing, smoky tendrils highlight the crystallised rock, close to Oro's old resting place. *"Mama, I found it."*

"Good work, son." We communicate through the mind. On Fury's island, I promised him that I would show him where I produced his egg. The place we once called home. Our trip is now tainted because of the three devious Gods who have only ever known destruction.

"Will you tell me about my father again?" Every chance I get, I remind Oro of his beginning, of the dragon who risked everything to save him.

So, I tell him, and hope the last of the loyal Gods of this realm saves my one and only friend. *"It all started a millennium ago, when Orion forged the first creatures of this land…"*

FOUR

DOVE

The pain. It's excruciating. There's no end, and I'm unsure of its beginning.

It's numbing, my body nothing but a weightless form—no longer tangible, but an immense void. The moment of light when I crack open my lids no longer makes sense, my surroundings a hazy blur. Piecing my body and my mind together right now is incomprehensible.

I never could've prepared; being ripped away from them, my three protectors. Gideon, Rivern and even Fury slowly carved out homes inside my chest, and my efforts to ignore them were fruitless.

I had finally begun to see how we could all fit. It would be tricky, but with those last moments together, all four of us, I couldn't imagine being apart. They had become everything to me. Their companionship. Their support. Their unwavering willingness to stick by my side, no matter the consequences.

This rhythm... It's too big, the disconnect an expanse too far to travel.

I no longer feel them.

I no longer feel anything, the pain too much to bear.

If this is it for me—my death—I should still feel them. *Shouldn't I?* Together beyond the great unknown, whatever that might be. *They need to be by my side.*

Instead, I am alone.

Completely and utterly devoid of connection.

My three lifelines stripped.

My body is nothing but a rag doll to the whims of three Gods—the Gods who stole me. Eyes firmly shut, I feel the indent of something pushing against my side. An amber eye with ripping scars flashes through my mind. *Mine.* Just as soon as I try to grasp his face, it's gone again, my body pliable to whichever God moves it now, jostling me about.

I knew it was them, their power lingering and snapping at the threads of my soul, pulling my protector's connections from my body. The excruciating burn. They are the only ones powerful enough to take my bonds from me.

If I've learnt anything about magic and the power of the Gods over the last several turns, it's that there's no love lost between Fury and his God counterparts. And I've just become their greatest adversary.

FIVE

WRATH

She sleeps. For three straight turns. Her soft, inconsequential form is almost lifeless in the crumpled heap I left her in on the cold, unforgiving floor of the stone dungeon. Above us, Oona, Osear and Oriel move around in the splendour of marble floors, golden decals and silken tapestries.

Down here in the darkness, rock, dirt and grime reign supreme.

I sit on an icy rock, watching her chest pull in and out, her long eyelashes fluttering against pale skin the colour of moonlight in this underground dwelling. To the eyes of the humans who toil above this place, it is hell, so black no light peeks through. Only the Gods and I can see the intricacies without the light.

As usual, it falls upon my shoulders to monitor this place. Oona has been down here once in all her rotations on Atla, citing it too ghastly for her soul. I was surprised she still had a soul. So, I was left to torture any of the people stupid enough to defy the Gods in their city, Atla—an island territory created in the image of the three Gods. A place where humans seek utter reverence and devotion in the entities who fell from the sky with magic never seen before.

I know of the lands the Gods played with before they arrived here. The different creatures they made. Upon arriving on these interconnected island shores, they were going to wipe out the lingering humans. Until they witnessed how far they would go to serve them.

The Gods, in turn, abandoned plans to forge any of their own creations, except for the godlins and me—the servant created in the likeness of another.

My onyx feathers ruffle behind me as I think of him.

Pert, pink lips puff out cold air on the hard ground below. I can't help the glower that takes over my features.

I never asked for this. To be created in his image. To serve the Gods. To be labelled a monster by the humans. Yet here we are. And she is my prisoner—technically, Oona, Osear and Oriel's prisoner, but they won't be the ones to undertake her punishment. I will.

It took all three Gods' strength to pull out the tethers of the bond with Orion that held the little human together. And not only did she have one God bond, but she had two, which Oona immediately stripped her of as soon as they landed in the marble palace.

However, I still sensed lingering threads of another soul on her, hovering around the periphery. But that was created by the fates, not of a God's hands. No God can sever a fate's will. So, it lingers still. *Could it be why she still lives?*

We expected that pulling the threads would be her end, but this connection—the one the fates granted her—is keeping her alive. *It has to be.* No human could ever survive having a God bond pulled from them, let alone two.

A strangled whine comes from the human on the floor. I scowl. Her body jolts, and I kneel before her prone form just as her eyes begin to open, the small movement stalling me. My knees hit the ground next to her.

I expect her to scream or cry. Instead, she lies paralysed, her green eyes open. Her heartbeat remains oddly unchanged until my feathers flap behind my form, and she breathes in deeply.

"Fury." It's barely audible, more of a dry cough. I know who she notices in me. The opening gives me a moment of pause, an idea forming in my mind. One that will make me not only look like the monster they claim me as, but *become* that monster.

Without a second thought, I grasp onto it. *Maybe I can finally have something of my own—a human to worship me. Just like the humans of Atla worship the Gods. Down here, I could be my own God.*

And so I answer her by reaching out and touching the softness of her cheek. "Yes, Flower. I will keep you safe."

Six

Fury

My heavy footsteps echo down the winding corridors of the Haven manor. Usually, I would relish the element of surprise, but this turn, I want everyone to know I am coming. I need them to feel the inextricable ache in my soul that reverberates throughout my whole life form, screaming out for her.

Dove... Aurora... Goddess... Mine...

My reason for falling.

The Gods will never rest easy again. Not until they are ashes between my fingers.

Bursting through the intricately carved double wooden doors of the old king's bedroom, I greet everyone with a menacing scowl. Gideon and Fenrir stand next to the old king's healer—an elderly man who looks about as thin and gaunt as a piece of willow bark.

"So there is nothing you can do?" Gideon flicks his eyes to mine for a movement before going back to the man, whose hands are shaking.

"I... I have done my best, Warden Gideon." The old man's voice trembles as he speaks to the wolf shifter towering over his slight frame. "He is beyond the human form. I do not know the fae. I cannot say if he will live to see another turn or if this is his undoing. All my tests prove him to be well, yet he is in some eternal slumber."

Gideon's face twists in barely concealed rage. I see the way his hands ball into fists at the news—the same news I gave him this morning, yet he still sought a *"real doctor's"* opinion because a God doesn't cut it in his books. If he were anyone else, I would have laughed in his face. Yet, he is my creation, and the staunch protector of the owner of my soul. So, I'll give him his petty jabs if they make him feel better.

With the painstaking conversation over, I let my eyes wander past a stone fireplace to a four-poster bed dripping in deep blue silks. Silver candelabras stationed at each side light the golden figure lying prone on the sheets below, like he is some fucking angel lighting up the darkness.

The air whistles beside me as the healer rushes past, a gasp coming from his retreating form. I pay him no heed. Instead, I move to the bed and look for changes in the fae prince's immobile body. When Dove was torn from us, taken by the three Gods who will forever be the walking dead, Oona pulled the bond that connected the fae prince to her.

Within the same moments of rhythm, the three Gods caught us by surprise and started the process of stripping the tethers of my bond from Dove as well. The process was unlike any I have experienced. Worse than death. Pain, the likes of which I never thought I would know as a God. But that is why I fell. *To feel.* To know *her* more deeply.

They pulled and tugged at the tethers joining us. My body contorted to their will. Yet, we were so joined, so interwoven that they could not reach everything. They could not cut her away from me completely. I'm sure the cocky arseholes think they did. It must have taken them all their strength to cut the bond of another God. What they didn't expect were the measures I put in place.

The tiny silver, gold and black threads I stitched together and surrendered to the fates. A piece of the puzzle they could never unravel unless they bonded her themselves; one last standing connection that lets me know she is still alive. The only thing giving me hope. I know what their goal is. They want me to follow. By stealing Dove, they expect I will come for her—for them.

And they are absolutely right. I will come for them. And I will tear them limb from fucking limb. But they expect me to come alone.

How wrong they are.

"The doctor says he is well enough to move. I want to go tonight. I can't wait any longer. I feel my body changing the longer she is away from me."

"From *us*," I correct the wolf shifter.

His teeth snap in response.

"You're the one who wanted a second opinion. I would have been gone this morn—"

"Don't start with me, Orion. You know if we let anything happen to him, she'll never forgive us." Gideon stretches pointed claw tips at the fae on the bed. Ever since Dove was taken, he's been fighting to control his beast side. The longer she is gone, the more parts of him shift into the wolf he was always born to be. The now-extended pointed tips on his fingers, ridiculous furry ears and elongated incisors point to the rapidity of his change.

He is right about one thing, though; I won't let anything happen to Rivern. However, I am not going to admit that. I'm a God.

"We leave now." I gesture towards Gideon's doppelgänger. "Fenrir will look after Haven, as planned. Release the manor's food to be rationed out to the people. And until we return, you will act as reigning monarch." I glare at him. "You let this kingdom collapse into further disarray while we are gone, and it will be your end."

Fenrir bares his fangs in exasperation. "This is my kingdom, Orion. This place will look unrecognisable when you return." My eyes shade to full black. "Fuck's sake. Calm down, oh, precious Godly one. I'm true to my word."

"You're lucky I don't care for such formalities. I should've put the fear in you as pups." All my creations know I never cared for my God status. I have always wanted to be one of them; to walk among the tall grasses of the meadows and swim in the lake of reflections. I want to fall in love, like the love I gave them all. I spoilt them until the others stripped everything away from us.

They may have hated me once, losing mates and lives they all took great pride in. Now, with rhythm and circumstance, they know who the real enemy is.

"You mean, instead of giving us everything we could've ever wanted?"

"I regret none of it." Halting the conversation with those words, I make my way towards the body on the bed, the only thing defining life being the soft whistle of breath.

There are only a handful of people I would go out of my

way for like this, and they are all in this room, except for her —my pet. Oona was the creator of the bond connecting Rivern and Dove, so it was in her power to strip it away. The golden-lined fae fell into a deep sleep right there on the cobblestones when Dove was taken and stripped of their bond.

He has not awakened since.

Long eyelashes flutter, his eyes moving behind heavy lids as if he is dreaming. I can only hope that's all it is. I know what Dove feels for this male. If she comes back to find him in this condition—or worse—she'll never forgive herself. I don't know what would be worse: losing her or living with her hatred for eternity. Because I never intend to let her go. The thought of never touching her again is one I simply cannot bear.

Each turn without her sees my soul slowly leaking from this body, like it's trying to find its way to its one true owner, drifting over the sea, back home to her. I wish it would take my body with it.

I can't stay here without her.

I thought I knew loss before.

I was wrong. Nothing can prepare you for what that four-letter word means to your life energy, mortal or immortal.

It's like drowning in the pitch-black. The only light I see at the other end is her. That tiny, lingering tether within her body continues to draw us together.

I'm coming for you, my Goddess. Hold on for me. First, I have to deliver this fae male back to his people for safe-keeping while we are gone.

I can only hope Dove hears me while she waits.

SEVEN

DOVE

Everything aches. Bleeds. Radiates a deep need.

Soft, warm hands take my chin. A cold metal cup fills my mouth with small sips of warm liquid.

I want him to hold me. Thirst and hunger are on the surface. That's not what I need, though. It's something else—or three someones—I need to control the deep, raking chill and ache in my soul.

Rivern is gone. I don't feel him. Instead, I see him in my dreams.

Gideon is too far to communicate with, but the mate bond is still there, his wolf claiming me completely. The Gods cannot steal that from us—my only salvation.

Fury is a whole other matter. He claims to be in front of me, yet my body no longer craves his presence as it once did. The threads we once held have been ripped away, except for a niggling tug in my lower stomach.

"Drink." It's his velveteen voice coasting over my skin, whispering for me to take my fill again.

I cough. "That's enough. Please, Fury." His hands jerk off my face. Tears well in my eyes at his retreating form. Since I became aware of his presence in this dungeon, he has been cold. I want him to take me in his arms. I want to rest on his chest. Yet, he has brought me a pillow and blanket, which I can only assume he produced from his power, much like he does my clothing. The buttery-soft fabric is worlds away from the grimy, cold dungeon floor. The mildew in the air makes me constantly sneeze.

I cannot bring forth the strength of words to tell him, "Lie with me." My eyelids shut before I have the chance to piece together the strangeness of our situation and the tangle of my fragile mind.

This is only the third rhythm I've awoken since coming to on the crisp stone floor of the darkened place I now find myself—*us?*—in. I'm starting to wonder if Fury is a figment of my imagination. A trick of the Gods who stole me. Usually, when he is near, I feel fire... rage. He's my ember in the darkness. Now, all I feel is emptiness.

The first rhythm my body roused from slumber, I could barely keep my eyes open, but I heard his voice like a magnet, drawing me to my other half, hopeful of what it may have found.

The second time, I woke to broth being poured down my throat, followed by the comfort of a pillow being positioned under my head. His hands barely made contact with my skin, as if I were poison to him.

Now, on the third time, my body feels slightly stronger, yet forever in need of sustenance. *What's new?* My mind can't help but wonder if this isn't yet another way for my subconscious to process the devastation my human form has been privy to.

"Don't be stupid, Dove." The words spring from the tangles of a long-forgotten voice, and I flinch.

It's not real. None of this is real.

Regardless, I try to summon him back to me. "Fury?" I murmur into the darkness. Seeing him would grant me some comfort, yet I have no vision within this place to ground me —just his voice. "Fury, please..."

Even if he's not real, having a voice to hold onto, to keep me going... It feels like everything to my barely beating heart at this moment.

That plea holds so much... Too much. I don't know how to say everything I need to say when the two other people who should be here are gone.

So, I wait for him to respond.

With something.

Anything.

"Dove." His voice fills me with reassurance. I sit up, gripping the sheet to my chest, my head suddenly woozy from rising too quickly.

"Will you"—I cough—"sit with me?" It feels odd to ask him something so basic, which makes me think he must be real. *The Fury of my mind would just know, wouldn't he?*

We are broken. Whatever is now between us doesn't seem right.

An audible sigh comes from the endless black before me.

"Rest. You need to build your strength. I will return with food." His tone, his timbre. They scream Fury. This... This coldness. It's more than physical.

"Where are you going?" I try to stand, barely making it onto my hands and knees, my body swaying uncontrollably. Or *maybe the spinning is in my head?*

"Flower." It's growled. Two hands come to grip my hips, sharp claws finding purchase on bones. "You are weak. Rest, and I will return with more food."

My head continues to spin. It hasn't gone unnoticed that he has dropped his pet name for me. My stomach automatically sinks. *Pet.* That silly name I hated, but grew to love because Fury said it—he claimed me with it. That name meant everything. Now, suddenly, because our bond is almost gone, that's taken from me, too. My eyes begin to water, my body a bag of uncontrollable emotions and incongruities. It's hard to trust that this is not another dream.

I reach out a hand and, as luck has it, find a stony forearm. "Take me away from here, Fury. Please." *My Fury would've taken me from this place already. Surely.*

There's a deep rumble within the chest of the God before me.

"You are not well enough to leave. Once you are stronger, we will move." That's the end of it. He has that same clipped tone I've heard when he expresses the finality of his statements.

"I'm fine." Pushing my body up again, I barely make it so my lower back is lifted off the ground before a firm hand is gently pushing me back onto my pillow.

"You've lost two God bonds. It's a miracle you're alive," he gruffs.

My head lands on the softness behind me, the rest of my body lingering on hard, cold stone. I shudder as his words sink in.

I haven't lost one of them completely. Fury is still here. He's still here.

I've spent so long pushing him away. Maybe this will be the end of us. What if, just as I've started to fall for him and all his oddly endearing characteristics, he's decided he doesn't want me anymore? What if this is him trying to pull away from me? What if he thinks he owes Gideon, and is only keeping me fed and alive for his sake?

I'm sleeping on the frozen, unforgiving ground. He can't even make me a bed! Goddess, can everything wind back a few sunrises to when we were on the isle of Fury, safe and together?

My thoughts are a lead weight on my chest. Hope for our future, that we can mend this, slowly trickles away like a leaky faucet. *If he has fulfilled his side of the bargain, then maybe this was always his plan, and the other Gods just sped it up for him?*

I'm the pawn.

He's been using me to get back to them—his Gods. Could I be part of his revenge plan? My mind continues a downward spiral, unable to think of anything but the worst possible scenarios.

"Did you kill the king?" *I have to know if his part of the deal has been fulfilled. I have to—*

"What king?" His voice is far away, yet everywhere at once. He may not be visible to me, but all I see is his face. Those black eyes with swirls of silver. Grey, flawless skin. Striking silver hair and onyx-feathered wings. The God who has been haunting my dreams forever, protecting me. Who saved me from death. Now, he is colder than ice.

"The king of Haven—the one you said you would kill in exchange for me bonding with you." It feels odd to have to explain this to him, like he doesn't know the intricacies of the arrangement between us.

"Oh, yes, him. He's dead."

A creaking can be heard, followed by a loud clank, and I know I'm now alone. *What is going on here? Horus is dead, and Fury is acting like I am nothing to him.*

The parts of me that once found themselves gingerly pieced back together from a certain fae prince, wolf shifter and fallen God drop away.

Strength. I can no longer latch onto it for resuscitation. The willpower that I found through them is nonexistent in this exhausted state. And instead of letting my heart break all over again, I sleep, knowing Rivern will find me and fix some of what Fury has undone.

WRATH

I can't do it.

I can't be like them.

My body feels like a lead weight at the idea of destroying something—*someone*—so innocent. I don't even see the godlins who move past me in my haste down the glistening ivory and gold corridors of the palace. My mind is on one person, in a full shutdown of everything that isn't Dove.

All she ever did was love the wrong people. I envy that kind of affection.

It was a flawed idea from the start. I was never like them.

Me, seduce a human—a broken human, at that. I can't muster the strength beyond the clipped replies she requires from me in my presence.

I'm a coward.

Some "monster."

Her voice is brittle, strained. Each rhythm she speaks to me, I can't help my reaction. I want to wrap her up in the finest silks and barricade her in my bedroom and force-feed her. She is nothing but skin and bone, her eyes devoid of the life that should dance through them. Seeing her small and cold, down in the dungeon, is burning a hole through me, wearing away at the sliver of common sense I have left.

I feel like the worst sort of wretch, preying on her vulnerable state.

However, Oona is keeping tabs on me. Each night, I've been summoned to her chambers, and each night, she asks of her prisoner. She may not want to lay eyes on her, but that doesn't mean the Goddess won't have Dove tortured to her exact requirements. Unfortunately, Oona still places trust in me where it is no longer due.

I told her what she needed to know to be satisfied: the human's fragile nature, that she thought I was Fury and the psychological toll it was taking on her mind. Oona loves mind games, so, for the time being, my news and the plethora of bone-rattling orgasms I provide to make her forget are satisfying her. She doesn't know about the warm broth I smuggle past the guards, or the pillow and blanket I took from my room. Small things, yet I've never provided such luxuries to anyone else before.

The smuggled contraband requires a distraction to slip past the vigilant shields in gold armour guarding the many palace doors. Oona doesn't trust anyone, so she created her shield; a network of devout God worshippers. They are no match for my brute might, but what they lack in muscle, they make up for in sheer numbers. Her spy network is unmatched. Everyone within Atla knows the shield is more than a force of protection; it is an enforcement.

And if that isn't enough, the godlins—palace servants—

are always hiding in the shadows. Small, stout creatures, made of pure gold. At three feet, they often slink around the castle unnoticed, blending into the walls.

It is time to face my maker, my feet carrying me across the long, gold-veined marble corridors of the palace, taking me to her chambers. The closer I grow, the more I slow, my heart picking up to agitated heights, the likes of which I've never known before.

The little human flower is affecting my composure. She is so delicate yet undeniably strong. A contradiction.

She confuses me.

My racing heart punches my ribs at the thought of her gaunt, dirty face and wide, green eyes staring back at me, unblinking.

"Fucking idiot."

I whirl, bashing a hand against my chest. Oona will punish me. The Gods only know what creative way she will hurt me. I *had* to feed the human a proper meal. She will perish without sustenance. Oona has to see that. I am already running late to see the Goddess. She summoned me to tend to her immediately. I ignored her original command, going to see Dove first. I had to know if she was awake, which she was. The girl was parched. Now, I am late, and I will run even later because I couldn't leave without feeding her. Turning on my heel, I speed back towards the dungeons.

I am going to regret this.

No one defies Oona, least of all her creations.

Nine

Gideon

A constant keening looms in my head, like a silent alarm no one else can hear. It's deafening, my wolf side making my human half painfully aware that we are without our mate, the woman who stole our heart. The woman I knotted. The only woman I've been with in centuries.

To reflect on her and not see the colour of her sparkling spring irises or the delicate curve of her neck is tantamount to torture. I have to push her aside, or I will go insane. Not forever, just long enough for Fury and me to find her. She is my sole goal, my only dream in this life, and I won't be without her.

Not now that I've had her. Tasted her sweet, honeyed skin. Kissed her petal-soft lips. Felt the warmth of her soul wrap around mine. She isn't aware of the measure of my commitment to her. She will soon find out. I am not a creature who will last a mere century. I am millennia old. She will be mine for eternity.

Forgetting her is like trying to forget that my heart has a beat. My body pulls me to be with her. My teeth ache to sink into her flesh for the final claiming.

Walking around with furry ears and my tail on full display, I try to shake the images of her that kept assaulting me, but it is no use. My wolf form isn't retreating, desperate to take over. Soon, I will be consumed by hunting her down. That doesn't bode so well when I am a land animal, and she has been taken over the sea.

We have to be smart about getting our songbird back. We have to have our wits about us. I can't sink into delirium.

Before we attempt any travel across the ocean, we have to visit the Kingdom of Osear. My broad paws pound through the hard, glinting sand. Each pound into the terrain of the Silver Sands brings a wave of tiny pinpricks into my fur-lined body, the pain a comforting distraction.

Fury is delivering Rivern back to Terra for safekeeping— a plan we decided would be in everyone's best interests because we can't yet trust the humans with a fae prince.

Rivern is starting to grow on me. His love for Dove is as plain as the sky is blue, and I could never take that away from her. As much as I thought my wolf would never attach to a female who was already bonded, I was wrong in my under- standing of that meaning. Rivern and Fury have become a part of my pack mentality. They are under my protection. We work together. It goads me that it is Fury, my maker, at the end of one of those bonds. But that is because of what happened before, in the God wars. He has been punished. His rhythm on that island was enough to send anyone mad. Now, all I care about is keeping Dove happy and safe.

At the edge of the Kingdom of Osear, I find myself trying to shake off a change in front of one of the many entrances into the kingdom proper. From my considerably short turns spent here previously, I know the city doesn't possess strong barriers. Instead, it sticks out like a sore thumb, screaming for entry. Sandstone walls glitter, creamy material billows where roofs should be and winding corridors invite exploration. The people inside are a matter all in themselves, warriors itching for battle—the true obstacles.

Running here in my wolf form is risky, especially since it's a struggle to return to my human state—a bet I wasn't sure I could win. It is necessary, though. Saff couldn't fly me out here, Oro being her main priority, so I had to use the fastest means at my disposal. My wolf form has the agility and speed necessary to travel long distances in short periods.

Sand sticks in my tail, itching my skin, the sensation strange when I'm no longer completely in my wolf state. I try to brush it out with clawed fingers. It's no use in this half-transitional phase, so I try my best not to think about it and move through the white walls of the Silver Sands city.

Being in this place again reminds me of Dove, her body writhing underneath Rivern's—the moment she almost touched me. The sight was incomparable, nearly on par with looking into her eyes as she shattered on my cock. The further I walk down winding corridors or shimmering sand, the more I expect her to walk out in front of me. *Wishful thinking.*

A breeze whips around the curved wall in front of me. Lifting my head, I scent the person I'm here to find—a crisp, earthen heat mixed with the salt of the ocean.

Around me, mers mix with silvers, darting through thin, winding, circular streets of Osear's kingdom. I can only surmise that the breeding program is in full swing. The mingling smell of two females guides me towards the same room Moyrie brought us to when I first came here. Stopping at the billowing beige curtain, the sounds inside tell me I'm correct.

I may not be able to speak the languages of the mers or silvers, but the moaning coming from the other side of the rippling material is obvious. Standing before the arched door, I pause for a moment, wondering if intruding is the best way forward—

The thought doesn't linger. My wolf takes over, pushing me through, taking charge of my decision.

Damned insane wolf.

Upon entering, I can't help the tilt of my head at the sight before me. Moyrie lies spread on the bed, legs wide open for a blue mer with pink hair to feast upon her. I don't need to see her face to know who is making a meal of the Silver Sands princess. It's the queen of the mers, Calypso, which explains the slight salt on my tongue when I was following Moyrie's scent to this room.

When you've lived as long as I have, nothing is shocking. *This is definitely one way to see two kingdoms come together.*

Light, powder-blue eyes land on mine, going wide. My incisors extend at seeing a female who is not mine this way. *Relax, you incessant beast. You're not ripping anyone's throat out. She will help us find her.* A smirk takes over Moyrie's luminescent features, and I escape just as I hear the final climax behind me. The only woman I want to hear in the throes of ecstasy is Dove. No silver. No mer. No other human. Just my songbird.

I focus on the reason I'm here, my claws elongated, nails digging into my skin from the tight grip I have on my palms.

A hand lands on my shoulder, making me flinch. My tail whips out, and a curse comes from behind. The smell tells me who it is before I even need to turn around—Calypso.

TEN

MOYRIE

I flop back on my bedsheets. The orgasm Calypso just gave me was mind-altering. World-shattering. Osear, did she know how to use her tongue and mould it to hit the right spots of my inner walls. I have been putty in her hands ever since she got me alone under the guise of "feeding me."

She is feeding me, alright—orgasm after orgasm.

At this point, I understand mers and silvers aren't that different. We crave physical connection. The breeding program will be a natural consequence of our two species coming together. It is the right decision.

The mers can access the ocean through the underground lake where we produce our snake tonic, which they are also fond of.

A glass of the green liquid rests on a gleaming bone inlay table to my right. The pearly white setting of the circular design sends my mind into a state of vertigo as I grasp the copper cup and down the poison inside.

It takes immediate effect as I sink back into the pillows.

When my eyes open again, wicked sharp teeth are all I see, blue lips smacking together as if I'm about to be devoured. My pussy weeps at the sight, my eyes finding Calypso's on a shuddering sigh.

"Wolf, meeting." She says the words in my tongue. We've been trying to learn each other's languages instead of just relying on body cues, which often lead to us being tangled up together—like we are now.

I nod, trying to will myself to get up. Calypso pushes back, a delicate but biting touch. I fall onto the cotton of my mattress.

"Soon." Her pink hair drapes over our faces, shielding us from the outside world. I have never thought of being a one-female sort of silver, but for this fierce queen of the mers, I might just be.

"Soon." I graze my lips against her cheek, my hands gliding the length of her patchwork of blue before latching back onto her lips and delving back into her essence.

The wolf will have to wait.

ELEVEN

RIVERN

The memory of the soft, silky waves of her hair. The melodic sound of her laughter. Her striking stare when our eyes lock just before our lips meet. It's all a never-ending loop in my mind.

It's all Dove.

Everything is a symphony of her.

Her smell.

Her voice.

Her touch.

It's also sorrow, anguish and bone-numbing pain.

Agony was all I knew at the end, and until I see her again, agony will be all I feel.

"Rivern... Love..." Her voice is a graceful hum on the breeze that brushes against the tall grasses of the meadow we are cocooned within. My eyes close, my head lolling back against the earth. Everything about this moment is as if my wildest dreams have taken root. Just her and me. No pain. We are one again.

"Rivern?" Dove's voice grows more insistent now. A hand comes to grip my chin. The knowing of her body flush against mine as she straddles my lower half is unmistakable to my cock, which immediately springs to attention.

My eyes go wide at the sight of an angel smiling down at me. One made of honey and gossamer—delicate but tough. Woven from an unbreakable fabric. So strong, not even a God can break her.

If I believe in anything, it isn't Oona, or some other dispassionate God who wants to try their folly among humanity. No, all I believe in is her.

My love.

My bonded.

My Goddess.

Her nose comes down to graze mine, a shiver raking up my body.

"If this is all we have left, I never want it to end," I say while grasping her waist and pulling her closer to me. Dove pushes back slightly to give me a knowing look, her hips grinding against my tip, making me groan involuntarily.

"This is not the end, Rivern. This is us building strength."

Looking at her light, her goodness breaks something in me. A tear tracks down my cheek. She leans back down, running her tongue along the offending liquid. Where she touches, my skin burns for her.

My hands trail down to squeeze her arse. She lets out a slight moan before coming down to suck on my earlobe, the spot a direct line to my need for her—only her.

"This is forever." She pulls back to whisper, "Never-ending. Infinite. Evermore." The softness of her tongue moves over the lines of my neck, and now it's my turn to moan without restraint. "You came for me. Now I will come for you."

With our chests flush, our breaths ragged and our eyes back on each other, I take in her words. They didn't break us. No one can touch what we have. The strings may be severed, the Gods having stripped us of their ties, but what they didn't bet on was our connection beyond that.

This time, I take over. I roll the angel straddling me onto her back. Her body spreads out before me like a feast, her form clad in a dress of sheer, fine violet cotton, the dips of the fabric moulding alluringly to her curves. A breeze blows past us again, ruffling her tangle of tawny waves. The scent of vanilla rose invades my senses. A deep, primordial grunt comes from my chest as I place my arms on either side of her head, a brilliant smile greeting me, my wheat hair curtaining us from the shining suns.

I trace a lone finger from her cheek to her heaving chest. Every part of her is perfect, including the scar that weaves around her collarbone and up her neck. Dove's breath catches when I continue the tracing of my finger downwards, pulling at the top of her dress to rip the fabric and expose the swell of her right breast.

My mouth waters at the sweet, light pink bud. Like a beast locked in a cage for too long, I pounce, sucking and licking her nipple, making her writhe and squirm beneath me.

God tethers be damned, the pull I have to this woman is paramount to breathing. She is woven into the very fabric of my soul, and there's no extracting her.

Fury called her a Goddess. He's right. She's my Goddess.

My lover. My lifeline. The only thing keeping me grounded to this plane. Without her, I would be at one with the soil.

Nails dig into my hair, pulling me back, interrupting my inner musings.

"Rivern." Dove's cheeks are flushed, her lips rosy red. "I need you inside me," she pleads.

I'm torn. I want to devour every part of her in slow ecstasy. Feel every part of her body against my lips until she is beyond begging me to take her across the edge. I want her to be so enveloped in us that she forgets where she is.

This is all we have: the hope that we will find each other again.

As much as I want to bring Dove to a sweaty mess of rapture, all I can do is roll us into a tangle of limbs, her on top of my body, the skirt of her dress fanning out around us.

"I'm here." I hold her face in my hands, our skin melding together. Long lashes flutter over deep, pooling moss-green eyes—my favourite colour. "I'm here."

She shakes her head, her hands coming to punishingly push mine against her cheeks to an alarmingly bruising level.

"Make me forget." It's a pained echo in my heart, the sound of her thumping chest grounding me. I refuse to be anywhere my Dove isn't.

Sitting up, I swiftly manoeuvre her so she's in my lap. With glassy eyes on me, I mash our lips together. Our hands grasp onto any free expanse of bare skin.

It's hurried and rushed.

Time no longer feels like it's on our side.

It doesn't take long for her hands to push through my breeches and release the hardness. Within moments, she is on me, pushing against the skirt of her dress and sinking her core deep onto my cock.

Our mouths still locked, we groan as one, our bodies joining wholly, movement barely our goal. But the animalistic need of our baser instincts takes over, and I'm guiding Dove, with hands on her arse, to move excruciatingly slowly up and down my length, never wanting this to end. Until, finally, we are breaking around each other.

Unable to move out of our utter state of bliss in our meadow cocoon of sweet, whispered nothings, we hold each other closely, still clothed. I know our rhythm is lacking. She will wake, and I will be pulled away to the darkness without her—the place I wait. For now, we soak in every moment the fates have blessed us with.

Twelve

Fury

Leaning over the edge of the bed, I watch inquisitively as Rivern's eyes dart furiously underneath his eyelids.

"Step aside, Sir Fury. I need to apply a compress to his forehead." The fae woman—who looks strikingly like Rivern, but without the golden lines—pushes past me. Her nearness grates at me, so I linger back, watching as she fusses over her brother, who lies still in his bedroom, a fireplace warming the cave-like space to feverish heights.

The journey from Haven to Terra was uneventful. I flew to the mountains and teleported within. It had been a shock to the fae when I arrived, but once they saw I was bringing their only prince back home, they were accommodating enough.

I was still an unplaced enigma to them, and that's how I continue to keep it. They can sense my power. Now that I am no longer imprisoned and bound, the energy that radiates off of my body is electric. All they need to know is that I will destroy them with a flick of my fingers if I wish. The fae aren't stupid. They never seek to harm, which is surprising considering Oona is their creator. Free will is ever-present here. Their creator might be a daemon, but it doesn't mean they have to be.

Rivern's mother has yet to make an appearance, his sister, Freya, stepping in instead. With the fae prince firmly within the holds of his family, I'm eager to leave. The hole I'm wearing into the rug is growing bigger by the moment.

A loud exhale comes from the bed. I look towards her out of propriety. If it were up to me, I would have left already. However, I know it is essential to share some news to avoid further conflicts. *I'm not a complete menace.*

"I've never seen anything like this before." Freya takes one of Rivern's hands in her lap as she looks up at me expectantly.

I go back to whittling a hole in the floor. "It's a side effect of being stripped of his God bond. He will hopefully improve once they are reunited."

"Reunited," she murmurs the word under her breath, like it sours her tongue.

"Yes." I cease my pacing to face her. "The bond was not severed at the will of both parties. It was ripped from them. They will need to be reunited if you wish for him to wake up."

Dark violet eyes meet mine, and Freya huffs before going back to fiddling with the compress on his forehead. "She's a human, is she not? My brother told me of her before leaving to go to the Silver Sands to be wed. I didn't think they were still involved."

"The Silver Sands is no longer a concern of Terra. They

have released you from any bargains made. Rivern chose to be with Dove."

A sneer vibrates from her lips.

"You do not approve of your brother's bond?"

Freya turns, ire in her eyes, though she cowers slightly when she takes in the full expanse of my wings and horns. "Why would the Goddess ever bond a direct heir of her line to a human? The very same who drove us out of Haven centuries past? It doesn't make sense. She has to be some sort of siren." She lowers her head, looking back towards Rivern's still form. "My brother would never have gone against his people. Once he met her, he changed."

The string of my patience grows thin when she talks of Dove. She can say what she wants about Rivern. To insinuate Dove is a siren is laughable. The trivialities of the fae are their own.

"I will not have you speak about my bonded in such a way," I all but growl at Freya.

She blanches at my tone. "You are bonded to the human as well?"

"Yes." I don't give her anything more, angered and annoyed by this fae. She's Rivern's sister, not mine, and I will not stay here while she berates her brother's choices. "I trust you will keep him safe."

"Of course. He's—"

That's all I need. I pivot and stride back through the door. Dove has been too long without me.

THIRTEEN

SAFF

Oro digs his talons under the scales of my back. His small claws pinch, but the sting is bittersweet. For so long, I've wanted this.

The little human is gone, and I can't do anything about it. My job is to stay and raise my son. He relies on me for nourishment. Our bond is sacred. The food he needs to grow is beyond even what I need as a fully formed dragon. As an adult, I'm used to only eating one large meal every several turns. When I was with the silvers, they would often feed me fish. It was a diet I grew fond of, so I began hunting on the surface of the sea for Oro, only going inland to forage for rabbits or deer when necessary.

It wasn't until a few turns of skimming the edges of the void, my face being sprayed with salty ocean water, rocky cliffs surrounding us on both sides, that a blue tentacle shot out of the water, grasping one of the biggest grey fish I'd ever seen.

I'd halted before the kraken, unsure of his motive until he reached into my mind and told me it was a gift for Oro. Food for my child was not something I was going to refuse, especially from one of my God's creations. My son needed the energy the meat provided to grow the muscles that would propel him into flight.

Gods, was he already starting to weigh my back down. Carrying a dragon backside was completely different from carrying people. Oro had untold mass in his scales. They were protective, but weighty, especially for the creature carrying him.

Since that daylight in the void, we've been meeting Ken, as the kraken likes me to call him, on the beaches by our cliffs, where he has been helping me fish.

I keenly watch as Oro trots along the beach, trying to flap his wings into flight, only to fall to one side or the other, his deep purple scales sparkling in the light of the setting suns.

Smack. An orange crab lands on the burgeoning pile of squirming aquatic animals at my feet. A blue-suckered tentacle retreats into the water.

"Thank you, Ken. That should be enough for today," I reach out through our minds.

"You need more. In case." His answer is cryptic, making me pause and move my attention away from my stumbling child, fully focusing on the bobbing, dark blue head in the crashing waves before me. He faces away, yet I know he's waiting for my reply.

"In case what?"

"The tides are changing. Our God will call." Once again,

his words are puzzling. *"Our God"* can only mean one creature.

Fury.

FOURTEEN

WRATH

I find Oona, blonde hair dripping, fair skin glowing, in the luxury of her circular, golden bathtub located in her suites. It is placed proudly in the centre of the floor-to-ceiling marble-covered room three times the size of my own bathing space. She giggles at a comment one of her two companions makes. Her copper irises twinkle as they reflect the light of two crystal chandeliers.

We both know she senses that I've entered the room. The mist of the heated tub lingers in the air, stagnant, a pungent aroma of bitter grapefruit making me wince inwardly. The display she puts on in the bathtub, the two women washing her, their lingering glide of skin against skin, shouting, *Look what you missed*, sends an electric current to my cock.

You don't stand Oona up. Especially as her creation. It's the highest form of insolence. I let my desperation to feed Dove take over without care of the repercussions.

Now, as my eyes linger on the tub, my onyx leather boots

padding softly against the white marble, I notice the crack in my Goddess's facade, the slight twitch of her blonde eyebrow giving her away only to me. The two human women doting on her are completely unprepared for the reckoning that's about to befall us all.

She won't mention that I'm late. Instead, her eyes flick to mine for the briefest of moments as I stand, towering before the tub, taking breaths through my mouth and not my nose to avoid the coiling, sickly bitter scent coming from the perfumed water.

The shapely redhead notices my appearance, staring at me hungrily for a moment too long. She must be new to Oona's revolving door of conquests. The pretty, dark woman to Oona's right doesn't take her eyes off the Goddess. She's been here before and understands the rules. In the Goddess's presence, you can only have eyes for her, unless she grants you permission to look elsewhere.

A bruising hand comes to grasp the redhead's jaw. "You want him?"

I inwardly groan, knowing how this is going to end up. *Don't show weakness.* If only I could whisper the words into the poor woman's head. Her frightened eyes dart towards the other woman in the tub. *She can't help you.*

"N-nnno." It's a breathy stammer.

Oona knows it's a lie. Many of the humans of Atla dream about the turn they can share one of the Gods' beds. It's the ultimate prize. Only those blessed with incomprehensible beauty are chosen. However, the underground whispers of sharing the monster's bed are surprisingly even more coveted—mostly surprising to me, as I have no idea why there is a comparison between myself and the Gods.

The only thing we share in common is our wings. Their beauty is unmatched, all soft and feminine. My body is a ruinous, sharp-edged sword.

I'm the monster in the darkness, undertaking the Gods' dirty work. Yet that only endears me to the humans. A fact that Oona is highly aware of, often using it to her advantage.

She releases her grasp on the poor woman's reddening face. "Go to my *monster*." Upon finishing, her eyes flicker to mine. *Monster*—the slap she intended it to be.

Trembling, the naked redhead pulls herself out of the bathtub like a newborn baby foal finding its legs. Droplets of water fall in delicious waves across full curves. She can't be a turn past twenty. Every part of her body is pert and perky.

My cock jerks instantly in my fine white trousers.

I'm my Goddess's creation; a hot-blooded monster with a constant need to please.

Scared but inquisitive deep emerald eyes flick to mine, the woman taking tentative steps my way. Without warning, a vision crosses my mind of soft, sad green eyes and a face covered in dirt. I clench my jaw.

"Wrath." Oona's seductive, teasing voice pulls me free, and I find gold, metallic, lifeless irises looking back at me. "You know what to do." A smirk is on her full red lips. Her finely spun golden wings shudder. She may look beautiful, however, Oona is as heartless as they come.

"Yes, my Goddess." I bow my head slightly. She is after my pain, my collapse, and I have no other option but to give it to her. My Goddess knows how much this part of my nature tugs at my soul. The problem is that the humans give themselves to me freely, and my body cannot refuse. She made me this way—sick in the head, constantly at war. And Oona loves to see me suffer.

I walk away from the redhead, making my way over to the inbuilt ivory vanity. Through the oval mirror perched atop it, I can see the eyes of all the women on me. Including my Goddess's, those cunning eyes approving of my movements. It doesn't take me long to find the scarlet velvet rope —its colouring stands out. I don't want to think about that; how it was chosen because of this specific shade.

Keeping my eyes on the far wall, I stride back towards the lush, naked body of the woman standing beside the tub. As if she has finally realised what is happening, her body is frozen to the spot.

I stand behind her, a tremble raking its way through her bones. I can't promise I won't hurt her. That's not the purpose of this specific exercise. I can only try to make it as painless as possible.

"What is your name?" I lean down to whisper in her ear. My eyes dart to Oona's as I say it. Her window for tolerance is short tonight. I can read it in the crease on her forehead. Thankfully, the other woman in the tub is keeping her occupied. The Goddess's eyes flutter shut on a moan. *Small mercies.*

Now that we are standing back to front, the size difference between me and the redhead is a lot more noticeable. I've yet to come across someone who matches my height. Even the Gods are a foot smaller, which is exactly what Oona wanted when she created me. She would be seen by the humans as an ethereal, delicate Goddess who requires the services of her terrifying monster to keep her safe. Little do they know, I'm not the real monster here.

"O-Opal," she stammers.

I release a pent-up breath of air, which trickles across the flyways of her amber tresses. It's a pretty shade for a human. I can see why Oona chose her. My cock is straining in my pants to get at the warmth of her heat. *Calm down, you ravenous beast.*

It becomes increasingly harder to play my part with this constant need working its way through my body. Oona saw to it that, upon creating me, my body would be up to the tenacious need of servicing her and any other who required it. At the time, she had no idea what that meant. For me, it means my cock has a mind of its own, a harrowing throbbing waiting to be filled constantly. The only relief I get is within the confines of the dungeon, the darkness a safety.

The woman currently living down there plays on my mind, my cock twitching.

"Fuuuuck," I groan.

Opal gasps loudly. I need to forget about Dove for right now, but there's something about her. A singularity that brings me just as much contentment as the cold, barren stone walls of the underground passages. Maybe it's because I have this sense that she might be the first person who can understand my plight.

We are both caged, after all, my walls slightly different than hers.

Forget about her, Wrath.

A solid thumping comes from my engorged cock, bringing me out of my thoughts. Looking back towards the bath, I notice Oona hasn't noticed my standstill, the Goddess currently in the throes of ecstatic pleasure, the woman on top of her sucking on her nipples, her arm underwater, between her separated legs.

I seize the wrists of the woman before me and place them behind her back. "Bend over, Opal," I growl out, bumping her with my hardness. A small squeak comes out of her mouth at the sudden movement.

Her back is blemish-free and exposed to me. When Oona has her way with this girl, this canvas will be unrecognisable. The worst part is that Opal will thank the Goddess for her markings and call them a blessing because that is the way.

Trailing a hand down her smooth flesh, I tie her hands together at the small divot in her tailbone.

Casting a shadow over her body once more, I ask, "Have you ever been fucked before, Opal?"

Another mousy squeak comes from the girl.

It's not Opal's voice I hear in response; it's our Goddess's. "The girl is as fresh as they come, my monster. A present for you."

Fates, have mercy on me. I close my eyes and buck against the backside of the bound woman before me. She may be green, but I will not take an unwilling human on my cock.

Grasping her hair, I pull her back enough to whisper, "Do you want this…" I rub my hardness against the heat of her core, wetting my trousers.

Suddenly, all squeaking ceases to exist. "Yessss," she moans. Her breaths come in sudden and shallow.

I flick black eyes to golden ones. Oona raises her brows as if to say, *See? I told you so.*

Gods, sometimes, I want to slap the smug smile off her face. These people would follow her off the cliffs surrounding our palace if given the opportunity. I would happily watch them fall for their lack of original thought, too.

Pulling down my pants, I expose the hardness that is already dripping. Hidden behind the shivering woman before me, I grip the sash around her wrists, line my cock at her tight entrance and push forward, seating myself thoroughly inside her wet, suffocating cunt.

I don't stop when her groans turn into screams, echoing through the steam of the bathroom.

I don't stop when a part of me shrivels inside for needing this savagery, a clawed nail opening a line on her back before Oona takes her pound of flesh.

And I certainly don't stop when I hear the melodious sounds of Oona laughing from her place in the bath, the woman I'm seated inside shuddering around my cock, yet still begging for clemency.

I'm her monster.

Fifteen

Wrath

Fingers trail my erect cock. I'm barely conscious, however, that's a trivial consequence when it comes to how my body reacts to someone touching it. Opening my eyes, I see thick mahogany hair draped over my abdomen. A wetness takes me from root to tip.

The groan that leaves my lips is involuntary. Off to the side, I hear faint sniffles. Tilting to the side, I find the virgin, Opal, on her side, her welted and bloodied back facing me, her shoulders shaking in soft sobs. I notice the depth of the cuts first. Some wounds are still bleeding.

She's made a mess of the poor girl.

Everyone in Atla knows this is Oona's dirty little secret. When she fell from the sky, she loved to indulge in pleasure. However, she soon realised that pain was far sweeter. Now, a horde of human Atlans possess the markings of the Goddess. That's what they call them anyway: chosen markings, a blessing of Oona.

What they really are is torture.

Teeth make an appearance down the underside of my shaft. *Fuuuuuck.* I grasp a lump of curls from the woman going down on me and push her further until she is choking. Her throat contracts sporadically around my hardness.

Soon, my groans and the woman's exaggerated moaning take over the room.

"Wrath," the sing-song voice hits my ears just as I'm about to come. The woman from the bath, who I was just about to blow my load in for the fifth time this moonlight, stalls at the voice.

Opening my eyes, I spot Oona in a practically see-through wrap dress in a gauzy silver.

"Wakey, wakey, I have a present for you." My eyes travel from Oona's full chest, covered in my bite marks, up her thin neck—*so breakable, if she weren't a God*—to her smug smile—a smile speaking of utter delight.

What are you up to?

I've only ever seen her this pleased once in our immortal lives: when she witnessed heartbreak on a human's face for the first time. It was at the beginning of Atla's creation, when she was starting to take lovers. She'd had a man refuse to come to her bed, stating that he loved his wife. Oona then proceeded to use her God powers to convince him that *he* was *her* wife. So, unbeknownst to him, the man fucked her in front of his true partner.

After that, the humans never defied the Gods' orders, and over time, they came to see it as a ritual. Only the most favoured are chosen. That's how they see it. I am starting to think the humans are getting dumber and dumber, century after century.

Her finger crooks, pointing at me.

I unhand the woman on my cock and get up from the comfort of Oona's bed. I am still as hard as a rock, and my balls are a deep blue. She doesn't care.

"Come," she leers, swiftly turning on her heel, her delicate wings fluttering behind her.

Because all of my choices belong to her, I go, following like the obedient dog I am behind flowing, gilded hair, ignoring the raging need between my legs.

She takes me past her chambers, down the wide, colonnaded staircase, and to the formal dining room. Two ten-foot bronze doors swing open to reveal a gold-veined, white marble table that comfortably seats thirty guests. When I enter the space, I find someone who shouldn't be at this table because they should be down in my darkness.

My flower. Dove.

Oona glides into the room without a care. "I thought it was high time I took some measure of your progress, Wrath." She turns to look at me accusingly. "It's been four turns, and still not a peep from our prisoner," she goads me. The Goddess knows Dove only woke up a turn ago.

She's jealous. That didn't take long.

Dove sits at the head of the table in her tattered black corset, the strings loosened so she can breathe, her breasts just contained. The sight in the flickering candlelight only fuels the need in my groin. What dampens it is seeing the dirt and grime on her ivory skin, her hair in utter disarray.

Despite her appearance, she sits upright, her hands placed before her on the table, tied together with a thin copper chain— a speciality of Oona's in the bedroom when silk isn't enough. A silken band covers Dove's eyes so her surroundings are hidden.

I pause at the threshold, extending my hand to grasp Oona's forearm, halting her progress further. At the electric sizzle of flesh touching, hard eyes fall on mine. "If I am to work on her mind, it will take time. It has only been four turns." My voice is hushed. I don't dare look directly at the woman beyond Oona.

"It is taking too long." She pulls her arm out of my hold. "I have other plans." A red mark remains on her porcelain skin. A sick desperation within me rises at the sight, to grip tighter next time, to finally take her in the way I have been dreaming of for so long. "With the trials coming up, I will need a champion."

That piques my interest.

Oona now stands next to Dove, lifting a piece of limp, dirty hair and letting it fall. The human sits ramrod straight against the back of the hard stone chair. Her pink lips open slightly, holding back her breath as if she is trying to remain small, quiet.

She could never be forgotten.

It's at this moment, with sparkling eyes goading me, that I step further into the room and break all pretence. This is part of the game Oona wanted. To Dove, I am Fury. To know I am with the Goddess will break her. In truth, below, in my dungeons, I had no idea how I would've broken her. I thought tricking her would be enough, stringing her along, having her as mine forever.

When you're raised in sin, it's all you know. It's all I've come to expect, and I wanted to take her as mine, to revel in her. I was naive to think Oona would forget, would let me have something for myself.

I quite enjoyed taking care of Dove, feeding her and bringing her comforts.

Seeing my Goddess next to her, a damning smile on her lips, makes my stomach flip—an odd feeling that spurs my next words.

"But I am your champion."

At my voice, Dove's head jolts to face mine, and even though she is blindfolded, I can still feel those sharp greens, her mouth a thin line.

"But now I have a new toy to play with, and I wish to see what all the fuss is about." Oona walks to Dove's side and takes her chin in hand, bringing her back to the Goddess. "Would you like that, human? To be a God's champion?"

She hasn't spoken. When her lips break to spit at the Goddess in front of her, I freeze. Humans have been whipped for far less.

Instead of raising her voice, Oona laughs at the insolence —a cackling, wicked sound that rocks me to my core. The sound catches the static air in the room and booms off the walls.

"I'll take that as a yes, *witch*." And like a slap to the face, Dove recoils back into the dining chair. "Clean her up. I need her ready for the opening ceremony tonight," Oona adds, strolling past me, a waft of pomegranate trailing in her wake.

The urge to gag takes hold, yet my cock jerks at being left alone with the human. *Gods, how I wish Oona had let me finish what the human upstairs started.*

SIXTEEN

DOVE

Witch. I hated it when Castor used that word. Hearing it again is a dagger to the gut, reminding me of all the turmoil I have already experienced in Haven, only to now face it once again in a new land—with a threat far more dangerous.

The Gods.

And this rhythm, there aren't three as I suspected. There are four.

Fucking Fury.

No, that can't be right. The slight chains holding my hands together clink gently as I push them against my throbbing forehead. *I'm not in the right frame of mind. Fury isn't here. It's all some dream, and now I'm imagining his voice everywhere I go.* It's growing more and more infuriating to know that now, after I've found my bonded, I'm losing my mind.

My heart had instantly kicked up speed at the sound of his voice again. Hearing him beyond the dungeon only solidified my state of delirium. *Maybe Fury is the new Wren.* I am officially going crazy *again*. Realising that is a lot more comforting than the possibility that Fury is actually here. *No, it is definitely just wishful thinking.* A warmth in the unexpectedness of this situation.

What if this is another dream? Like the ones I've been having with Rivern. Goddess, why?

"I'm going to pick you up now," Fury's voice, all smooth lines and chilling notes, greets me. This time, I let myself have it—have him. I'm barely holding on after nearly being stripped of two bonds. If this is all the comfort I get before I die, I'll take it.

Two hard arms come around me, lifting me with strong hands against a smooth, naked chest. *Even his hold reminds me of him.* The only noise that can be heard is the jingle of the tight chains around my wrists, indestructible in their delicate nature.

I close my eyes behind the blindfold, breathing in a strange scent of metal and black pepper. The combination reminds me of the turns I've spent in the darkness of the Gods' dungeon, in and out of consciousness. It bites at the back of my throat.

My body is jostled slightly as the person beneath me moves. I have no idea where we are going. My energy to fight back is nonexistent. The part of me that was once a flaming furnace is now just coal, and I don't know if I have the strength to flame it.

A door creaks, and before I realise what is happening, I'm placed on a cloud. I know it can't be a cloud—unless I'm dead. That's just what the softness beneath me is akin to. Compared to sleeping on a cold stone floor, this is the ultimate bliss. A deep groan works its way out of my throat, and I let my body sink.

I drift in and out of consciousness, my stomach growling, desperate for more of the delicious stew I was fed earlier.

"Sit." It's a command, fathomless in its ending. The vibrations want me to rise. I stay still, my muscles too sore to move, the will I have to continue this fight no longer raging inside me. Gideon is there on the periphery, the tugging low in my abdomen, but I keep wondering if that's enough if Rivern is gone to me. He was my first, my everything. There's something to be said for the first person you give your heart to. They awaken you to a side of yourself you've never met before. I hadn't allowed myself to love for so long beyond childish dreams. He broke down my barriers, regardless of the God bond. He renounced his duties to help me and my people.

I can't imagine being without him now. He's so ingrained in me, he's all I dream about when I close my eyes. It's the only place I feel connected to him.

"Flower, you have to sit up so I can feed you."

That voice again—Fury's voice. I open my eyes. This time, I'm not met with a blindfold or darkness. Instead, light filters through large, curved windows. At the brightness, I instantly shut my eyes. Hands come around me to move my body into a sitting position against a cushioned wall.

"You don't need to open your eyes, but you do need to open your mouth." The sharp sting to his tone, like I'm a petulant child, taunts me. Fury always knows how to get under my skin.

My eyes flutter wide again just as the bed dips beside me.

I have to blink multiple times to adjust my eyesight because what I'm seeing can't be real.

"Fury," I croak. Outlines of a grey figure with black-feathered wings hold me in a vice. "It's you." My saliva is nonexistent, and I almost choke on the words.

His silver hair is pulled back, all the cutting lines of his face visible to me, his black lips thin and unmoving. I follow his straight nose up to his eyes, the blackness all-encompassing.

"How?" I choke back a sob, somehow finding the energy to launch myself at him. I catch Fury off guard, and he holds a bowl of steaming hot liquid to the side and lets me plaster my body to his. Finally, since being taken by the Gods, I cry, letting every ounce of me bleed for everything I lost right when I finally found it.

I'd almost believed I was going to get my happily ever after—the kind you hear about in stories. I should've realised happily ever after was a lie.

His skin is warm as I nestle into the crook of his neck, my hands finally free to throw over his shoulders. Sniffling into his very real and tight, naked upper body soothes but doesn't fix the cracks in our bond—the bond the other Gods broke.

I pull back from him, an idea forming in the fragments of my consciousness. This all feels so unreal. His skin is smooth and taut beneath my skin. Looking up into his eyes, the first thing I take in is the onyx; complete darkness, the silver that once ringed his pupil gone again—the first visual sign we aren't connected.

My heart aches for him, for us and this ultimate undoing. The embers within heat up. No black dragon makes an entrance, no voices from my past spur me on. Just me and one of the three men I've fallen for. His existence is enough to spur my light into being.

"Bond us." I pull our bodies back together, bringing our noses to touch. "I don't know what is going on, but—" A clawed hand finds my tattered corset and pulls me back. "Ooof." I hit the bed with a thud, Fury now on the opposite side of the room, pacing, the soup discarded on the floor.

The erratic organ in my chest bucks, alarmed. *What in the name of the Goddess is going on?*

My features twist in concern. My Fury would never miss an opportunity to bond with me. I would hazard a guess that being bonded to me is his favourite thing.

Pushing to my knees on the plush comforter, I watch as he walks back and forth on cream stone before three large, curved windows. His sombre mood against the brightness of the suns feels wrong, or maybe it's just the white linen pants he's wearing.

As I puzzle over his attire, he turns and storms over to the bed, the V of his hips flexing tantalisingly in my line of sight. A clawed hand comes to cup my cheek, pulling my eyes up to meet his.

"Take your clothes off and go have a bath. I will be back with more soup."

With those last words, he is gone, and I'm left by myself —again.

———

ON WOBBLY LEGS, still recovering from the effects of the God bonds being severed, I explore the somewhat bare room

I've been left in. A rug made of soft red threads lies before the sunken, burnt-orange velvet bed frame dressed with similarly toned sheets. Two golden-marbled bedstands sit beside the bed, holding thick candles in varying states of melt.

Turning, a heady rush unsteadies me, and I place a hand on the wall, only to find myself falling onto a hard, cold surface.

"Ouch," I groan, rubbing my side. *That's going to bruise.* Massaging my sore hip, I find myself in a space much like the temple hot springs, but without the glow-worms and green moss. Steam rises in the air, and the smell of rosemary comes from the end of the bathing room, where a deep pool sits overlooking the vast expanse of open sea.

My eyes go wide, witnessing the endless crashing waves beyond. It's gorgeous, the spring below the vista calling my name. I start by crawling until I get to the lowered edge of the hot water. Seeing the rippling liquid of the large bath overlooking the crashing waves of the ocean below makes my bones throb. The hot water represents a pleasure I haven't experienced in several turns.

Uncaring of any consequences, just running on pure want, I strip out of my skintight pants and corset, finally sinking into the water. "Goddess." I moan loudly as each inch of my sore body sinks beneath the surface.

The mist hides me from the expanse of the room, memories of my old life taking route. *Gods, I hope everything is okay back in Haven. Fury is here, so it must be, right? He truly is here to rescue me. Right?*

The questions linger. The more my body repairs itself,

and the more I come back to consciousness, the less sense all of this makes.

Are we safe?

Is Fury getting us out?

Is this part of his plan for revenge against the Gods?

Where are Gideon and Rivern?

What of the Gods who took me? And that woman with the melodic voice, calling me her champion?

My mind spins, and I sink further into the water, almost floating. The smell of sulphur and sweet, earthy rosemary lulls my eyelids back into sleep—the only thing I seem to be good at these turns.

"Are you feeling better?" He startles me. My body jolts, creating waves in the water around me.

Fury's shadow looms overhead, his eyes not on mine, but at the lapping current on my chest. My first instinct is to cover myself. Then I remember this God has been in my head. He's my bonded. There are no secrets between us, including my body.

He takes a beat too long to travel back to my face, his features impassive, his jaw hardened as he grits his teeth.

"A little," I reply, answering his question.

"Good," he clips. "You need to eat." He bends his tall body to roll his pant legs up before dangling his feet in the edge of the bath. His wings stretch behind him, fluffing out. I get the urge to touch them, to run my fingers through the plush raven.

"Come closer." Fury's words sear through to my core, my body lighting up for him. That's when I see the bowl in his hands. "You need to eat."

My stomach grumbles, and he raises his eyebrows as if to say, *What are you waiting for?*

I come to sit beside him, his leg and my arm a breath apart from touching. Reaching out for the bowl, he replies by scooping some soup onto his spoon and holding it out for me.

"I can feed myself." I cross my arms over my naked breasts. The coals of my inner fire feel safe in their beginnings, now that Fury is here and I'm starting to get my bearings again.

"I know you can, but you don't have to. Open up, little flower."

My mouth automatically opens for him, and as I'm swallowing the first bite of utter deliciousness on my tongue, I realise he still hasn't dropped the name *Flower*. *What happened to Pet?* The endearing name I loathe. The name that somehow wiggled its way into my heart.

Brow furrowing, I roll my gaze over the lines of his abs, the thick veins of his neck throbbing with darkness. Continuing my perusal, I find the tips of his ears, glossy hair and eyes that are glued to my face.

"Why do you keep calling me *Flower*?" The spoon comes to my lips again. I don't hesitate, opening my mouth for the sustenance my body is craving.

"Because you are as delicate as you are beautiful, but in that beauty is constant renewal." My brain stalls, and my heart skips a beat at his answer. "Would you prefer I call you something else?" His eyes don't leave mine as we speak, like he's trying to burrow back into my soul. The answer is not at all what I was expecting.

"I... Well, it's certainly nicer than *Pet*." I yawn, exhaustion taking over my body. A phantom tug pulls at my chest, violet eyes washing my vision. "Are Rivern and Gideon okay?" I add, never forgetting about the fae prince and wolf shifter who should be here with us.

"Drink. You need your strength." He ignores my question, and when the spoon goes for my mouth again, I close my lips.

"Open." I shake my head, moving to the other side of the bath, which looks out over the azure sea below—a space he cannot reach unless he joins me.

"Answer my questions." I splay my arms over the small lip against the wall and window. A slight ledge at the perfect height to sit holds me up, my breasts fully exposed to the dark God. His eyes wash over with complete darkness.

"Eat." His voice cracks, and he tries again. "Fuck," he murmurs under his breath. "Eat your food, and we will talk."

"Answer my questions, and I will eat." I hold firm. I don't know why he's denying me the information he knows I need to feel better. *Why is he here, and Gideon and Rivern aren't? None of this makes sense.*

A growl comes out of the daemon God before me. Without preamble, he enters the water in his pants, holding the bowl above the surface, making his way over to me.

Godsdamnit. Of course water is no barrier for him.

"Eat," he says, holding the food before me.

"Where are the others?"

He sighs, his hypnotic onyx eyes drawing me in. "You eat, and I will answer your questions."

"Fine." I open my mouth, drinking down the broth, waiting for him to answer, raising my brows.

"Gideon and Rivern are not here." I open my mouth again, and he continues. "I have made a deal with the other Gods that will keep everyone safe."

Dread forms in the pit of my stomach. *This is the God who was hell-bent on taking revenge on the others, not pandering to them. These are the same Gods who ripped the bonds from us. They are not our friends; they are our enemies!*

Fury must notice the change on my face. He places the bowl on the edge of the bath and grasps my cheeks between his claw-tipped fingers. "It is the only way. To get out safely, you must win the trials and become Oona's champion."

Champion? "What?" None of this is making sense. *Why isn't Fury outraged? Why isn't he ripping heads from necks? Why isn't he burning this place to the ground for what they have taken from us?* The rage within is starting to grow wings, finding places to take hold and fester.

Everything I've ever wanted has been ripped away from me. The love I never thought possible was taken on a whim. Now, my God stands before me, water dripping from his chiselled chest, and he's saying they require more of me.

I try to pull away, but I meet a glass wall.

"This is the best way, my flower. It is the best way to guarantee your safety."

If the furnace within was a mere ember before, it's now a roaring, raging, flaming crater. All thanks to the fallen God standing before me. The fallen God who looks like Fury, but isn't acting like the all-obsessive daemon I know and love.

I take a step into his space, knowing the only way out of this bath is through him. Placing my hands on his hard chest, I look up into his eyes. "You are not the daemon I was falling for. He would never allow this."

At my choice of words, something within Fury snaps. I see it in the way his jaw stiffens. His incisors elongate. *That's new.* He breathes through his nose, his eye twitching. Broad hands come around to grip my arse, pushing me further into his chest. I don't give him the satisfaction of letting him know how he is affecting me. Every part of my body yearns for his touch, and when his skin meets mine, it calms the call. There's still an undercurrent of want, like something is missing, a niggling at the edges, but that must be because Rivern and Gideon are not with us. And our bond is holding on by a thread. There are so many extenuating circumstances. With my body still recovering, having his hands on me, sedating some of the anguish, is enough for now.

Our bodies press so close that an unyielding hardness presses against my lower abdomen.

"And how would you prefer I act?" His voice is hoarse against the upper curve of my ear.

"I want you to take what you want." *The old Fury would've bonded with me already. We would be sharing his power. He would feel—*

He growls, pushing me away, ending my thoughts. "Get out and dress yourself in the clothes I have left on the bed. I will be back to collect you when the suns begin to set."

Without giving me another glance, he stalks from the bath, his dress pants dripping as he leaves me gaping after him in disbelief.

SEVENTEEN

GIDEON

Silvers bring in trays and trays of food as I wait in a secluded alcove in the Silver Sands kingdom. I sit on a bench seat of creamy-coloured cushions, my body taking up most of the hidden area. My torment must have been written all over my face because, upon seeing me, Calypso immediately ushered me to this space to... wait. Without Fury here, I have no way to communicate with either Moyrie or Calypso, but my creator is meant to be meeting me here for those purposes once he has dropped Rivern off.

This was the best idea we had. The suns have already moved over us multiple times. I am getting antsy over the rhythms spent away from Dove. My wolf is raging to be free, but we have no way to get across the water. *I didn't. I should've let Fury go.* Instead, I stopped him after he woke from getting his bond stripped. It is smarter for both of us to go. We need backup.

We need a kraken. It will be our fastest mode of transport beyond the decaying ships of Haven. And Saff. The dragon would be the perfect choice if she didn't have a baby attached to her back at all times. Oro is several turns off of figuring out how to fly, and even then, he doesn't have the capacity for long-distance travel like his mother.

Without knowing what we are going into, the kraken seems like the best option. Anything on land will have to be dealt with by me or Fury regardless.

With varying platters of meat, fruit and bread before me, I take it as my last chance to refuel. It's hard to digest, and most of what I eat tastes like sand, but I'm also a warrior, practical to a fault; my pack won't be safe if my body isn't fuelled.

With bread halfway to my mouth, three sets of footsteps catch my attention. As they grow closer, I know he's here without having to see him. An ashen scent along the breeze wafts my way. The scent of Orion—the aroma most would associate with death. Yet, from ashes grows life. He's the catalyst for beginnings, just as all the Gods are.

I chew on my bread as they come into view. Fury's eyes are steely as they take me in. "Are you finished?"

Calypso and Moyrie stand on either side of him. The Silver Sands princess, barely tall enough to reach his chest. Calypso, in all her cobalt beauty, nearly reaches his shoulder. It has always been odd, seeing my God among the people of this world. His ebony wings and horns are enough to deter anyone. Yet these females stand next to him, unperturbed.

Getting up, I rub my hands on the black pants I changed into after shifting.

"Is everything alright in Terra?" I address Fury.

"It is." That's all he gives me. "Calypso believes we will

be able to reach the kraken through the waterways under the Silver Sands. Come."

He wastes no time, which I appreciate. He has tunnel vision, unable to hide his impatience. Every moment away from her is agony. We are on the homestretch of finding the songbird now. I have no qualms about his pace.

When the luminescent people of the Silver Sands see us coming with the winged God leading the way, they move for us to pass easily. Blue females dot the assortment of shimmering bodies until we arrive at the tunnel that leads down to the snake pit—the very snake pit I jumped into to rescue Dove.

The hair all over my body rises at the memories of losing her and knowing she is close to being lost again.

Never again. I'll never let her be lost to this world. She was meant to be safe with us. I know Fury has the same feelings. As soon as I found out he'd bonded her, I knew that was it for him. Gods create bonds *for* the humans; they don't bond *with* them. From what I know of the Gods from the great wars, they had no interest in sharing their power, especially with mortals. Orion gave his away freely to Dove, as if it cost him nothing.

And then he proceeded to accept Rivern and myself as parts of her. It gave me a new appreciation for the man behind the creator. He is harsh and blunt, but for her, he is soft, and that's all that matters to me.

We walk through the dank underground tunnel and past the snake pit without thought. No one lingers in this place. Fury mentions that they are using it as a thoroughfare for mers to gain access to the Silver Sands territory for their breeding program, which is going better than expected, since the silvers and the mers have much in common.

The news does not surprise me after seeing Moyrie and Calypso together.

Reaching the edge of the water, Calypso jumps in, and Fury continues to talk to Moyrie in another language. My bare feet touch the water, my tail flicking out between the ripped inseam of my pants. *Fuuuucck.* I want to turn and run to Dove; it grows with every moment she is gone. Every moment she's not impaled on my knot makes my groin cramp. I've never felt such maddening unease before, my centuries of restraint coming to a full head because of one human woman.

I feel like I'm going insane. When I was first mated, it was never like this—like I would maul everyone in my path to get to her—yet, here I am, in her orbit, uncaring of the consequences once I find her.

EIGHTEEN

FURY

The energy rippling off Gideon is a beacon. I understand it well because it also radiates through me. I raced to be here after leaving Terra.

Gideon doesn't know what I know, though he is smart. He senses the other Gods' depravity. I know that going in blind is akin to suicide, even though that's all I want to do—run to her. And I nearly did until Gideon talked me out of it when I was in my mind-altered state after waking up from the bond being ripped from us. They already imprisoned me on an island. They could do it again. I am not stupid. This rhythm, it's more than me. It's Dove. It's Gideon. It's Rivern. And the final part of the deal I fulfilled before we left the island.

I place a hand on the wolf's shoulder, hoping it provides some comfort to us both—some sense of normalcy to ground us before I step into the water rippling across the light-coloured sand beneath our feet.

Regardless of how far my creatures are from me, I still

have an inkling as to their whereabouts, and with my God powers, I can send them messages. I don't abuse the power. This is different. It is Dove, and Ken likes my Goddess. And I would kill for her. As soon as I told him I needed him to meet us here for her, that was it. He was on his way.

The water before us parts to make way for him—the kraken, a deep sapphire-blue beast with eight tentacles and two endless, knowing eyes.

"My God." His voice is in my head, talking with reverence. Out of all the beasts, this ocean dweller is devout. He held faith in my return, where the others had seen parts of my humanity he had not yet.

I step further into the water. "My creation, I need your help to save my Goddess."

The cavernous space around us is lined with bronzed wall sconces, highlighting the cerulean beast before us. Differing shades of blue shadow Ken's body.

"Our Goddess. She is gone?" he questions in my mind. Our small entourage looks back and forth, only hearing a one-sided conversation.

I take another step into the lukewarm water. "Yes. She was taken by the other Gods."

A rumble breaks the surface, small waves coming from the vibration of the large creature before us. *"We will kill them."* It's a statement, not a question of how or why. He understands the importance of our mission before we even set sail.

"Hold your breath, my God. We dive deep to get to the surface."

Slippery suckers seal themselves to my bare chest. "The

wolf, too," I add, before I'm whisked away by the urgency of my creation.

"Others?" he asks as another tentacle comes to wrap around Gideon's tawny skin. The wolf swears at the process, the odd slimy sensation unusual even to me.

"Just us two," I answer.

With both of us in his grasp, Ken gives us no warning. The great giant ducks under the water, Gideon and I going with him. Moyrie, Calypso and the cave are long gone in a matter of moments.

Nineteen

Dove

My survival instinct is strong, because the first thing I reach for when Fury leaves is the bowl of stew he left on the edge of the bath. I slurp it down in silence, trying to keep the furnace inside me alive.

Fighting with Fury always does that. However, this still doesn't sit right. Something about it—no, *him*—is off. The God who practically stalked my dreams wouldn't have walked away from a chance to kiss and touch me.

I was naked. He wanted me—

And what was up with his teeth? I've never seen them grow like that before. *None of this makes any sense.*

Finishing the flavourful beefy liquid and quickly scrubbing my skin, I feel like a brand-new person, except two very important parts of me are missing, and I desperately want to touch them, to feel their hearts beat next to mine. Gideon's connection is growing stronger the healthier I get. *Does that mean he's close? If Fury is here, maybe Gideon is close by.*

I need to find them.

Once I'm out of the bath, I wrap an exquisitely fluffy white towel around my body and head through the arch doorway connecting the two spaces. Now that I'm more lucid, I can appreciate the full outlandishness of this room. If I thought Terra or the Haven manor was extravagant, this place really takes the cake. Everywhere I look, the stonework is made to look like art. The ceilings and doorframes are wide enough to fit giants, and the linens draped over the columned arches that lead to an outdoor patio, where the ocean crashes below, are mesmerising. It's almost peaceful here. Idealistic.

As I walk closer to the bed, I realise I'm still waiting for the other shoe to drop, and I have a sinking sensation that it's coming in a Fury-shaped package.

A finely spun, practically see-through dress is waiting for me on the bed. "I can't wear this. I'll be naked." The divine material slips through my fingers as I pick it up. Underneath, I spot creamy, silken undergarments edged in lace that match the colour of my skin. *It seems I won't be completely exposed to onlookers.*

Without options, I drop the towel and put on the underwear. I'm so used to being dressed by Fury or in rags that the novelty of slipping on silk is a small blessing in this fucked-up situation. When it's on, the material feels like I'm naked, it's so soft. Not surprisingly, the fit is perfect. I'm not fond of the string wedged between the cheeks of my bottom. The need to pluck it rubs at me, but the material is so smooth, the sensation goes away after I put the dress on.

With my hair dripping wet, I probably look like a dressed-up drowned rat.

A breeze from the open windows draws me to the

balcony. Stepping past the threshold and watching the two suns move below the water's edge in an array of yellow, orange and red feels surreal. While my body was piecing my sanity back together after the bonds were torn from me, I hadn't acknowledged the gaping hole that sat firmly at the centre of my heart. Grief—the kind that numbed me, the only kind I've ever known—was seeping through every crevice of my being at the sudden stillness.

Out in the distance, a creature jumps through the waves, another one following, their skin glistening in the setting light. *Goddess, it looks so freeing to frolic in the water without a care.*

Gripping the hard stone balcony, I let a tear slip, knowing it won't be the last. It certainly wasn't the first. To crumble now isn't an option. To lie down when I have people to fight my way back to isn't an option. That fire in my core—the one stoked by Fury, Gideon and Rivern, the one that said I was powerful and strong in my own right—means everything to me.

My three protectors saved me from myself. They helped me see myself beyond a mute servant to a fake God. They shared parts of themselves I never thought I'd have the privilege of witnessing in this life. They never wavered in their confidence in me. And now I have to show that I will not waver.

I have to trust Fury.

The air changes when he is near, the wind suddenly stilling with bated breath for him to speak behind me. I don't turn. If I see his face right now, I know my one tear will turn into one hundred.

"You look exquisite, Dove." He uses my name, and my heart skips a beat at his lowered tone.

Blackened claws encircle my waist, a solid gold, criss-crossed belt wrapping around the dress. He then takes my right arm, sliding on a wide but thin shimmering gold bracelet that covers one third of my forearm. He places a matching one on my left arm. A slight sensation of power passes through my wrists. It's gone as soon as my brain understands what's going on, and I brush the feeling aside.

Once he finishes adding the golden adornments, he says, "Come." I want to question why, to scream at him. *Where is Gideon? Where is Rivern?* It's hard to voice the words when everything in me wants to follow this male, take him to bed and repair our bond.

My stomach turns in unending knots. I've never felt such inner strife. *I'm a mess.*

So, I follow him back into the bathroom. The fog of the bath is subdued, the white marble inlaid with gold standing out on the walls and floor. Before me, Fury stands by a dresser with a gilded mirror.

He motions for me to sit.

My face in the mirror says it all, a quizzical look expressing my sadness. Suddenly, I feel so exhausted. My brain spins, trying to match my Fury of the past with this one. When Fury wants me dressed, he blinks, and it's done. This is not my God.

"Where are Gideon and Rivern?" I hold my ground against the man I love.

He huffs in exasperation. "I told you they are safe."

Looking up at him, I stare into pitch-black irises. No

twinkle, not even a glint. Something in me feels shallow, like his answers. He's not going to give me what I want—*them.*

There have been moments in my life when I've had to make the choice: to fight or to surrender. Never in mind, but in body. *Now is one of those times,* I realise, looking into the depths of eyes I once thought I knew.

I suddenly understand that if I want my men back, I'll have to play the game Fury has set.

"Humor me," he says, reaching out for me.

His onyx claw lures me. I have to take it. When I grasp his palm, the warmth he emits confuses me. Before, he has always been so chilling to the touch, like a burn. I can't place it, but something continues to feel wrong about this. Old Fury would be pushing against me at every turn.

If he will not push, I will. Because as much as I can surrender to the outside world, I can't surrender to him. My fire forbids it.

Letting go of his hand, I push into his chest, my nails digging into his hardened muscles. When I look up, his wings are out, incisors on show.

"Please tell me what is going on."

His nostrils flare. "Sit, and I will explain," is his guttural reply.

I aim for pain, digging my nails into his skin, trying to draw blood from the blackened veins within. A smirk crosses his dark lips.

His hand comes to encircle my neck. "Don't tempt me, little flower."

I push my chest against his body. "Why aren't you calling me *Pet?*"

There's a slight knit to his brow—one he thinks I

haven't noticed. *He's hiding something.* "Would you prefer I call you *Pet*?"

"I'd prefer you stop playing whatever game this is and start talking, or our bond will stay permanently severed." At my statement, I expect the full force of his fury or even a sarcastic remark. It's usually one or the other with him. That's not what I get.

Fury eyes me curiously, taking my chin between his thumb and pointer. "Sit down, *Pet*." He overly exaggerates his nickname for me.

There's a feeling of security when he calls me that, like it isn't just a pet name he has for me, but a symbol of our promise. Our forever.

Eternity with him used to seem like the worst thing in the world. Now, I can't imagine the rest of my life without him. However long that is. I'm so used to seeing his face most nights in my dreams that I can't bear our bond staying severed. Not when I now understand the gravity of his feelings for me.

I have to get to the bottom of his sudden shift in mood. That's the only thing puzzling me about this whole situation.

Complying to his demand, I sit on the plush-cushioned stool before me. I should know by now to expect the unknown with this fallen God. Since meeting him, it's been surprise after surprise. *Why is this any different?*

He takes a golden brush from the vanity. Gold seems to be such a plentiful resource in this land. It truly seems fitting for a God realm. The ornateness of it—unlike home, which is filled with deep, woody browns and greens. I can appreciate the beauty of this place. It also solidifies the fact that I don't want to stay here.

The bristles of the brush scratch my scalp as Fury glides the comb through my hair, the itch an aphrodisiac to the trauma of the past several turns. So much so that a groan exits my lips. Hands still in my hair not long before a whisper lands like a delicate tendril at my ear.

"Stop testing me, Flower." His tone has lowered an octave, and he's gone back to calling me *Flower. Maybe I can get used to it. I was a gardener at the temple. It makes sense.*

I close my eyes to his continued ministrations, opting to try to control my breathing as a wanting need pools in my underwear. *He can probably smell me.* I'm not embarrassed about my desire for my three protectors anymore. I've been inside their minds, hearts and souls, as they have mine. There's no room for decorum between us.

"Done." That's all he says as he lets my hair go. I have no idea what he has done or why he hasn't used his magic to do it, but sitting before Fury and having him fuss over me is pure euphoria. I almost feel normal for a second, like our bond wasn't completely ripped to shreds, and we are back home in the safety of our kingdom. What I don't forget is who is missing.

Opening my eyes slowly, light catches on the golden threads having been woven through my hair in intricate braids. It's stunning, and I'm left slightly speechless.

I look from my hair to the raven-winged male standing behind me in the mirror. Anyone would run for the hills, seeing this broad, muscled, horned God coming for them. He's the epitome of *if looks could kill.* Yet, here he stands behind me, having made my hair the most beautiful it's ever looked.

My hand automatically goes to the pain in my chest—the one telling me something is wrong, that we aren't connected the way we should be.

That raging furnace within spurs me on. I stand and turn, stepping onto the small stool, slightly stumbling to the side. Fury catches me, leaving his hands on my hips.

At this new height, I reach for his face, cupping his cheeks.

"I know something is wrong. You're not acting like yourself. Please, Fury, tell me what's going on."

Looking deep into his swirling darkness, I see something change in him. It's only a movement before it's gone just as quickly as it comes.

"I'm trying to keep you safe from them. They are powerful and deadly. Like this"—his gaze sweeps down my human body, lingering on my chest—"you are exposed to them."

"Then bond with me again. Make me yours. Share your power, and we can escape whatever this place is and go find Gideon and Rivern." I pull him against me, our noses touching.

"No." He speaks as if that's the end, like he forgets who I am.

"You don't get to say no to me, Fury." I grip onto his hair, keeping him close. The air shifts suddenly around us. He wants to run. He's not going anywhere. "You're mine." An odd taste of burnt pepper hits my tongue. *Strange.* It only makes me flinch for a movement before I dive in and kiss him.

Not gentle or sweet, because we are neither of those things.

No, this is rough and raw.

It's destruction and consumption.

My core drips for him. For his hands on my body. I get my wish when he gives into my nipping, grasping my bottom and hauling me up against him so I'm no longer straining my neck.

He plunders my mouth, his pointed tongue sweeping between my open lips. I bite down on it. He doesn't back down. Instead, he lets me suck, our teeth scraping, a particular sharp tooth hitting my lip, a copper taste igniting me further, and I sweep my tongue into Fury's mouth.

It's instantaneous, the change in him. The shift when every bone in his body freezes. His pointed claw tips dig into my arse, his mouth frozen over mine, his breathing heavy, laboured.

The air in the room goes cold, stagnant. The body I'm touching, though, is far from cold. It's heated and warm and... new. My brain can't figure out this change.

I look into my God's eyes. He doesn't blink, his incisors having doubled in size.

"What happened to you, my *love*?"

Something in my words sets him off. He's trying hard to maintain his composure. It's not enough. He throws my body against the vanity. My head cracks against the glass, and the last thing I see is Fury walking away from me as my eyes close, my head pounding.

TWENTY

WRATH

Her blood is driving me—the sweetest nectar to grace my lips. If I hadn't left when I did, I would've drained her.

When Oona created me, she made my longevity dependent on the blood of the humans. Every moon break, I require a feeding to keep the hunger at bay. Since *her*, my flower, I've resisted.

I don't know why.

Oona tried to get me to feed on the women the previous moonlight. She made the redhead bleed so much, it tried me to no end. I ended up licking her wounds, the desperation in me hungry for the smallest drop of blood.

I've never gone this long before. Drinking from the humans is a necessary evil that keeps me sane. I'm *not* the monster the humans like to call me.

Drinking from my flower isn't an option. Not only do I take blood, but I also drain the soul. You can't repair a soul that has been ruptured in such a way. Once I finish feeding off the humans who come to me, they leave a shell of themselves, addicted to my touch. It is not uncommon for anyone I've fed from to go missing after a feeding. They lose themselves. During trial periods, Oona makes me round them up to use as bait. She calls it "culling the weak." If you can lose yourself to blood loss, you don't deserve life.

I would never forgive myself if I did that to my flower. She's bright and fiery and strong.

And I left her hurt. I was so fucking torn, I threw her against the vanity to keep her *safe. I hurt her to keep her safe.*

The Gods are expecting us for the first trial in the arena, and now, she's a crumpled mess on the floor in the clothing Oona instructed me to place on her. Clothing that will in no way help her during the trial. The first trial, where I—not *her*—should be Oona's champion, fighting against the humans.

But I have no way to help her. If I smell my flower's blood again, I will drain her.

Here I thought I was so clever, that I could have this one thing. This one human for myself. Dove suspects I'm not him. She knows it. I may look like Fury, but our ways are not the same.

While Oona is alive, she will always control me.

"FUCK," I growl, punching the hard marble wall. The hall leading away from my chambers, where I've left Dove, seems endless.

The pull to go back to her is mightier than anything I've ever known.

Her best chance for survival now is if I distance myself. Pulling away from the wall, I force my legs to move towards the waiting Gods.

TWENTY-ONE

DOVE

M y head hurts. A dull, throbbing pain at the back of my skull pulls me under again and again. It's constant until a loud, booming sound catches my attention.

"Welcome to the Rotational Trials of the Gods. A rhythm for celebration and a rhythm for three of you to prove yourselves as champions. As you all know, each rotation of the suns, the Gods give the Atlans the opportunity to become their personal champions through three different trials. Pain, pleasure and sacrifice. It is a blessing that sees the winners living alongside each of the Gods in the palace." There's a pause. "To begin, each God requires one champion to compete on their behalf. Let's meet our God-chosen."

Shouting and an uproarious beating wake me with a startle.

Godsdamn all of them. The last thing I remember is Fury throwing me against the vanity and leaving—*walking away from me.* The knowledge that he would hurt me and leave me cuts deep, even without our bond connection. This is the God who went to extreme lengths to protect me. Now, suddenly, we are back with the other Gods, and he hurts me.

Numbing grief looms. *I can't lose him—not now. Not after everything.* But this isn't right. *He* doesn't feel right.

My Fury would *never* hurt me.

There's an unease in my stomach that tells me not to believe what I'm seeing. How I wish Argus and Wren were here to lean on again. Right now, I don't want to be the strong one. *I want my childhood imaginings back. I want to be home, in Haven. I want—*

My body is pulled from its prone position on the floor. I sway on my feet, a harsh voice hissing in my ear, "You are a fucking God champion. Compose yourself, human."

"Let me introduce you to Oona's champion, Dove. Zero rotations." My body is lifted from behind, and my head lolls to the side like a rag doll. I try to right it, opening my eyes. The flickering lights and my pounding head cause me to squint.

A collective boooo goes up around me. "Hush, Atlans. It is not the monster, but in Oona, we must trust. This rotation, there's a genuine opportunity for the first rhythm in centuries—a new champion for Oona. For an Atlan to beat this human woman Oona has chosen and be the Goddess's champion in her place. This is a gift from our Goddess. Remember, it's about winning the Gods' favour in each of the three trials."

Again a loud, raucous thundering surrounds me. "Goddess," I mumble, bringing my hands to my ears and holding them.

Opening my eyes again, I blink them to gain some mental clarity. I'm not prepared for the overwhelming sight I see. I open and close them a few more times to make sure I'm not living in my worst nightmare.

Upon peeping open my eyes again, I see the same sight: a stadium of people. I've never seen so many people in one place before. The gatherings we used to hold at the one-Goddess temple in Haven could never compare.

This is something else. Above the stars, shining bright, the moon is big and round. And when I pan my head slowly around to avoid more trauma to my throbbing skull, rows and rows of seated people are cheering. The rows are continuous; they go around in circles that end at the platform I stand on. Looking below, there's a large, circular pit of some sort. On either side of the ground seem to be gates. With my tender head, I narrow my eyes witnessing a large bonfire in the centre, the firelight matching the flaming pyres dotting the seated area.

My stomach twists from straining my eyes for so long, and I buckle forward, vomiting up the stew I ate in the bath. That seems like a turn ago instead of moments.

A large hand comes to cup under my elbow, lifting me. "Don't show weakness." I grumble something unintelligible at the hard-edged voice, moving to my full height. "They will eat you alive to gain a spot as Oona's champion."

Oona's champion? "What—"

I turn to the person next to me. Just as quickly as the words are spoken, the calloused hand is removed, and the man standing next to me is looking forward.

"Everybody, make some noise for Osear's champion, the incomparable Bear. Eleven rotations." The man beside me—

the one I swear just spoke to me—steps forward and waves to the people, thumping his shining breastplate. He's wearing golden armour, a helmet under his right arm, a mess of brown waves curling around his face.

He doesn't acknowledge me again. When the crowd has finished their shouts of approval, he steps back, making way for another man wearing the same golden armour.

I obviously missed the dress code.

"And last, we have the ever-enchanting Lune, Oriel's chosen. Six rotations as champion." The golden-haired man plays the crowd, blowing kisses with his free hand.

Gazing down at my see-through gown, I wince. *How are these men in full armour, and I'm in a gown that leaves nothing to the imagination? I'm totally fucked. Fury has fucked me.* He was the one who left me in this outfit and helped me get ready.

The only conclusion I can come to is that he lied. He's been lying this whole time. Fury *doesn't* love me. He *doesn't* care about me.

Everything has been one big lie.

Gods, it sends a dagger through my shattered heart to even think such a devastating thing, because I know it's not true. When he opened himself to me before leaving for Haven, I saw inside his heart—his soul. He hated the other Gods with the sort of anger you reserve only for your worst enemy. And he loved me beyond rhythm and space. It felt eternal, unbreakable.

He would kill himself before he hurt me.

Something is wrong. It has to be. He isn't himself. They have altered him. Just like the Silver Sands aphrodisiac that made Rivern, Gideon and me act out of character. There has to be something sinister the other Gods have done to Fury.

The ache in my heart and the tug in my stomach demand it. He isn't himself; even the temperature of his skin is off, and his smell—pepper. *Where is his ashy darkness?*

Moving forward, I will be his strength and find a way to get us out of this. He has saved me so many times before. I might have freed him from his island prison, but if we are truly counting score, I still owe him. In reality, the score doesn't matter because he belongs to me and I belong to him. And I will do whatever I must to keep him safe, even if that means facing off against Oona, Osear and Oriel.

Just like Gideon and Rivern. All three are my end. If I have to die saving one of them, that is what I will do.

Thinking of my three protectors gives me the boost I need. The love they have shared with me, expressed, felt, every inch of my skin they have licked, fuels me. Suddenly, the throbbing in my head doesn't feel as bad.

Standing tall, I push my hands through my hair, trying to assess the wound at the back. I find a wet patch, but it's small. Nothing I can't manage. Abruptly, a memory of harsh, punishing hands shaking my small, childlike frame grips me. *My head hitting a wall behind me.* I flinch. My father could never control his liquor intake, and if we didn't give him the right answer, he'd pick a fight with me, my sister or my mother.

Fear was a powerful motivator in my family. It seems impossible to count the number of rhythms I've hidden in a cupboard or closet to evade him. And the last time, when I watched as Wren was forever lost before my eyes... The smell of burning flesh fills my nose. *As long as this trial doesn't involve my body near that large, burning bonfire in the middle of the field, I'll be fine.*

I'll be fine.

The licking of the flames below holds my attention. I breathe in deeply.

Please let me have a reprieve. It's a prayer I send up to the fates, because I know the Gods down here aren't listening to me. Not anymore.

I'm all alone.

An odd whirr rolls through my ears from side to side, making me feel adrift for a moment. I shoot a hand out to hold onto the balcony before me. I have this overwhelming sense of being watched, everyone's leering gazes on me. Turning my head, I find the God champion, Lune, inclining his head my way. His handsome features are scarred, but somehow, it adds to his magnetism.

Catching myself staring into his blue eyes, he winks at me. I ignore him, quickly gaining my balance just as the ominous voice booms out of the sea of people again.

"The trials!" it announces. "The three trials are the backbone of the Gods' games. They sort out the weak from the brave. Only someone of immense mental strength and fortitude can serve a God. The Gods require sacrifice in their chosen, and that will be seen on the battlefield today."

Battlefield? Are they kidding? Of course there's a battlefield. The Gods are sick. They thrive on violence.

"Trial one is of pain. Not only will this trial test your capabilities with a weapon, but it will also test your cunning and strength. The last contestants and champions standing on the battlefield when the bell rings will progress to the next trial." There's a large pause as the crowd mulls over the words of the announcer. I barely make it through the part where he mentions weapons. Down by the sides of the two armoured men next to me are swords—the kind of blades that would cut off one's head in a single strike.

I rub my hands against the gossamer of my dress. *What is my weapon? Kill them with exposure.* I have a feeling these Atlans are very familiar with the carnal flesh. After all, the fact that my body is mostly on show will not stop anyone from slicing me in two.

The ominous voice continues into the void, "As is customary, all Atlans have the ability to compete in the trials to become the next champion of the Gods. However, to become your chosen God's champion, you will need to kill the current champions, Bear, Lune and Dove." When the voice says my name, my heart falls. "Humans competing for Oona's favour will wear a gold band around their wrist." I raise my wrists to see my matching gold bands sparkle in the moonlight. "Humans competing for Osear's favour will wear a silver band around their wrist. And humans competing for Oriel's favour will wear a turquoise band around their wrist. Our first trial will begin momentarily, so please take your seats."

At that end, I hear more whoops and cheers from the people sitting before us. "Move," a gruff guard decked out in all-gold armour like those Bear and Lune wear is pushing me to follow the two other champions moving beyond the balcony we are being displayed on and to an indoor staircase that goes down.

At the end of the staircase, I'm pushed through the curved doorway big enough to fit the tall men before me. I place my hands in front of my body to catch myself as I run into Bear.

"Sorry," I mumble, crashing into his metal armour with a thud. He turns, face impassive and unreadable, looking down at me with dark brown eyes.

He continues to give nothing away as he pushes into my body and leans down to whisper just for me, "Take this. You'll need it." A shiver prickles my skin as those same calloused fingers that propped me up back on the balcony place something hard in my hand. I grip it tightly.

Turning, he advances towards the bonfire, standing before one of the large, arched metal doors.

Bringing my hand before me, I finally see what Bear has gifted me with: a dagger, my only weapon in this trial. I want to thank him. This blade might be my only salvation in this war against the Gods.

Fury isn't magically coming to save me. Neither is Rivern, nor Gideon. I'm alone here.

I take a step forward, my bare feet not liking the harsh bite of the sharp rocks against my exposed skin. *Sorely underdressed* is putting my state mildly. My head still throbs lightly. It's more manageable now. I've had broken bones before. A slight throb is doable. It doesn't compare to my heart screaming for its lost connections. Including my mate bond with Gideon, which is still fully intact and calling out for him. It's the rhythm and space wearing me thin, causing me pain. It feels like my skin is physically rippling to find him, constantly searching for him in a room I know he's not in. If he were here, I'd feel my wolf before I ever saw him.

"It looks like our newest recruit needs a nudge in the right direction." The voice without a form notifies everyone.

I do not know what I'm doing. *What does this place want of me?* "Shall we play a game of hot or cold?" The group stomps their feet. "Very well, then. Dove, Oona's champion, listen to the rules. If you are close to your place in the trial field, we will say *hot*, and when you are far, we will say *cold*. Move!"

My body jolts into movement at the loud voice, running on pure adrenaline.

"COLD." The people in the stands shout and laugh as I take a step forward. I understand the premise of the game. Wren and I used to play something similar when we were young. It's not the game that is the problem. No, it's the inferno at the centre of the field—the one the people are shouting at me to go towards—that is giving me pause.

Endless blue eyes blink into sight. "*Save me,*" they scream.

I stop. The heat from the fire pricks at the scar on my neck—the one that has seemed to vanish along with my insecurities. Now, it's back with a vengeance, letting me know old hurts, old wounds. They never fully disappear. They're always under the surface. It's how you cope with them in the present that defines you. Flashes of my father escape the confines of my heart to assault me, Argus no longer the barrier before my cave of secrets, forcing them to stay hidden.

How will I let this crippling experience define me? Will I let my abusive father ruin my present? He killed my whole family; my mother, my sister and nearly me.

It was pure luck I wasn't dragged back within the vengeful flames. I may have landed on the doorstep of another devil, but the high priestess's cruelty was more mentally draining by nature than physical. The woman never laid a finger on me and never lost her cool. That didn't stop her from taking pieces of me.

Each step towards the blaze is stifling, like I can't breathe, the workings of my cave of secrets fully open to the elements, entirely exposed to me for the first rhythm in a long time.

Thanks to Argus, I never fully experienced the grief, rage or pain of what the losses in my life equate to.

Now, as the Atlans shout, "*Hot!*" and I stand mere feet from the torrid smoke and flames, I can appreciate what this is. It is beauty in its wildness. It is strength in its boundless limits. And it is courage in its force. Since seeing Wren being taken from me, I see her smiling in the fire, happy in the sticky heat. I can find beauty in this inferno, just like I find in Saff's and my own.

Finally, I turn my back on the once-tormenting sight now behind me, and look at a giant metal door.

"Your time starts now. Let the games begin," are the last words the speaker announces before all hell breaks loose.

TWENTY-TWO

DOVE

My first thought is to run, and my eyes dart around for a way out. Stone walls are erected around the circle before us, with three large metal doors firmly placed at evenly spaced intervals in the arena. One regular-sized door we entered through previously is firmly shut and no doubt locked. The only ways currently not locked to us are the three large chained gates that are slowly rising to allow access to the people I see standing beyond them—the people who are going to fight us to become the next God champions.

There's no way out of this hell. I'm stuck, and so are the people who plan on joining this "trial." We will all be stuck in this raging inferno together.

I clutch the dagger I was given firmly in my fist, hiding it in the folds of my dress, down by my leg.

"Godsdammit, Fury," I hiss under my breath. *He's here. He has to be.* He dressed me for this event. Since I find no way out down here, I look up.

Up is not much better. The stone walls are scaled so high that there's no way even Bear or Lune could climb them. Above are the humans, hanging on a collective gasp, waiting for the gates to finish rising.

The people in the stands are dressed in a mix of colourful fabrics—a veritable rainbow. Seeing these people in such colours speaks of their ability to afford the finer things in life. In Haven, all people could afford was muted, secondhand material, not like the brightness that currently blinds me.

With the moments ticking by, I quickly scan the circle above. That's when I see her. *It has to be her—Oona.* She's the most beautiful woman I've ever laid eyes on. If I thought the colourful fabrics of the Atlans in the stands were blinding, this woman is dazzling. A golden halo practically surrounds her. Wings as fine as silk, hair flowing to her hips, tall and lithe. Her sparkling irises are on me, lips upturned like she knows a secret I don't yet understand.

If the secret is that I'm going to die in this arena at her hand, it's not much of a surprise.

A flash of grey jolts into my periphery. I do a double-take of the person now standing next to Oona. It takes a moment for my synapses to fire on all cylinders.

When it registers, it's an agonising stab to the heart, like I've taken the dagger Bear gave me, pushed it into my chest and twisted in a full circle, not missing an artery. It is followed by throwing my whole body into the pit of heated dispair behind me.

Next to Oona stands *Fury.*

Not the stoic Fury. Not the angered Fury.

Next to Oona stands a Fury I've never seen before. One

who has reached his arm around her waist and pulled her tightly into his side. One who whispers in her ear and kisses her cheek.

Fury isn't himself, I repeat the phrase in my head again and again. *She's somehow got her claws into him.* However, it doesn't stop the anger that boils within the pits of my soul, higher than the tallest fucking inferno, at the sight. The fire at my back has no bearing on what I'm holding inside.

He hasn't noticed me yet, or the rage in my bones that rattles to be set free.

If he were in front of me, he would know pain. This dagger would see the inside of his heart—the one I thought I knew like the back of my hand.

Oona's gaze is still on me, but it's not her attention I want, or the other Gods'. I want Fury to notice me. I want him to look up and lock eyes with me. I need to see his soul; only his eyes can tell me how far he is gone now to the Goddess.

Finally, he does, dark orbs of indifference finding mine. I tug on the lingering thread still connecting us, the last frayed vestiges of our bond still holding out hope for the fallen God who spent his whole imprisoned existence protecting me.

He looks towards the crowd as if he doesn't even know me, like I'm the silly little human speck on his shoe he hopes to be rid of momentarily.

The Atlans around us suddenly scream, *"Pain."* My thoughts whir in a tangled knot.

I dismiss the Gods on the balcony and look towards the gates, where a mass of Atlans are using hammers, carving knives and fists to beat the surrounding people. I'm momentarily stuck on what I just witnessed on the balcony. The people slicing into each other barely register until the sound of people screaming out, "*Pain,*" is all I hear.

They think this is pain. I will show them pain.

Ire boils inside of me like never before, itching to be seen, to be known. A blurred figure staggers towards me with a crimson tipped carving knife. Blood trickles down its blade, the woman holding it crinkled in the face. I'm surprised she made it this far. Her bones are visible through her sagging skin.

She has a slight limp to her gait, but it doesn't stop her. The blade comes out, aiming for me, and I step back. The older woman sneers at me. She looks like a beast, a blood-stained yellow dress falling off her right shoulder.

I've been on the precipice of death multiple times in my life. This barely registers. The woman before me doesn't see it coming when she pushes forward again. I move to the side and dig the point of my dagger through her. The old woman's knife lashes out, catching my thigh and slicing.

"Fuck," I wheeze through gritted teeth, pain only amplifying my anger.

Blood trickles down my leg, but the woman advances again. We swing our blades, mine slicing her cheek and hers cutting my upper arm. The wound stings, though it's nothing compared to what I know is going to come if the people behind keep advancing.

I won't go down without a fight.

Both of us bleeding out, we go to attack again, the pointed tips of our blades covered in blood and ready to strike.

A glint of gold catches my attention from behind the woman, and her head is unexpectedly gone. Lune is there, then vanishes. *He saved me.* The woman's body takes a moment to crumple to the floor. I still think I could have taken her, even if Lune hadn't intervened. His glinting, armoured form slices through other Atlans as he stalks around the bonfire, unfazed.

The throbbing pain in my leg and arm numbs any other emotions, except for the anger that continues to fester.

I could die in this arena. Fury watching.

Death at the Gods' doing.

None of this is right.

A lump forms in my throat, and all I want to do is scream at the top of my lungs. Instead, I throw the dagger at the ground. The crowd must be watching, because a collective *"Ooooo"* rises through the stands—the first noise I've heard from the Atlans since they shouted, *"Pain."*

If this is how I die, I'm going out my way. For an instant, I'm reminded of the song that saved me so many times. Her song—*Oona*.

Just thinking her name ignites the licking flames inside of me, and I pull. I gather and tug and draw on that lingering, fraying thread in my stomach that belongs to the God who refuses to see me. With all my ire, I imagine it knitting back together, my flames welding our bond back in place —one that should've never been destroyed in the first place.

The one created from a deal, now one of my most favourite possessions. A possession no one is taking from me. I will no longer let others take what is mine. The Gods will rue the turn they brought me to this place. If I have to claw the magic back from Fury to do it, I will.

Before me, men and women inflict pain on each other as

they edge closer, blood raining down on the dirt. A iron, ashy scent clogs the air.

The smell spurs me on, that sooty aroma of an island prison, of my Fury before. The one who was going to share a lifetime with me. I tug harder at our thread, seeing it fully formed in my mind's eye, feeling the power I have experienced through my veins before finding me.

Like a spark igniting, I sense its completion. But is it enough to save me from this chaos the Gods have put me through? *Just another pawn in their never-ending game.*

All around me, people are clashing, calling for blood. The unnecessary fatalities, the way these Gods are asking for death in their name, is my undoing. I've spent the last four-teen rotations wishing for my sister back, and these people eagerly ask for death. There's no salvation here. Only destruction.

I fall on my knees, and an eager, brawny-looking man with an axe comes my way.

"Pet." It's a whisper in my mind. A recognised syncing of our beating hearts. The bloody man before me lifts his axe, a menacing incline to his cheeks.

"PET." This moment, it's a scream. And I know I've made a terrible mistake. Power pours through me at our slight connection, like he's trying to push everything he has into me. The furnace in me runs hot, stoking to scalding at the power flowing through me.

When the axe comes down, it shatters on impact. Shards of steel fly out around us.

I don't dare look up, knowing the man with the axe will use his hands next.

"Dove, answer me right now, or there's hell to pay. We are

coming for you." With my head bent, I focus on his voice. *My* Fury's unmistakable need for protection. *He won't be able to save me. None of them will.*

DONG. A drum rings, and rhythm ceases to exist.

I push back tendrils of my hair and look up to face the axe-wielding man. He's not looking at me. Instead, his eyes are on the balcony, where three Gods reside.

"The first trial is finished," the disembodied voice announces.

All that can be heard from the onlookers is silence. The muscled man before me drops to his knees, exhaustion written all over his face. I look up towards the balcony that houses the Gods, noticing Oriel and Osear, just as beautiful as Oona. I don't linger on them. They are not who I am after. Instead, I find "Fury." Grey skin, curved, onyx horns, feathered wings. He is every inch of him, yet he is not.

"We are coming for you, Pet." Just to solidify my suspicion, *my* Fury's voice is in my head again, the tether in my stomach pulling tighter and tighter as if my body knows he is gaining. I stand, my brows coming together, my lips pressed to form a stern line.

I must be a sight, bleeding, dishevelled and angry.

Now, I know that this fallen God lookalike, the exact replica of Fury standing beside the Gods, is not mine. He never was.

My Fury would never hurt me. He would burn the world down to get to me. He would give me all of his power, even if that meant he was left with nothing. His love is endless. His love is unconditional. He hates his fellow Gods with a passion so strong there's barely any room to move. And he would never let them trick or coerce him.

I was wrong.

"*Liar,*" I mouth the word at the imposter. I don't know how she did it. He looks exactly like him.

"*To all the fates, answer me, Pet.*" That's my Fury.

"*Thanks for the save,*" I reply through the small connection I threaded back together between us—one built on anguish and pure rage. His presence is growing, and so is my wolf mate's. Now that I've opened the floodgates to them, they are barrelling in full force.

"*To your right,*" are Fury's clipped words before the beast of all beasts comes bounding through the gates opposite Bear.

"Gideon." Pure relief washes over my body as my mate-bound wolf shifter comes hurtling towards me at untold speeds in his full wolf form. His black fur glimmers in the moonlight, his amber eyes solely on me as he pushes past any human in his way.

He slows down just before he reaches me, swiping me around the midsection with a paw and holding me aloft, tucked up against his chest, standing tall on his back legs. In his fully shifted form, he's the biggest creature in this stadium.

Sandalwood and warm spice lull me into safety, the thudding of his steady heart the best sound in the world.

"I missed you so much," I murmur into his fur, gripping it tightly. He grunts, lightly flexing his enormous paw around my waist.

Power continues to thrum through me, searching for its true match. The solace I feel in knowing Gideon and Fury are safe leaves me breathless and once again utterly exhausted.

A combined gasp rolls through the stands as they see him. Fury, the God, in all his godly power, is walking with purposeful steps towards us, his hair looking slightly damp. Silver strands drip down onto his bare chest.

I melt at the sight of him. Luckily, my wolf keeps me pressed close to his chest, because having Fury this close with his power running through my blood, looking like he's about to eat me alive... A noticeable silver thread around his irises could be my undoing.

He stops before us, and Gideon growls.

"Come on, big boy, we are on the same team here." My wolf continues his imposing stance.

Fury huffs. "I thought this would happen. Lover beast here has had a hard time controlling his wolf form since you've been gone, so we may be stuck with him like this until he realises you are safe."

My eyebrows quirk. "I don't know if you've noticed the blood, but I wouldn't call this place safe."

"Riiiggght." He takes his eyes off me for a second. "And just so you know, 'Thanks for the save' is not an appropriate response to your demise."

"What would you rather I say?" I retort, missing our quips.

"*I love you. Thank you for coming to my rescue. You're the only God for me. I want to worship at the altar of your cock.* Take your pick." He holds his hands out.

"Are you serious right now?" I squirm in Gideon's grasp. "If I were closer, I'd slap you."

Fury smirks. *Gods, I missed that mischievous smile.* "I'm as serious as the guards surrounding us and the three Gods currently staring venomously at my back."

This male has the ability to make me forget about everything else, except for the wolf holding me, and the fae prince I still haven't seen yet.

He's right, of course. I totally missed the golden ensemble of armoured guards surrounding us.

"Welcome, Orion." When the voice reaches my ears, it has a body. I look up to see Oona, with fake Fury standing next to her. Following Gideon's lead, I growl. He huffs a bit, and I hope that means he approves. It didn't sound as menacing as his.

"It has been an age. I see you have found a way off your island." Fury doesn't look at her. He keeps his eyes on me, using me as his compass so he doesn't lose his head.

"It would've stayed an age if you hadn't taken my bonded Goddess." My eyes flick from Oona to Fury. She doesn't like that he called me his Goddess. Her whole body goes rigid.

"It seems we have a lot to discuss. How about we do it over a meal?"

"Do I have a choice?"

"No." Her twinkling voice lingers around the stadium. "If you notice the golden cuffs around my champion's wrists, they will keep her bound to the trials until she either finishes them all or dies. Essentially, you will not be able to leave Atla. Out of respect for my champion, I offer you a meal and accommodation. Wrath will show you to your quarters."

What the actual fuck? I raise my hands, the bracelets on either wrist twinkling in the moonlight. At the mention of her champion, cuffs and not being able to leave, I practically see the steam rising from Fury's ears, the silver in his eyes blowing out to black. "Fine."

"Excellent choice. Shields, back to your duties." With one flick of her wrist, the sea of golden armour circling us is gone, and a black-winged Fury lookalike is flying down to meet us.

"Wrath, I presume," my God grumbles, looking his replica up and down.

"Correct." Wrath nods at Fury, ignoring me completely. The lack of any need to communicate what happened between us and what he did to me leaves the erratic organ in my chest heavy.

Sensing my downer mood, Gideon tucks me into his hard muscles and carries me out of the arena. With two of my protectors back in my orbit, I can almost relax. *Almost.*

WRATH

"Follow me," I instruct the God, human and beast at my back. Oona gave strict instructions to take them to her guest wing, not that we ever use that part of the palace.

She planned this as a contingency. The shock on her face said she thought it wouldn't be so soon. She wanted it to be after the trials, when the human was either dead or so worn down, she was unrecognisable.

None of us expected Dove to wield Orion's magic. The bond is meant to be severed. Apparently, it isn't. Oona, Osear and Oriel have never tried to bond with a human, let alone share their power. That was unfathomable.

Power belongs to the Gods, not to the humans.

Even my longevity relies on my feeding on the lifeblood of others.

The Gods are singular in their creation, and they don't share.

However, the God following me through the guest wing, silent and full of hatred, is an anomaly to me. Everything Oona has expressed about Orion has been spiteful. She told me he is cruel, a killer and has to be stopped. That if he were free, he would spare no human life.

That is at odds with the God who shares his power with a human. A fallen God who forsakes his own life, going up against Oona, Osear and Oriel—who imprisoned him—to save one small human woman.

Not just any woman—Dove. Given the opportunity, I'd also want to share my life with her. I *was* trying to trick her into being with me, after all.

None of what Oona told me is right, though. Over the centuries, I've learnt to discern her falsehoods from her truths. They are always woven together in an intricate tangle. This one seems, from the outset, to be another lie.

It doesn't surprise me. I barely trust her anymore. If I had the chance to leave, I would. For me to leave would be death, and I'm not sure I'm ready for that. For once, I want to experience a true connection with another before my demise comes to pass. It is idiotic of me to think that I could convince the human to feel for me like she does for Orion.

The more and more she pushed for us to be closer, the more I felt a sickening turn of my insides. I never wanted her to love me as Fury. I wanted her to love me as Wrath.

The bloodlust is also another unforeseen consequence.

I need to feed before sunrise.

Coming to a set of white double doors, I turn the bronze handles and push them open, facing my twin. *Gods, it's like looking in a mirror.*

"This will be your quarters. I will fetch you for your

meeting with the Gods of Atla when the suns have risen to their highest peak. If you require anything, call on the godlins." I gesture inside the palatial guest suite, where a small army of short, stubby golden servants prepares the room for guests. The gold-lined marble twinkles in the moonlight streaming through the open doors beyond, and a soft ocean breeze trickles through, masking the stagnant smell in the air.

The black marble walls and the sides of the palace are situated on a cliff face, granting every bedroom ocean views. I have always loved watching the waves in the light of the moon, how they tussle and race against each other.

Tearing my gaze from the windows to the open bedroom door, my thoughts immediately race to them sharing one bed. Dove in another man's arms all night long. My eyes flit to her curled-up form in the powerful embrace of the prickly wolf who stands on two legs, cradling her.

Orion takes a step closer to me. "Don't even think about laying your eyes upon her again. She's mine, and you are nothing but Oona's lapdog," the God spits his words at me, the power radiating off him palpable in the surrounding air. *If I had that kind of power...*

Holding my ground, I stare into his swirling silver irises —the same colour I sometimes find mixed with the light, stark green of Dove's. "You don't need to worry about me, but you should know that the other Gods want your head. And they will kill your bonded for sport."

There. It's all out on the table. Now, he can't say I didn't warn him. The nicety of giving them a suite over the dungeon is purely for theatrics. Oona loves a show.

The darkness of his eyes bleeds through the silver. It's

eerie, watching yourself stand before you with the power you wish you had.

"Noted," Orion bites back, ushering the wolf inside, slamming the door in my face.

GIDEON

MATE.

MINE.   MINE.

SAFE.

BITE.

BITE.   BITE.

MATE.   SAFE.

MINE.

SAFE.   BITE.

MATE.

MINE.

MINE.

BITE.   MATE.

BITE.   BITE...

FURY

She created a fucking clone of me. The stone archway I hold between my hands crumbles with the force of my anger. I step back from the debris to look at the oversized wolf curled around our Goddess. Only moments ago, he was licking her wounds clean.

When I look at her now, *fragile* is the word that comes to mind, however, I know she's anything but. My Goddess is stronger than any God I've ever known. That human lying in the arms of my beast brought together the whole of the Forgotten Lands and solidified the last string that still wove us together. *Fates, if they have hurt—*

I can't think about that. Gideon must know by now. His mate bond is strong. Her pheromones are sweeter than I've ever smelt, more honeyed than before. It's addictive. As much as the anger of the turn runs through me—my hate towards the other Gods, and the vengeance I want to partake in—I can't see past solidifying our bond to its full strength. It currently feels sluggish, like she is there, but also far away. I want her to be right next to me. Now more than ever, it's a hunger.

Dove knitted the one thread that still connects us back together, but there's still thousands more to go. That one thread is strong enough for her to have drawn power under extreme stress. It's not enough to protect her. And those cuffs around her wrists present another complication.

I pace. *If I am to complete the bond again, will Oona just seek to strip Dove of it once more to punish me?* To risk her like that again would be selfish. The moment I touch her, I'll be gone, unable to stop myself. I know it. So, for now, I will watch her sleep. Keep her safe. And never let her out of my sight again.

Twenty-Six

Rivern

The pointed needle in my hand draws a deep groove into the line of my forearm. Sitting on the ground in front of my fireplace feels tantamount to prayer, except my Goddess is Dove. Each mark represents my connection to her. We may no longer be bound by Oona, however, she is bonded to my heart and soul for eternity. Fated by the stars.

"Are you going to do me next?" the sound of her sweet, husky voice calls to me.

"You're back." I neglect the needle at my arm, dropping it to my side.

"I'm back." She grins down at me.

Every rhythm Dove returns to me in my subconscious, she looks even more ravishing than the last.

She lingers over my shoulder, looking at my handiwork. "It's silver."

"It's you." I hold up my forearm. The fireplace before us crackles loudly. Silky hair falls next to my face. Soft fingers trail over my arm where the silver meets the gold, weaving vines dance around each other, wisps and roses emerging.

"This is me," her breath whispers over my skin. Blood mingles with the silver. She smudges the red with her finger, bringing it to her lips.

"Yes, you and me." Her lips linger.

"Mmm, can you do me now?"

"Sit." I tap the place between my open legs. She sinks her petite body between my outstretched thighs on the plush green rug beneath us. Dove is dressed in my tunic. It's way too big for her, so it falls to her knees.

She pulls her hem up, showing off her thigh. "Start here," she instructs.

"Tell me if it hurts," I murmur as she adjusts her body between my limbs.

Her milky skin is mesmerising, and I lose myself for a moment, my thumb rubbing back and forth. "Well, I wouldn't say it hurts."

We both chuckle as I bring the pointed end of the needle against her flesh. Her skin is more delicate than mine, so I know I will not have to be as heavy-handed. Just a prick should be enough to pierce the skin and place the ink underneath the surface.

"Oh." She flinches when the needle hits her flesh, and I stop instantly.

"I don't have to keep going. There are many other ways we could have fun." I squeeze her thigh.

She shakes her head. "No, I want this with you. I want your mark on my skin." Taking my hand with the needle, she draws it against her skin. "Tell me what's going to happen when we are back home, and I get to touch you for real."

When she utters those words aloud, my heart practically bursts in my chest. It solidifies the fact that we aren't really together. Instead, we are separated by vast ocean waters.

"I can do that." I kiss her head, continuing the spirals I'm making on her thigh. Suns, vines and roses of gold and silver begin the picture of us.

Sitting in silence while I focus, the crackling fire, I finally speak everything I see for her and us. "The first thing I plan on doing when we are together is folding you into my arms and never letting you go. But I know I will have to eventually because of those other two brutes." She huffs and takes a deep breath as I drag the needle across her skin. My lips reach for her temple, a sigh escaping her.

"After we make love"—her hand reaches out for my thigh and squeezes hard, nails digging in—"we will start our lives together. Just the four of us, in a cottage we build. Or, most likely, that Fury conjures out of thin air."

"I like the sound of you all chopping down wood and building it with your bare hands better." Goddess, I'd kill to do that for her.

"Hmmm. That can be arranged." I rest the needle, letting her have some breathing space.

"You're finished?" she asks, surprised.

"Not even close. I just wanted you to catch your breath."

Turning in my grip, she gets on her knees before me.

"Careful. Your thigh." I place my hand on her freshly tattooed leg.

"Okay, but first, I want you to promise me something." Almost eye to eye, her big green pools stare at me with hope and wonder.

"Anything." Dove already has me, and when she's in my arms again, I won't ever take her for granted.

Her arms weave around my neck, pulling us closer. "Promise you'll build me that cottage when we are together again."

I'll build her one hundred cottages. "I promise." Her face lights up with the most glorious smile, and I pull her waist into me, bringing her lips to mine and sealing our promises of forever with a kiss.

TWENTY-SEVEN

DOVE

I wake to unrelenting heat and the sound of heavy snoring. Opening my sleep-crusted eyes, tufts of black fur tickle my skin. Taking a deep breath, all I feel and see is Gideon—sandalwood and spice. *Heaven.* The security I feel within this dyre wolf's arms is incomparable, except to that of my fae prince and fallen God.

Yet, the dream of Rivern weighs heavy on my soul. *Where is he?* I need to speak to Fury right after I deal with the pressure in my abdomen.

"Gideon," my voice is ragged as I say his name.

A snort comes between his warm breaths that tickles the back of my neck.

"He's sleeping." It's Fury—the *real* Fury. The tug in our last remaining thread confirms it. I don't know how I could've been so wrong. Being with him is unparalleled. His lookalike barely scratched the surface of my draw to the fallen God when I'm in his presence.

"What do you need, Pet?" Gods, do I want to wrap my

arms around him and never let go. After pushing him away for so long and being on the cusp of losing him, all I can think about is finally having him in my arms again.

"I need to go to the toilet."

"Hmmm." He sighs. "Gideon's wolf is unwilling to let you go. Maybe if we replaced your body with a pillow?" All I hear is his voice as I stare at the heavy rise and fall of my wolf's chest.

"Is he sleeping?" I ask, trailing my fingers through Gideon's fur. Being in his arms is enough to settle every ache from our separation. It's not that I want to leave his embrace, but more that I have to. If anything, I want more of him now that I am rested. I need to feel our physical connection again.

"For the most part. Here." Pointed fingers snake around my ankle.

Fury tugs me down gently as I try to wiggle out of my wolf's embrace. It doesn't work.

Gideon's amber eyes fly open, and a low rumble moves through his expansive chest at my leaving. I've never seen him stay in his wolf form for such an extended period of time. *It has something to do with our separation,* our mate connection whispers to me. He needs us to be close so he can find himself again. And I want that too. Having him in this form for life isn't the most practical. Everything about him is huge.

"Gideon, I need to go to the toilet. Please," I plead. The hot exhalation from his nostrils caresses my cheek.

He stalls, as if thinking for a moment, and sinks his head down to his chest. I almost expect him to let me go, but of course, he doesn't. Stretching his limbs first, he then grasps his paws around my midsection. I try to wrap my legs around his waist to hold on. With the size of his body, it's hard to get my legs to fully encircle him.

A second lot of footsteps follows us into the bathroom, my face burrowed into exquisite warmth.

Once we are beyond the threshold of the stark white-and-gold room, I drop my legs to slink down my dyre wolf's furry, muscular stomach. The big beast reluctantly lets me go, my body shivering in our extraction. I may be tired and hungry, however, that hasn't stopped the desire I have for any of my males. They set off a magical spark that ignites my core. And it's never at convenient times.

Turning in his grasp, I try to ignore the throb in the lace underwear I still have on. We stand in a similar bathroom to the one I got ready in with the *fake* Fury. Bitterness seeps through my marrow at the thought of Oona's spy. *Don't think of him. He lied to you.*

The light of the rising suns streams through the windows. Stone and marble cover the walls and floor, and a deep bath filled with trickling water from a spout by the windows beckons me. On the opposite wall of where the bath waits, there's a large, tiled expanse with a walled seat, and above that, some type of strange, glinting bronzed chandelier.

Still in Gideon's grasp, I ask him to let go. His reluctant grunt tickles my hair. "I'll be fine. You can still see me." I point to the golden seat tucked into the corner of the room. He lets out somewhat of a pained groan before I'm released.

My body feels like it's missing a limb as soon as I'm without him, and I almost consider running back into his arms. I don't, though. Not with the toilet in sight. Seeing it spurs me on tenfold.

Before I sit, I quickly strip off my underwear. They are beautiful and butter-soft, but hold the blood and dirt of the trial. I no longer want to be reminded of the crazed men and women who fought for Gods who no longer served their interests. Gods who never served *anyone's* interest.

With my chin in my hand, two violet orbs linger in my field of vision. *Rivern.*

"You still haven't told me where Rivern is yet," I say to the glossy marble beneath my feet.

"He's in Terra, waiting for you." Fury's velveteen voice causes my skin to prickle.

"Is he okay?" Since our bond broke, I have no inkling of his health or safety. It's a constant weight on my mind, thinking of him. Fears plague me; his face is shallow and pale.

"The prince hit some complications after the bond was severed." *Complications?*

Liquid spray jolts me to look up. The wide chandelier on the other side of the room streams droplets of what looks to be water on the floor, where it seeps into the ground. I blink again to make sure what I'm seeing is real. *Rain is falling from the ceiling?*

"What complications?" I ask, standing, ready to run. I don't know where to—Rivern, I suppose.

"Nothing you can't fix with your mouth."

"Fury!"

At that very moment, I notice my naked God duck his head under the spray, and I'm frozen in my tracks. My eyes are wide. My mouth is salivating. My chest is beating erratically. The tug in my stomach desperately urges me to go to him. My lips tingle to kiss every inch of his toned, glistening body.

Gods be damned, he's hot. This is the first rhythm I've seen him on display for me in such a way. No pants, just pure, unadulterated grey skin stretched over sinuous muscle. His wings flex behind him, like some erotic tease. His arse is so tight it looks like stone.

He turns at that moment, his black-night eyes locking onto mine.

"Come here." His voice is low and smooth as honey. My breathing comes in ragged.

A force of untamed natural power suddenly blocks my view—all black fur, white canines on display. Gideon lowers his head.

I walk up to him, closing the distance between us, to touch the face he has lowered to meet mine. "You know Fury isn't going to hurt me." I stroke the side of his hard jaw. His lids close as I scratch. "You'll be right here, watching." His eyes open, irises swirling.

What if he never turns back into his human form? Will he be like this forever now? Staring deeply into his amber orbs, I know I'll never forsake him in any form, even his wolf. If this is how he is to be, then this is how I will love him. It will probably look different. I can't imagine how we would meld together with him at his wolf size.

He steps back, allowing me to pass. I drop my hand. By the Gods, do I miss his heat already, and he's barely a couple of steps away. He goes to stand by the door, guarding me.

Then I see my God—the one who has made me his

equal—and I quiver. His imposing body is before me, his legs slightly parted, his erect cock on full display.

"Do you like what you see, Goddess?" he asks. I gulp.

"I..." I don't know whether I should take a step forward or a step back. My legs decide to propel me forward of their own volition. I have no say in the matter. Before I know it, I stand before a heated stream of water. It separates us like a clear wall.

"Look what you do to me, my Goddess." He's moved his black-tipped fingers to grasp his throbbing grey cock. Black veins highlight the hunger he is experiencing for me, the tip black, like the ends of his clawed fingers. He reminds me more of the daemon I once thought he was than a God. He looks every inch like possession, lust and power. And I want him to seize my body. Take command of me. Use me to his will.

Surely, it's wrong to think such things. I almost feel dirty. However, that only makes me even more aroused by the sight of him, my core throbbing.

His head tilts up. "Sweet fucking spring." He sniffs the air. "Fates, Pet, I want you like I've never desired another before. Before you, I was drowning in a fog of my own making. Seeing you, standing before me, all I see now is light. You're everything I wanted since before falling onto this forsaken place. And I will do anything to see you happy and safe. You are my end." He drops before me in the stream of the water above, close enough for me to touch. "I give you my power, my soul, my body. My everything."

I trail a finger along his arched silver eyebrow, his eyelashes fluttering downwards, skin as smooth as porcelain.

At this height, we are nearly nose to nose. He leans into my hands.

"I want you to bond with me again. I want..." In an instant, his body is on the other side of the flowing water, his shoulders hunched and his wings pressed tightly to his back. "Fury." I sidestep the stream to go to him.

Spinning, his pitch-black eyes find mine. "Don't." He holds out his hand.

I stop in my tracks. *What is going on?* One movement, he was declaring his love for me, and now, he's wanting separation, like I've stung him. The fire deep in my body turns into an inferno. For the longest rhythm, this male has wanted me, and now, I give in to him, completely naked, and he runs to the other side of the room.

Godsdamn him.

"I *finally* want you to touch me, to bond with me, and you run!" My voice is pitched high.

At my distress, Gideon growls behind us. Fury prowls back towards me, but stops before touching me.

"I'm not running." He looks angry—angrier than I've ever seen him. It isn't directed at me; it's this situation we are stuck in. "I'm protecting you from undergoing the same fate I put you through once already." His hands go up and down, like he wants to touch me.

I step into him. He steps back.

"Stop." He holds up his hands, placating me.

"Why?" I push back.

"Because if I touch you, that'll be it for us. You'll be mine again. I won't be able to resist bonding with you again." He clenches his fists at his side, his abs flexing. "If I resist bonding, I can keep you safe from them. If they know we are bonded—and they will know—they'll strip you of it again, and I don't know how much your human form can take. Next time, you might not wake up."

I take a step forward, trying to process what he is telling me. It makes sense the more I think about it. *If we suddenly bond again, who's to say the other Gods won't just strip us of it?* The consequences of that could be devastating. My indignation diminishes just a tad, now directed back towards the three Gods who deserve it the most.

"You're right. We shouldn't. Not when we haven't figured this out yet." I focus my attention on the one imperfection in this room—a chipped stone on the ground before me—letting the reality of the situation sink in. Oona has placed us in luxury. I can't help but worry it's more because she is providing us with a false sense of security. The Gods have more power than we do. There are three of them and only one of Fury. In the fight for power, they win every time. *How do you beat that?*

Fury takes a step forward, so we are a mere foot apart. Eyes squinting and brow furrowed, he seems to be in physical pain. "You have no idea how excruciating it is to have you here right in front of me, naked, and not be inside you."

I can't help it. I reach out for him, finding his length. He's still hard and throbbing, and my hands grip him tightly before letting go, his eyes rolling back into his head. "I think I have an idea."

"Just wait until I kill them. Their corpses won't even be cold before I'm weaving our souls back together."

In all his godly beauty, grinning like the cat that got the cream, I can't help it; I grin back. "I can't wait."

"My Goddess." He grunts. "Finish washing yourself

under that stream while I watch. My self-control with you is finite."

Fury doesn't need to convince me. I head straight for the warm stream of water and let it fall over me, accepting a bar of soap from my fallen God. The soap slips in my hold, our hands barely grazing, and his back is against the wall again, his gaze never leaving my naked body.

In our current states of undress, it feels like I'm putting on a show for him and Gideon. To make them squirm, I lean down, cleaning all the dirt off my legs, my arse facing them. A loud groan comes from his direction. A heavy grunt from somewhere else in the room. I continue to ignore them both, scrubbing all the parts of my body in the luxury of this indoor waterfall.

With Fury's heated stare, and knowing Gideon is watching by the door, care and warmth flood through me. It allows me to relax, letting go of some of the pent-up stress I've held since being here without them.

The constant unknown. My anxiety. The strain on my body from the bonds being severed took a heavy toll on me both physically and mentally. It's hard to pinpoint where the individual soreness comes from, so it vibrates under my skin.

The red and brown that runs off my body reveals a white scar on my thigh. *How?* I raise my eyes beneath my eyelashes to catch a heavy-lidded Fury watching me, touching his cock in even strokes. I sizzle from my toes to my core. *Goddess, do I want him inside me.* I extract my eyes from the Fury tunnel of need I'm spiralling down and run a finger over my new scar—another one for the trauma bank I'm building in my cave, yet, when I continue to linger on it, my finger brushing back and forth, it's not the trial I'm thinking of. Instead, it's a wide canine tongue flicking along my skin.

Gideon.

My mate.

He had something to do with healing me.

Mate. The magic four-letter word draws me to him, and with the last of the soap and grim off my body, I head towards the dyre wolf standing by the door. *My mate.* Without speech, he knows what I need, wrapping my dripping body up in his arms, his scent my undoing. He nuzzles his wet nose into my neck, and I let my heart bleed for the fae who isn't here. *I'm coming for you, Rivern.* I send the thought down the bond. Regardless of our fractured connection, I still feel him right next to me.

TWENTY-EIGHT

DOVE

"Why isn't he changing back?" I ask Fury as he finally comes out of the bedroom—only after I got dressed in another barely-there gown Oona has requested I wear to a meal in her honour.

Wrath delivered it. Hearing his name is enough to make my hackles rise. *I can't believe I was so easily tricked.* My teeth grind just thinking about how he let me think he was Fury. *What if we'd had sex?* I don't even want to think about that. Now that I know who he is, how I have been treated makes more sense. Fury would've never kept me in such a place.

"His wolf form has taken over. The strain on the wolf mating bond made him succumb to his most natural instincts in an effort to protect and find you." Fury answers my question as we wait for our escort in the sitting room.

I push at the see-through crimson fabric of my dress. Intricate flowers are placed over my breasts and pelvis, with matching panties. My body is thoroughly exposed, especially since the fabric clings to me, long sleeves draping down my arms.

There's no jewellery except for the gold bands locked around my wrists, placed there by Wrath, impossible to remove. Fury says they are imbued with God power. To show I belong to him, he has cultivated a black velvet choker out of thin air that sits snug around my neck, an onyx dragon head dangling from the centre, reminding me of the best friend I left behind.

My hand glides over the charm's smooth edges. *Please be safe.* I will never forgive myself if something has happened to Saff or her child since I was taken from Haven.

"So he could be like this until we find a way out of this place?" I've already succumbed to the fact that we are all prisoners here. Well-kept prisoners. Nevertheless, still prisoners.

One peek out the door reveals several guards. Our rooms also overlook a treacherous drop. Fury could always teleport us. He's done it before. Gods, there's too much to take into consideration with this predicament.

"Yes—" He pauses for a moment, sitting forward in his chair. Instead of his usual black leather pants and no shirt, he's wearing black linen pants and a linen shirt, with spaces for his wings at the back. He's even tied his hair up. No matter what this male wears, he looks devastatingly hand-some, and seeing him like this is no exception.

He leans forward, one elbow on the armrest, chin in hand, staring at me. Having all his attention is panty-melt-ing, making me squirm, my pussy dripping for him. A pointed tongue comes out to taste the air. *He knows exactly what I'm thinking.* My cheeks burn. "Or you could try to convince him you're safe through other means." Leaning back, his teeth are on full display.

The air vibrates around us. *He's up to something.*

"I'll bite. What do you mean?"

His smirk only widens. "You could convince him with your body that you are his. That he's yours." I must look puzzled because he laughs. "Pet, your face."

"What's wrong with my face?" I ask, bringing my hand to my cheek.

"You look fucking radiant when you're confused." He continues to bask in my *radiance* while I roll my eyes at him.

He tsks.

I poke my tongue out.

He growls. "Don't make me bend you over my knee."

Gideon growls.

Now it's my turn to laugh. "You want me to what? Have my way with him in his wolf form?"

"Well, well, well, I was just going to say let him mark you with his bite, but your plan sounds better."

"Argh, you're so annoying." It's not my best comeback, but it'll have to do because all I can imagine is how big Gideon is. A bite mark from him in this form would cover my whole shoulder. It wouldn't be pretty—

That doesn't matter. I want Gideon to feel in control again. And I want him to bite me. I crave it. The thought alone has my clit throbbing, my blood vibrating and my pussy clenching.

Gideon is at my side in an instant, nuzzling at my palm, noticing the instant change in me. Fury notices it, too, judging by the sudden readjustment of his cock above his pants.

He sits in a lush, burnt-umber wing-backed chair, and the contrast against his skin is utterly tantalising. Who am I kidding? If it weren't for the three Gods holding us hostage, I'd be riding him right now.

"Why don't we just teleport out of here?" I dig my fingers deeper into the fur pelt of the wolf sitting on the floor. He sits like a man in his wolf form, his bottom on the ground, his legs bent before him to meet his chest, like he is tucked in on himself, trying to be small, when he is the most obvious thing in this room.

"That would've been my first course of action, yet those cuffs around your wrists are tied to Oona. I can feel her magic in them. Which means she'll know if we leave." He almost burns a hole through my wrists with his penetrating stare. "We'll play her little game for now. As soon as she's dead, those cuffs will fall from around your wrists. Without her power fuelling them, they'll be useless." *Easier said than done.*

"How are we going to kill them all? Can Gods even die?"

My questions are interrupted by a knock at the door. Staring deeply into each other's eyes, we ignore it for a moment. A punishing thud comes the second time, and Fury groans. "It's my doppelgänger."

Goddess. Wrath.

Do I want to see the creature who pretended to be one of my bonded?

Fury extends his long legs, gracing us with a tantalising stretch before heading over to answer. He's not quiet in his anger with his lookalike. I can hear it in the tone of his voice, which has lowered to a menacing degree.

Within moments, I am ushered behind Fury and before Gideon as we follow Wrath through the winding hallways of the manor, though it's like no manor I've ever seen, bigger than anything we have in the Forgotten Lands.

After walking down the curved marble staircase, gripping the gilded railing tightly so I don't face plant into Fury's wings, we find ourselves at a doorway that stretches high into the ceiling. Bronze doors creak as golden godlins part the way for us. Wrath leads the way to a thirty-seater dining table that seems to stretch far beyond its capabilities until I notice my red dress reflected in a mirror at the end—an entire wall of mirrors.

Gleaming eyes watch me intently from our reflection.

"Please, sit," a feminine voice imparts graciously. Fury doesn't budge, his eyes roaming the three winged Gods at the head of the table—gold, silver and blue. A trifecta of wings hover on the backs of the imposing figures, their wings unlike Fury's, instead reminding me of those of butterflies, delicate and intricately woven.

"We have much to discuss." The voice is distinctly masculine—Osear.

A grumbling Fury turns to face me, taking a wide step to bridge the gap between us. I desperately want his hands on my skin. He reaches for me. A claw grazes my waist, catching in the fabric before he pulls away. We shouldn't be this close. It's too tempting to touch and kiss. His ashen scent will have to do for now, so I take a deep breath.

Without physical contact, he does the next best thing, giving me a reassuring wink. Looking over my head, I can see in the mirror around Fury's broad shoulders how Oona's face shifts at our display, her eyes narrowing. I try to ignore how it curdles my stomach, opting to keep my face neutral.

Fury brushes past me, leaving Gideon at my side. My fallen God stands towards the middle of the table, close yet far enough from the three Gods at the head. Not that distance makes a difference with any of these ethereal beings.

Every word that comes out of Fury's mouth next is a threat, disguised under a cadence of indifferent friendliness. "I'm not here to pretend what we are to each other. All I require is my bonded back, unharmed, and we will leave this place." What he hasn't mentioned is *how* we will leave this place.

The three unworldly beings at the head of the table mirror his look of indifference. No one is willing to give anything away. This is the first rhythm these four Gods have come to a head in centuries, the air pulsing with their power. It's electric and euphoric. The connection I opened back up between myself and Fury drip feeds some of his power to me now, like he can't bear the thought of me being without some form of his protection.

Oona's face is the first to fall into a sinister turn of the lips. "It has been a long time, Orion. We would like you"— she glares at me now, with glinting golden irises, her intensity making me step backward into the warm beast guarding my back—"your human and your *beast*"—the last word is a hiss, like Gideon has somehow offended her by entering her dining room—"to join us for the last two God trails, pleasure and sacrifice."

Fury doesn't answer straight away. The way his hands fist at his sides tells me he doesn't like her response. "We appreciate the invite, however, we have pressing matters back within our own lands."

"Oh, don't be such a bore, Orion. Join us for the last of the trials." Oriel perks up from Oona's side. I look to Oona's right at the stunning, ebony-skinned God, her ringlets adding to her allure.

"As I've already said, we have pressing matters back within our own lands we need to attend to." Fury is firm in his words, emphasising, "I will require you to remove the bindings around Dove's wrists." His crinkled brow and tight jaw tell me all I need to know. He's displeased.

Oona's eyes widen at that. "Hmmm." Her chin now rests in her hand. "I just don't think that's something we can accommodate." She smiles when Fury's wings rise behind him, unfurling as if preparing for a fight. "Now, now, Orion, the binding will remove itself upon the ending of the last trial." Her hands go wide now, signalling the godlins I'd scarcely noticed dotted around the room. "So, you see you must attend our trials." She claps her hands, signalling the conversation's end. "Let us eat."

On cue, a small, godlin-sized door bursts open behind us. Two rows of godlins round the rectangular table, placing an assortment of food in the centre. Roast meats, potatoes, greens, gravy, pie, breads. Everything one could ever want, but I haven't seen in Haven for turns—not spread out like this.

With the dire food shortages currently plaguing my kingdom, this extravagance seems excessive. *Who am I kidding? This whole manor is excessive.* My stomach grumbles loudly at the display, my mouth beginning to water at the sublime smell of apples wafting from the sugar-topped pie. Fruit trees and bushes have always been my favourite to grow. They can feed whole villages straight from the branch. Plus, they are part of my favourite food group.

As much as I despise the Gods at the head of the table and want to send them to a fiery death, I can also admit my hunger has suddenly quadrupled at the delicious sight before me.

My hand rests on my stomach, trying to hold my grumbling in. I can't tear my eyes off the crispy-skinned potatoes. "Sit. Eat," Oona speaks, her voice echoing through the quiet room.

Fury's presence is behind me instantly, his hand resting gently on my wrist. That movement alone is enough to make me want to turn into him, let him have me now. My stomach complains again. *Actually, he can have me after I eat.*

"Come, sit." He moves around me and pulls out a bronzed chair, finely cut into the shape of vines twisting through the back. I expect him to take the seat next to me, but he doesn't. Instead, he stands at the back of my chair, my winged protector.

Gideon watches over us, surveying the space for any danger.

"Eat your fill. You will need your strength for the next trial," Oona's voice carries down the lavish table.

"And if we choose to leave?" Fury is composed in his question as he reaches over to place a rosemary-scented bread roll on my plate. I instantly go for the butter and slather it on, nearly groaning when the rich taste hits my mouth. Simple yet perfect.

"She will die."

That halts the procession of bread to my lips. The back of my chair cracks.

"You see, the cuffs placed around the female human are connected to the events of the trial. If she survives each trial, she will live to see another turn." Oona does all the talking. Fury is silently fuming behind my chair. "The subsequent trial is a favourite of our people. The loss of life is much less compared to the first trial."

I look over to catch her pop a grape into her mouth. *Much less.* These Gods are insane. They have no morality. No concern that they are harming real people with these horrid trials. I witnessed tens of people die on that blood-stained arena floor last night, and they did that all in the name of fun. I shudder to think of this next trial.

"What does the next trial consist of?" Fury growls the words behind me, my fallen God no longer composed. His lividness ripples outwards.

My bread roll no longer holds the same flavour it once did, so I put it down.

"Oh, you know," Oona says, waving her fork around as she stabs a bloody piece of meat. "The first trial was to test our potential candidates for their composure and strength when challenged through trivial inconveniences like pain and safety." I almost spit out the water I'm drinking when she says *trivial. They placed me in that arena without a weapon or protection, not to mention my concussion.*

"The second trial is all about pleasure and testing your endurance and willingness to please your Gods." She taps a finger on her slightly pointed chin as if contemplating what she is going to say next. "Since our long-lost Orion is back." *Lost.* I want to bark the word out in laughter. "He will join us." She claps her hands together again, as if it is a done deal, her catlike eyes narrowing on me. "I may even allow you to play with your little human toy. After all, I do have Wrath to keep me company."

At that moment, the doors opposite the three Gods and their table crack open again. Three males walk through them.

Bear and Lune are both in their golden armor, and there is a tall, grey creature behind them who looks exactly like the male at my back.

"My Gods." Bear and Lune bow at the same time before the end of the table. They don't rise until Oona speaks, directing them to eat. Gideon has released a menacing low growl, watching the two men intently. They move to the opposite side of where I sit.

A throb in my lower abdomen lets me know the God at my back is displeased with the situation. *I never thought I'd want this, but I wish we could still communicate through our minds.* I need to know what he is thinking. Oona has admitted that we are her prisoners. Obviously, these trials are a trap. Oona has some game afoot. She seems to be the spokesperson among the three Gods.

I'm actually surprised at how well Fury and Gideon are keeping their cool next to me. There's a part of me where ire brews, waiting for the perfect rhythm to release, but I know, after living at the hands of an abusive parent, exploding will do none of us any favours. Fury seems to understand that. His need for revenge is not as important as his need to protect me. I love knowing that. It feels like it gives me an edge on these all-powerful Gods. I have the one thing they can never have: Orion.

As soon as he opened up about his true feelings for me, I was stolen, heart and soul. Denying myself him was easier than admitting that a God wanted me. Now, I have a God, a wolf and a fae prince in my corner. *Godsdamnit, I just want to be home, snuggled up with all three of them, and for this nightmare to be over.*

TWENTY-NINE

FURY

Wrath sits at the end of the table, opposite Oona, Osear and Oriel. The other two champions are facing us across the feast. I have no animosity towards these champions or Oona's creation, even if he was designed in my image.

It was all her—Oona—and her minions, Oriel and Osear. They've always bowed down to her will. They have the same power, for we Gods were created equal. Here, on land, they show how susceptible they are to her persuasions.

When we were nothing but power, true Gods amongst the stars, living within imaginary worlds of our own making, life and death weren't as all-encompassing as they are in these bodies.

Finding the world of Maia changed everything. I watched the humans on this planet and saw how they would fall over each other because of *love*. What the other Gods saw was pleasure. Our vantage points were the same, our views completely opposite.

As a deity, all I felt was power... Emotions eluded me, and for the first time, I was angered about not being able to attain something that was so easy for the insects who lived down below.

From what I'd seen, I decided I wanted to create this phenomenon for myself in the form of my own beings. Not like the humans, but vaster and more animalistic, with the complexity of varying emotions, like mating bonds. Oona, Osear and Oriel all thought it was a stupid folly until they saw what I made. What life could be like.

From that point onwards, everything expanded. The other Gods created smaller creatures alongside my own, and feelings we'd never experienced before started to dictate how we made decisions. Oona was becoming angrier, and I sought love.

That was when I told them I wanted to fall. And Oona brought war amongst my creatures below in an effort to keep me. Not succumbing to her brutality, of which she had enlisted both Osear and Oriel into, I fell anyway, to save what was left of my creatures. But, in retrospect, all it did was make me vulnerable.

None of us knew what would happen once we fell to the earth below; if we would keep our powers or if they would leave us. I also never imagined Oona, Oriel and Osear imprisoning me on an island out of pure jealousy. Then, in my imprisonment, they created more creatures, and they themselves eventually fell on this new land called Atla.

I was always the one in our foursome who never followed suit. No doubt Oona thought she was done with me when she imprisoned me on that island. The way she flicks her eyes back to me every few moments to make sure

I'm here is nauseating. Her presence alone makes me want rip out lungs. Cut off heads. Watch her bleed for what she took from me. The only thing I ever wanted: love.

To keep some peace for the woman in the chair before me, I stand still, holding the frenzy of revenge inside. It bites at my inner walls, begging to be let out, but for her—for the spark that keeps us tethered—I will do anything, including halting my own plans.

The thin gold bracelets around Dove's wrists seem innocent. I know the truth now. They're deadly. Everything on this island is about lavish excess. These trials are another way to fill their need for power. They are killing for sport, and the people of Atla go along with it.

My instinct is to bite first, take questions later. This time, I'm biding my time. I will let the Gods before us have the passive side of me while I calculate and find their weaknesses. One thing I know about being a fallen God is that it doesn't come without failings. The woman I came here for is mine.

Getting Dove out of this kingdom of depravity may take time. There's only one option moving forward: death. And it will not be Dove's.

THIRTY

DOVE

After silent eating, the clashing of knives and forks hitting porcelain aggravates me. Oona sighs heavily. I don't want to look her way. Yet, I still do, for it is hard to ignore the trifecta of beauty at the end of the table. Her blonde hair falls in effortless waves around her shoulders, cascading over a figure-hugging dress.

The woman is blinding in her beauty and her accessories.

She motions gold-tipped fingers at the godlins around her for one of them to take her plate, her chair shifting back automatically. "The second trial will be held this evening. Wrath will collect you when the suns begin to set beyond the ocean." With those parting words, the Gods glide out of the dining hall.

At their exit, the room goes still. "We're leaving," Fury growls. By the looks of the receding suns through the windows, "this evening" is going to come around quickly.

"I will take you back to your rooms." The second voice jars me. It sounds like Fury. I know it's not.

Bear and Lune, familiar with this strange atmosphere, continue to partake in the feast before them. I don't know how they put up with deities who see them as less than. It doesn't seem right. Nothing about this place does. There's a constant undercurrent of wrongness circling us, ready to run at the slightest sign of danger.

Standing, I stumble on my feet for a moment, my equilibrium off. "I've got you." I lean into Fury's hard side. The ever-present thread connecting us pulls tight at my God's closeness. I want to wind my arms around him in an embrace. This close to him, the burn of his coldness seeps through our clothes. *Goddess, I want him.*

I close my eyes to the feel of being tucked up against him. Just as suddenly as he is there, he's gone, replaced by fur and warmth. My heart leaps at having them so close, even if we are stuck in this place.

Gideon picks me up, tucking me against his chest in a sitting position. His strength in this form is extraordinary. Not that I'm more than skin and bone after living in a perishing kingdom. Everything about him speaks to pure force and agility, muscles rippling on top of muscles. His sharpened incisors are constantly on display, ready to rip into the nearest person who tries to hurt us.

I've never had this solidarity before. Just the insects on my walls and in my gardens. Now, I have three men who have attached themselves to me for eternity. My soul sings at the knowledge. Even though I've lost my bonds with two of them, they still belong to me.

They helped me chase away all the daemons from my

past. They supported me when I thought I was all alone. They gave me the strength I never thought I could muster. However, not without the help of a dragon from my dreams and my dead sister. Now, they are tucked away in their rightful places. Gone, but never forgotten.

What the mind will do to keep one safe and sane is beyond comprehension. For the longest time, I kept my sanity by being able to control my voice. It was the only power I wielded. Now, I see that I can wield power through my words, and not my silence.

A twinge in my chest reminds me that Rivern isn't here with us. I'm glad one of us is away from this place. I want to protect them all just as much as they want to protect me.

Wrath walks before Fury. Every moment I see his onyx horns or feathered wings peek out in front, it's like I'm seeing double, and I rub my eyes to gain clarity.

Soon, we are back within our quarters, Gideon reluctantly placing me down.

"If you need to say something, speak." Fury's voice is hard. I don't realise who he's speaking to until I turn to face Wrath lingering in the doorway. He looks weary and, dare I say it, forlorn?

"I wanted to apologise to Dove." His words surprise me. *Apologise.* No one makes the effort to say sorry to me. I've always been the servant. Too low to care about. Until Fury, Rivern and Gideon.

Wrath takes a step into our sitting area. Gideon growls, moving to block his view of me. I step around him and place a hand on his hard forearm. "It's okay. I want to hear what he has to say."

It was devastating to think *Fury* had hurt me back in the

first trial. However, it wasn't my God; it was Wrath. I don't know him. He's not my fallen God. He's a weapon for Oona. So, I wait for him to begin in the safety of the two males who surround me. Oona wouldn't try anything with them around. *Would she?*

Wrath steps closer. He wears finely spun light linen pants and a shirt—his usual attire around the manor. I've only ever seen Fury wear black. That should've been my first giveaway.

"Oona instructed me to break you. I've done it before. I'm her helper in most things. *Her champion,*" he spits the last of his words. "She is my creator, and for the longest rhythm, all I've known is being under her servitude. Breaking you wasn't anything new to me. I'd done it to countless humans in the past." He shrugs his shoulders, which almost gives him a boyish charm. His mannerisms are so different from the God who is currently shooting a death glare his way.

"But it was different with you. I saw an opportunity to have something for myself. I saw familiarity in you. I thought I could play the part you needed me to play, and maybe have you for myself, for once in this place. And none of that is an excuse for my behaviour. I wanted to say sorry for my part in this. This is not a kind place, or fair. All the power lies in the hands of the Gods." His own hands come out before him, his blackened fingertips extended.

Gods, what he speaks is so much like my experience; trying to navigate the hand you've been dealt. It's not always an easy path to see beyond the corruption. The lies. If that's something I can help him achieve, then at least this whole kidnapping is not for naught. People are struggling on this land as well.

Life isn't easy, and we follow the compass we are given. Sometimes, the compass is given to us by liars and cheats. Sometimes, it's wrought in love and affection. Who am I to judge?

"Thank you." The two words come naturally to me. This isn't a rhythm for animosity. It's a rhythm for coming together and showing compassion. The embers within my gut still roil, but this is one of those times the flames lap softly, almost calming, like waves hitting the rocks off the coastline.

We don't exchange any more words after that, just a drawn-out stare into glinting, stark raven eyes before he bows and walks away.

"There's only room for one grey daemon in this four-some." Fury's snarky remark draws me towards him. I push a finger into his frigid chest.

"I make the rules in this foursome." My words are play-ful, but the way he grabs my wrists over the cuffs sears me.

"It is only a matter of time before you are mine again." I push into him, trying to taunt him into breaking, knowing it's a bad idea. His wings push against the wall.

"Pet," his voice is a roughened growl. "If you come any further, I won't be able to stop myself."

I place both my hands on his chest. "Pleeease." Looking up into his eyes, I see the pain there. The torture of having to keep his distance. The smell of salt and soot and a crisp winter turn fills me with hope. I lean my head on his broad chest, taking a deep breath of him.

Just him.

Once all I can smell is Fury, I pull back, taking two wide steps towards my wolf shadow. "All done." My smile is wicked, mimicking the one currently gracing his lips.

Fury takes two steps forward. His eyes are hungry. His teeth glint in the afternoon light—until a decidedly furry dyre wolf blocks his path. All I hear is my God murmur, "Well played, old friend, well played."

A snorting snuff comes from the beast in front of me.

BITE.

NECK... MATE.

CLOSE. SHE'S MINE.

FINALLY.

IN ARMS. MINE.

MINE. MINE.

BITE HER. PROTECT HER.

PLEASE HER.

PROTECT.

PROTECT.

PROTECT.

THIRTY-TWO

DOVE

Utterly exhausted from eating my weight in rich, decadent foods at mid-light, I find myself having whittled the turn away, sleeping against my furnace. I wake from a dreamless sleep, hard edges and soft fur surrounding me.

I push my backside into the shifter behind me. Everything about his frame is solid and sturdy. His body is large enough in this form to curl around mine, his snout leaning over my head. He walks like a human, yet with the body of an animal, his limbs a little longer than normal due to his enormous size.

The more I push back into him, the more a full, rumbling purr comes from his chest. It vibrates through me, lighting my core on fire. It feels unusual to be attracted to him in this shifted state, but he is my mate, and regardless of his physical appearance, I want him. Everything he does calls to the siren song in me that screams his name.

Gideon. Gideon. Gideon.

Continuing to rub my lower half into him now, my pussy growing increasingly wetter, the pleasure, after turns of fear, feels good. The purring rumbles further and further out, hitting my clit just as I feel a hard, pointed ridge hit my arse. My toes curl at the unexpected pressure.

It's bigger than it ever was before. Without laying eyes on it, I know it's beyond me. *Where has he been hiding that thing?* This is the first time I've felt or seen his cock make an appearance.

He pushes into me, the movement tempting me, calling me to want more. Gideon's clawed grip on my waist leaves only an inch of room to move. I use that give to turn in his embrace. The hand holding me automatically loosens. I sit in the circle of his curled body, looking down at the amber eyes roaming my face.

Even though we can't communicate while he's like this, I understand him. He's letting me lead. I have full control over this situation and over him. He's my beast. He belongs to me.

I trail a hand through the fur around his muzzle and up past his eyes to the tips of his ears. His lids automatically close as I continue my perusal down his furred back, the thick hair dense, white lines of crisscrossed fur lining his black, telling the tale of the harshness of his existence.

Finally, I shift enough to find my prize. The air in the room is charged with sexual tension. Gideon moves when my fingers touch his waist, manoeuvring to lie on his back, fully exposed to me. His limbs hang over the edge of the bed, but I can't bring myself to look further beyond where I've left my hand at his side.

The heat coming off him is leaving a drip of sweat on my

forehead. His wide, red tongue comes out to lick his lips, as if he can smell me in the air. My pussy clenches.

"Well, Pet, it seems like you've got your hands full." I jump, Fury startling me from behind.

"I..." I stumble on my words until I see the arsehole himself come into my line of sight on the opposite side of the bed. "If you don't want to see, why are you watching?" He always brings out the snappy side of me. I don't think I could hold my tongue with him if I wanted to. There are just some people you have to bite back at.

"I never said I didn't want to see." He's back in his no-shirt, leather pants look. The sight is strangely encouraging. "Anything involving you, I want to see." His silver eyebrows wiggle mischievously.

"Goddess, do you have inside thoughts?" My hands grip the fur at my beast's waist, not ready to look down yet.

"Only when I can talk to you in here." He taps his head.

"Figures," I mumble.

"I know we are here to save you, Spitfire, but I still feel it necessary to remind you that I'm not opposed to taking you over my knee."

"Gah... Of course you wouldn't be." Hearing that name again—the one he used before being stolen—makes the pesky organ in my chest speed up.

"Your wolf is waiting." His stare doesn't leave mine, like the bastard is goading me into touching Gideon.

I'll willingly admit I'm the first to break our stare down. The thought of seeing what Gideon looks like all over is too hard to resist. I'm curious by nature.

I look down past his waist. What I find is beyond anything I could've imagined. Something similar, but different from his human cock. Jutting out from his fur is a rounded base—his knot. Exceeding that is his full length, dark and ridged. Thick rings line his cock and stop at a bulbous end.

The last thing I try to comprehend is his size in his wolf form. The beast of a cock I see before me is meant to fit within another wolf, not a human, and definitely not one of my stature.

With my eyes freely roaming his most intimate parts, the purring from his chest starts again, the tip of his dick leaking profusely. So much so that I am intrigued to investigate how much it releases when he comes.

"Touch him, Pet." Fury's voice is low, husky. *Is this turning him on?* The idea excites me.

I reach out for Gideon, the obscenely thick length calling me. However, I pull back at the last movement. "It's not going to fit."

Gideon's hand reaches out for mine, guiding me back to the fur just above his hard cock. I find his ambers reaching for me, searching my eyes, his purr rapturous. Seeing his canines only makes me wetter for him. I want him to bite me —the one he promised when he knotted me.

"Whether it fits or not doesn't matter, Pet. Your mate needs to feel you, taste you, smell you. The more he feels connected to you, the more his beast side will be satisfied, and the man can come back."

I raise my head to Fury. The rise and fall of Gideon's body under my hand grounds me. "So, you're saying for him to turn back, we have to make love."

"Is that what we are calling it now, my Goddess?"

"Would you prefer I say *fuck*?" He licks his lips.

"Talk dirty to me, Pet, and I'll join you."

I roll my eyes. "Looks like you're just going to have to watch today."

My hand goes to wrap around the giant cock before me. On contact, both man and beast make sounds of utter delight. Like the rest of him, his length is boiling, my fingers not even close to touching all the way around his hardness. I run my hand up and down the surprisingly soft ridges. A loud, vibrating moan escapes Gideon's chest, his hips jerking.

The liquid leaking from the tip draws me closer. *Goddess, I want to taste him. Will it be the same as his human body?*

"Lick him, Pet." Fury reads my mind.

It's all the encouragement I need as I sit up on my knees and lean forward, the dyre wolf shifter surprisingly still underneath me. I don't hesitate, leaning towards him, angling his pointed length my way.

I lick the very top of him, my tongue flicking forwards and backwards, lingering for a moment. As soon as the taste of Gideon hits my lips, the amber spice of him takes me back to warm nights under the stars. It's intense, so I take another lick. The flavour he produces is addictive.

Gideon's clawed fingers find the underside of my red dress, skimming underneath ever so slowly. I groan, leaning back onto his length with my mouth, licking a drop from knot to head. Sharp fingers trace the seam, where my lacy underwear meets my inner thigh. A thought crosses my mind that I should be more scared about what those sharp claws will do when they hit the delicate skin of my pussy. Instead, I'm excited. *I'm so fucked around my bonded mates.*

My wolf would never hurt me. He is here for my pleasure, and I am here for his. This—our joining—is all that matters. After tasting him, I'm now afflicted with a pressure in my core that is crying out for relief, and he's the only one who can give it to me.

I whine and sink into the feeling of him teasing me, my hand running down his hard length. It's not enough, and he knows it. Soon, my beast has me gripped by the thighs, and my lower half is pulled over his face so my core hovers over his snout. My panties are soaked, thinking about what he could do to me like this.

A wetness that is not my own tickles up the inside of my leg. I giggle. The wolf under me grunts, his cock jumping before me. At this angle, the sight of it looks obscene. There's no way that giant cock is going anywhere beyond my mouth and hand.

In my current position, leaning forward on his rock-hard chest, I can barely reach his length with my mouth. There's a crackling energy in the room, and I know a lot of that static power is coming from the God lying in wait against the wall. I don't look his way. If I catch a glimpse of him, I'll beg him to come closer, and I won't be able to resist the urge to touch him.

We can't risk bonding right now. The consequences of potentially having the other three Gods ripping it from us again would be devastating, so I have to stay strong. Keeping myself distracted from the winged male isn't so hard when teeth scrape across my lace-covered core.

A shocked gasp of desperation comes out of me. *Goddess, I want to feel that again.* Feel that lush friction all over my body. His tooth catches on the fine lace and rips, exposing my dripping pussy to him.

Everything from my muscles to my skin cries out to feel his lingering touch on that wet heat. My wish is granted shortly after that singular thought, my fingers shaking in his coarse fur. A wet, rough tongue comes out to lick in one movement from my clit to my ass.

It's all-encompassing, so wide he doesn't miss a nerve. "Gideon," I groan breathlessly.

I will let him do that all turn if he wants to. Lick after lick soon assaults me from my lower half, my orgasm building quick and fast in my mate's presence.

"Please, please, please." I'm at a point where it's the only word I can utter on each moan.

"What do you need, Pet?" Fury finally speaks.

I take a gulp of air, another tremble rocking me as Gideon's tongue lavishes me like I'm his last meal. "I need" —I take another deep inhale—"to come."

Knock.

Knock.

Knock.

On instinct, my head swivels towards the sound, my eyesight blurred from the pleasure I'm experiencing.

"Ignore it, Pet." Fury's words pull me back.

My chest skips a beat. My toes curl. A line of electricity runs from my clit to every cell in my body. And a wolf's wide tongue breaches the wall of my pussy. I scream. Not a moaning, languid scream, but a loud, unexpected, *that was so good my body just turned to jelly, gushing all over the tongue of the wolf shoving his face into me from below* kind of scream.

THIRTY-THREE

FURY

The high-pitched wail triggers Gideon's cock into shooting large ropes of cum towards the woman riding his snout. I never thought watching my bonded fuck someone else would turn me on the point of almost bursting because she's still *my* bonded.

My dick jumps in my pants, the outline hard against the leather. Dove slumps forward, and the door from the sitting area bursts open, bashing against the foiled wallpaper. The bang is loud enough to draw her attention. Her body quickly shoots up, eyes on Oona's plaything.

He's not welcome here, and it brings out an instant need in me to shield her from him, yet I want him to see what he'll never have. She's already claimed, and there's no room for anyone else.

Wrath stands in shock, unable to take his eyes off the glorious sight before him. It's raw, it's animalistic, it's hot as sin. In the millennia of my time on these lands, watching one of my own creations with my heart was never something I would have expected. It was more likely that my thoughts would fly to ripping out the throats of anyone who dared touch what is mine.

This. Her. Is different. I want everything she wants, and I will kill anyone who gets in her way. Now that I have my full power back, the possibilities for us are endless.

First, I need to take my revenge on the Gods. Then, I will be the strongest power in this world, and I'll be able to keep us safe for eternity.

"Are you here to watch, *brother*?" I spit the last word in disgust. "I don't remember extending an invitation to you."

His blown onyx-black irises flash to greet mine. And that's when I notice his fangs. Not like the sharpened state of my incisors, his are more tapered and extend beyond his lips. *Fucking Oona.*

I see it in his vacant stare. It's a lust far beyond that of what he is seeing before him.

"Oh, Gods, Wrath," Dove squeaks. A roar alerts me to Gideon's awareness of the male standing just within the doorway on the marble floors. Before this turns into a bloodbath, I teleport over to Wrath and push him through the door, slamming it behind me. Dove will calm Gideon down. She's the only one who can.

"What the fuck are you doing?" I snarl at my doppelgänger. His stare is still vacant, his lips quirking up.

"She smells like paradise."

I punch him square in the jaw. No one is allowed to smell what is mine, except for Gideon and Rivern. The circle is small, and that's everyone within it. It does not include Wrath.

He falls on his ass, blinking rapidly.

When he looks back up at me, his whole demeanour has changed. Even his fangs have shrunk back into his mouth.

"Start talking, Wrath, or you're a dead man walking."

Even though he has exactly the same measurements as I do, he looks small on the floor. Innocent. The stark contrast to his features is a puzzle.

"I—" He looks away, his voice tortured. "I thought she was hurt." My face must say it all because when he looks back, he already knows how absurd that sounds. Dove is always within my or Gideon's sight. No one is hurting her in this place. Oona will have to go through me if she even thinks of going down that avenue.

"I'm sorry. Ever since she arrived here, her scent has influenced my senses. Usually, I can hold onto control of it, but not with her."

"And what the fuck does that mean? I want answers, Wrath, and I want them now." I loom over him, my wings stretched wide. We need leverage on the Gods, and if there's a way I can get that through Wrath, I'll do it.

"She wants to destroy you." There's only one *she* he could be referring to. It is nothing new. I'm also trying to destroy her. The possibility of doing that now is much greater.

"Keep talking."

"Only if you promise you'll keep her safe. That you'll save her from this place." He actually looks sincere.

"You mean my human bonded, Dove?"

"Yes."

"It's a given. She's mine. I'm hers. I will protect her until the last star dies." He nods. My gravity for Dove is inked onto my soul. She's the whole reason I'm breathing. When she no longer ceases to exist, I will no longer cease to exist. It's why bonding with her has always been the end goal. I want our souls tied together beyond recognition. When we disperse these constitutions, we'll be joined beyond rhythm and distance.

He nods, happy with my answer, standing. "She is jealous of you."

"What's new?" I mumble under my breath. "Her jealousy was the catalyst for every disagreement. Every war. She's a fucking viper." My wings ruffle behind me.

"Dove mustn't go to the next trial. She plans to bond with her…" Wrath continues speaking, but at his admission, I see red explode across my vision. An anger so deep and vast that my blood curdles.

She can't. Dove. Aurora. My pet. My spitfire. She's mine.

I'm cooking from within at this news, only aware of the woman and wolf shifter in the other room. She can't know. She's fragile right now. I won't put her in danger of losing the last part of our connection.

"You'd better be here with a plan, Wrath, or so help these lands, because by the time I'm done with them, there'll be nothing left." My voice is full of pent-up ire.

"Bond with me." *Hah.* If it were anyone else, I'd gut them for even suggesting it, but his eyes express unhappiness, like this is a necessary evil to him. He doesn't want this bond, but he would do it for Dove, to keep her safe.

"Tell me why." And as Wrath describes the innermost workings of his plan, I see how bonding with him might be the only way out of this mess.

THIRTY-FOUR

DOVE

When a gigantic wolf shifter has you pinned to his chest, you'd think the first thing you'd feel would be fear. Except, after our brief interruption from Fury 2.0, all I want is for Gideon to have more of me.

He's too big in this form for us to fully fit, so I do the next best thing. The one way we haven't claimed each other yet: a bite. I tilt my head to the side that holds my burn mark. The one I and so many others thought had ruined me. Gideon's exposed teeth glisten with my juices.

Goddess, I may be held prisoner, and I may be receiving a bite that will cover my whole shoulder, but this is perfect. He's perfect. My core flutters. My flames ignite with need.

All I can smell is hard spice, sandalwood and vanilla. It's cloying, making me drift into a state of completely relaxed bliss.

His snout pushes against my shoulder. I find his amber

eyes, coloured like the honey I used to collect when the bees were plentiful in Haven. The longer I look into them, the more I sense the part of him that's more than wolf at the surface.

"Bite me, please," I whimper. We may already be mated, but I want his mark on me—the part that will complete our union and show everyone I'm his.

He doesn't need any more from me. His mouth widens, and I turn my head to the side just as his teeth press down on my skin.

My body jerks at the pressure, expecting pain when he pierces my skin. Instead, when his teeth push further, breaking through scar tissue and fair skin, it's heaven— better than the orgasm I just experienced on top of him.

His bite is like floating in a galaxy made just for us, where I can see and feel every part of him in intricate detail, including his voice.

"That's it, Songbird. You're taking me so well. Good girl." His coarse voice finds me, and I weep. Tears roll down my face. Finally, after being dragged to this place, I hear him. My hands fly up to grip whatever part I can grab of him to pull him closer. *"It's okay, my mate. I'll never leave you again."*

I don't know when his teeth retract from my skin. It's apparent I'm drifting in and out of some drug-induced Gideon delirium of our full joining. Having his knot in me was one thing. His bite? That has completely changed our connection. It goes beyond touch.

A calloused hand glides up my thigh, leaving a trail of unadulterated lust.

"You brought me back to life."

His voice isn't in my head; it's outside of it, a gravelled growl, my head leaning back on a much smoother chest.

Quickly turning on Gideon's lap, I shake my head, not believing what I'm seeing. "You can shift again?" My excitement at being able to have him in his human body again makes me giddy. I throw my arms around his neck and place my lips on his in a bruising kiss.

I'm lost in him until I need air, and I reluctantly release him, resting my forehead against his. "I liked wolf Gideon, and that orgasm was epic, but I really missed you like this, too."

He chuckles. "You're my humanity, sweet mate. There's no way I was missing out on knotting you." The length between us is obvious. His cock is massive, but a much more manageable size—one I've taken and knotted before, and one I can't wait to ride again.

I wrap my hand around it now, and Gideon throws his head back and groans. After the bite, I'm a floodgate of need for him, so I lift my lower half up and sink my core down on his hardness.

The ridges on his length aren't as pronounced, but the girth and length more than make up for that fact. He fills me to bursting, my pussy so wet I slide to the start of his knot with ease.

"Can you take all of me, mate?" When he calls me his mate, my heart grows in size. *Gods, do I love it and him.*

"Yes, please. I need all of you. Please, Gid—" I don't have to say anymore because, in the moment it takes me to blink, he has me on my back, my legs open wide for him and his knot sliding all the way in.

Unlike the first time, my body expects the weight of him inside. It's like coming home.

"I'm going to breed you full of my pups," he grunts, thrusting deeper. Those words should scare me. They would've scared temple Dove. But the Dove who has travelled across the Forgotten Lands and fallen in love with three men? That Dove reveals in his words. I want everything with him, including his babies. *Not right now, though. We need to get back home first.*

Also, he might have to get in line behind Rivern.

But that future—the one I always thought I couldn't have, the one a mute servant girl in a dying kingdom couldn't hope to dream of—is coming true. And I'm finally giving myself permission to take it in both hands and hold on tight. I'm not letting this male above me go.

Pulling out slowly, he measuredly guides his cock back in, inch by torturous inch, and back out until I'm fully knotted. He does this over and over again.

In and out.

Inch after inch.

Until I can't see straight and I'm listless underneath him. A mess of heightened sensations. Finally, he hits a rhythm where I'm exploding around him. We groan in unison, his knot expanding within me, holding us together as he comes.

———

I'm jolted suddenly by the door bursting open. When I crack my eyes, all I see is a flicker of black wings and grey skin. "Rise and shine, lovebirds. This is no honeymoon, if you haven't noticed."

"Fuck off, Orion," Gideon grumbles, pulling me into him.

"No can do. It's time for my revenge." I swear, there's a slight cackle when he finishes, so I look up to him pacing back and forth. He seems to be doing a lot of that lately, I've noticed—a nervous tick.

"We have a plan. Now, I need you both dressed." He clicks his fingers, and both of us are sheathed in new clothes. *That's my Fury.* Gideon is dressed in fine linen, white pants and a tunic with gold threading. I exhale audibly at my outfit. Another see-through dress adorns my body, this time in gold thread, with thicker material hiding my most intimate parts and a deep V down the bust line. Getting off the bed, I notice the lack of underwear.

"Do I have to wear this?" I lift my arms, showcasing a draped part of the dress purely for adornment, leaving my entire arm bare, the sleeve reattaching just before the gold cuffs on my wrists.

Heat. It barrels through to my core as Fury examines me. "Yes," he growls. His face is pure lust. I'm drawn to him. *When am I not?* The glint in those dark irises. I take a step forward on bare feet, my hair out and draped over my shoulders. The light of the setting suns highlights the fallen God standing his ground before us.

"Stop staring at me like that," I mumble under my breath.

"Like what?" he smirks. A pointed tongue darts out.

"You know, like what," I parry back.

"No, I don't. You tell me." He takes a step forward.

"N-no!" My cheeks flush. He continues his charge, my

own back hitting the wall behind me. Eyes flitting towards Gideon, he looks back, unfazed. "Are you going to help me?"

"You don't need my help, Songbird." He's relaxed in his demeanour, resting against the feather pillows. I seem to be on the opposite side of whatever *this* is.

"Argh, fine! Stop staring at me like you want to eat me." I let my piece be known, Fury a foot from me, looking down.

"That's right. When the Gods are dead, you'll be mine to devour, from head to toe, and I'll savour every last drop of you." I try my hardest to grip onto the wall behind me, digging my nails into the gold decorating the opulent quarters we reside in. My heart is not made for these men who constantly surprise me at every turn. I almost want to reject his words as a lie. Old traumas try to weave their way back into my thoughts. The seriousness on his face tells me there's no lie. He will only ever tell me the truth. *This God is mine. Forever.*

I want our bond, now more than ever. At this point, we can't have it unless we want to risk destruction at the hands of Oona, Oriel and Osear again.

A lump forms in my throat, and I can't talk. His hand goes to my neck, touching the choker that still lingers there —the symbol of his claim over me. Oona may have cuffed my hands, but Fury, Rivern and Gideon have the parts of me that truly matter.

"It's time to go." His silken, alluring words linger on his tongue, neither of us wanting to part.

"Okay," I rasp out.

We stand there as if all rhythm has slowed for us until the spell is broken, Gideon leaping off the bed and boxing me in from the side.

"That's enough, Fury. It's time to go." Gideon side-eyes him.

The sudden boost of testosterone around me makes me weak. *Get it together, Dove.* I almost want to slap myself. Going from having zero to three males vying for my attention will always be an adjustment.

"You're right." *That's a first.* "It's time to head to the next trial."

"And are you going to share this plan before we go?" I ask.

Turning, he locks onto me. "Do you trust me, Pet?"

"Yes." There's no question about it. Fury has saved me more times than I care to admit.

"It's better if you both go in blind."

He releases my hold, and I sway to the side. *Why does he have such an effect on me? Even when we aren't fully bonded anymore.* Gideon steadies me with his hands.

"If he fucks up, you know I'll gut him." Gideon's growl in my ear is comforting.

"I'd welcome it," Fury interjects before walking out of the room.

"It's showtime, I guess."

"I'm right here with you, love. Always." I've never felt safer in enemy territory. My smile is so wide it feels like it stretches from one ear to the other.

"I love you." I grin up at him. The mate bond between us ripples in joyful exuberance.

"*I love you more.*" His voice in my head soothes my aches.

I don't bother retaliating. It's not true; everything about us is equal in measure. Our love, our respect, our understanding.

And with that knowledge, I plaster a smile on my face and walk into the viper's den, knowing I have *almost* everybody I need at my side.

THIRTY-FIVE

GIDEON

Trust. It's a tricky word. To trust the God who was my creator and kept our most precious creation on these lands safe, or to hold animosity against him for the potential future crime of breaking her heart.

Trust over failure in this situation seems like the safer bet. This indoor expanse we find ourselves in is a mood unto itself. Gold is stripped bare from this place, unlike the gaudy palace above. Instead, this place is full of blacks and reds, leather and silk. Colours, textures and luxury that invoke dark, gritty sensuality.

The pleasure trial.

This room is about a quarter the size of the stadium floor we found Dove in. Humans mill around naked, or in different shades of undress. Some in delicate lingerie, some in harsh leather straps. Multiple people have collars around their necks, with leashes tied to them, being dragged along. And some others lay back on red pillows, putting a long, tapered stick in their mouths, puffing out air.

It makes the open room smell like a mixture of earthy herbs, their notes of taste unfamiliar to me—too bitter to be viewed as a delicacy, in my opinion. I only thirst for honeysuckle, rose and vanilla, sometimes burnt into a crisp caramel at the edges. Every part of my mate's smells and tastes are all the aphrodisiacs I need.

Saliva pools in my mouth, filling my nostrils with the woman standing beside me.

"What is this place?" She has been practicing talking within my mind on the way here. Apparently, the link differs slightly from when she was bonded to both Rivern and Fury. Our connection relies less on threads connecting along heartstrings and more on a sensation of our souls touching.

What we are is more than God-bonded. I may have been created by a God, but we are not bonded by him. This human beside me is my fate-matched. It means our souls have chosen each other again and again, and they will continue to do so.

"It seems to be a space where all the most intimate secret pleasures of the Gods and humans may be entertained," I answer. The pleasure trial looks to be about fulfilling desires.

"What do we do?" Dove asks Fury, who stands to her right.

"We wait... Right on time." My gaze darts from Fury to Dove to a short, red-haired man standing before us. His muscles glisten with oil, a leather strap hiding his cock.

"Welcome to the pleasure trial, champion." The slippery man bows slightly. "Oona has asked that I receive you on the Gods' pleasure stage." His voice shakes slightly. Good, I hope Fury and I intimidate him. If it weren't for those God cuffs on Dove's wrists preventing us from leaving, we wouldn't be here right now.

If I achieve anything in this place, it's that these people see me with fear in their eyes. I want them to know I will do anything to protect the woman standing between Fury and me. Heads are going to roll for her treatment. All they can hope for is that they aren't on the chopping block.

What my mate needs right now is rest and food. She has no idea what is to come, what Fury bestowed on her before we left his island. This is not the time to drop a bombshell that will change our lives forever. First, we kill these mother-fucking Gods, and then we will go home and live our lives in peace.

Fates only know the Forgotten Lands deserve it.

We fall into a natural line of Fury at the front, Dove in the middle and me at the back. It's where I feel most comfortable, always watching her. The further we walk into this strange world, one could mistake the groans and gasps going around for either pain or pleasure. Lanterns light velvet alcoves, highlighting shadows grinding against each other. Even though this is called the pleasure trial, I have a gut feeling it goes beyond pleasure and into something more sinister.

Further and further we walk, humans milling around us. Godlins linger along the periphery, the only gold in the room zooming around, fulfilling differing requests.

As much as I want to take stock of what is going on around us, my mate steals me away with every sway of her hips in front of me. She doesn't understand the effect she has on me. The slight hitch of her mini dress as it inches higher every time she takes a step forward is torture, knowing she's bare under there.

The only thing currently saving these humans is knowing they do not have my senses. They can't smell her wet pussy dripping with our mingled essences from our knotting, but I can, my cock still at full mast after she fell asleep on top of me. The only thing that went down was my knot when I spilt everything I had inside of her. I adjust myself, unable to help giving myself a hard squeeze to alleviate some of the pressure.

As if knowing exactly what I'm thinking, Dove turns around and smiles, like she isn't cuffed to the Gods who stole her away, and we aren't about to, no doubt, fight our way out of this. Her smile is sweet and utterly disarming, making me fall in love all over again.

Fates, give me strength. I'm merely a shifter. I'm not a God with untold powers. My heart can only handle so much.

Walking up a set of three stone steps, we come face to face with three stark white statues, almost as high as the roof that extends several floors. I take in the pieces, starting up the top and moving down the naked figures, only to find my worst fucking nightmare at their feet.

Thirty-Six

Wrath

I wasn't sure if he would go for it—Fury, that is. I'm the one who shouldn't be trusted. Oona made me in his image as her personal slave. He doesn't hold any animosity against me, though. Oona, Oriel and Osear are another story. Fury wants them dead, and so do I.

We both have a common goal: freedom from the three tyrannical Gods.

The only problem is how to kill them. Gods are immortal, thanks to their power, but what if the Gods lost their power? It is unthinkable because there is no way to take a God's power. So that makes them automatically invincible, right?

Wrong.

An idea occurred to me around a rotation ago. One of how Oona had given me an ability I once saw as a weakness, and now might be her downfall. Bloodletting has always been the way I have fed, ever since I was created. It is the gift that provides me longevity, never immortality. The Gods only believe in having that within themselves—the only ones with any true power.

Now, they will see me as their downfall. Wrath, pretending to be Fury, or should I say Orion?

With Fury's power now running through my veins, I am stronger than ever before—invincible. *I'm not.* It would be foolish to believe that half of Fury's power equates to three Gods at full power.

Convincing him to bond with me had seemed like a long shot. After hearing my plan to trick the other Gods and pretend I was him, he surprised me and agreed. With a simple touch of his hand on my exposed skin, we were bonded, effortless, nothing to it. Except for the unimaginable toll of the force of his power as it is running through my veins. It's angry. Untamable.

It's like a doorway has been opened up within me, unnatural, spine-crawling. Fury's power flows through it, but only because he wants it to. It could be stripped from me at any moment.

"Oh, Orion, I'm so glad you've come to your senses." Oriel is mark number one. She will be the easiest to crack. We need her power to gain leverage on the others. There's no way she would give it to me. However, I know if I were Orion, she might let her guard down enough for me to strike. Whenever I'd found Oriel in a weak moment, she expressed her fondness for the lost God and how he was able to be his own person without the persuasions of the other Gods.

Her hands fidget in her lap. The royal blue settee we sit upon is barely big enough to comfortably hold our wings.

"After seeing what you've created here, I just knew it was

something I would want for myself," I respond, playing Orion. Her blue orbs sparkle as she looks up at me, her deep ebony skin truly breathtaking against her wispy, sheer wings. I've always found her more striking than Oona, yet I've never joined her in the bedroom—or Osear—due to Oona's jealousy. She can share me with the Atlans, but sharing me with the other Gods is where she draws the line. And they know it, which is part of my reasoning for needing to disguise myself as Fury—or Orion, as Oriel knows him.

She places a hand on my thigh, tapping her thumb dangerously close to my cock. "I'm so glad. I can help you talk to Oona about this new transition. I know the two of you haven't seen eye to eye, but that's only because you've never been with us, you know?" I nod. "If she sees you want to join us, I'm sure she will be happy." Her endearing smile quickly turns into a frown as she mulls over her own words.

I take her delicate hand from my leg, squeezing it between mine, the electricity of our power stinging as they meet. Blue meeting black. Her grin is back, a giddiness about her.

Leaning in close, our foreheads touch. "It was never Oona I was worried about. It was you."

"Me!" she says in surprise, pulling back. "Why would you be worried about me?" I've perfected bedroom eyes over the centuries. Right now, I let them do the talking.

"Oh... Oooo." Her free hand flies to her mouth. "Oh, Orion, you mustn't tell Oona. She would put you away again. You know how she likes to be the centre of attention." She places a fingertip to my lips. She smells like a cool ocean breeze and sweet lemon tarts on a hot summer's turn. It's a striking combination I find hard to resist now that I'm this close to her, my cock already rock-hard. Her moods always read kindness and sunshine, whereas her counterparts are cruel and glum.

She's probably the most likable being in this palace. It's unfortunate that she also has a dark side. You don't live forever without one. She just hides it better than the others. I've seen her lose herself to the point that she's ripped a human's throat out in exasperation.

It's a sore spot for the Goddess—and motivation for me to kill her, even though I find some parts of her endearing.

She tries to move her finger from my lips, so I bite the digit between my front teeth. "Orion!" She gasps, her other hand going to her mouth, a perfume of ocean spray filling the room.

My lips suck the finger in further, my tongue swirling around her skin, letting her know how much I want her. Her eyes are wide, wondrous, disbelieving. She has no idea how lucky she is. I'm going to spare her Oona's wrath. She'll be the first to go at my hand. It will be peaceful. Maybe even beautiful.

A smile snakes over my lips, her finger popping out.

"Let me taste all of you." My voice is growly and rushed. It does the trick, her face flushing.

"I—" Her breath catches in her throat. I take it as an opportunity to move to my knees between her legs, pushing her wide. The dress she wears for the pleasure trials is her traditional turquoise chiffon. Peaked, dark nipples are visible through the top layer. I push aside the skirts covering her bottom half. My claws finally find her thighs and dig in, making her gasp. "I can't be late to the trials..."

"I can provide you pleasure right here." I don't give her a

chance to back out. My head goes under her dress, and my mouth is on her ocean nectar in an instant. She's crying out from the first touch, like she's wanted this forever. Wanted Orion, not Wrath. No, she wants the power she feels through my blood. The lightning dances through our skin, making this cataclysmic

I almost get lost in her until my fangs drop, and the reason I'm here hits me full force. *Power. I want her power.* Within moments of that realisation, I'm sinking my teeth into Oriel's thigh. A scream rings throughout the room, hands trying to grab at my head through the skirts, but the venom that makes my bites irresistible to humans seeps through her skin.

As a rule, I'm not allowed to bite any of the Gods because we don't know the consequences. Breaking that rule feels better than sex. I moan loudly into her thigh, dragging her blood and her life force into my body. The weakness of the Gods is their life force, their power.

In a normal situation, I would stop before I drain the human. I take a little off the top, enough to only age them a rotation at a time. This is taking so much more; it's taking everything Oona has kept from me.

Power grows alongside Fury's. Like meets like; they dance beside each other before finally mingling, seeing the sameness within. The moment the two powers merge, Fury is in my head. *"Bleed her dry and be done with her. We are at the trial. You need to move quicker."*

With my bonded God's words in my head, I drink harder, faster. The moment the last of Oriel's power has left her body and entered mine, I no longer feel the need to suck, my teeth retracting.

I'm lightheaded from the sudden rush. The static whooshing through my veins is more than sharing half of Fury's power; it's now knowing the totality of a God's power within. I rock back on my legs, my eyes closed, stars forming behind my lids. It's a languid blink to open them.

Before me, I find the sunken face of a Goddess, her body shrivelled and aged, her indigo wings limp. She is no longer a Goddess. Instead, she's just a mortal woman on her deathbed.

I wasn't sure how this would play out. If taking her power would cause her death, or if I would still need to strike the killing blow. It seems the latter might be true. Her breaths are short and shallow, so I take the dagger from the back of my tight leather pants and strike true.

One swift, clean blow to the heart.

"Fury says hi," I murmur in her ear as I feel the life completely drain from her body. She croaks one last time before I sink back, bloody dagger in hand.

"I killed a God." It's disbelief that comes from my lips. Not malice or anger, but utterly sheer, crazed exhilaration that, for once, the fates are on my side. "I killed a mother-fucking God." *My plan might just work.*

THIRTY-SEVEN

FURY

The power from Oriel is a charge to my system. *Fucking finally*. I've already forgone half of my power to Wrath so the other Gods will believe he is me. Now, my power is fully restored, and then some.

I let a small amount of it ripple through the last thread in my and Dove's bond. She will not go without; my first priority, always.

The statues don't surprise me. The other Gods wanted more than their share of pleasure in all its forms when they fell. It's the three sacrificial-type slabs below each of the statues that fill me with dread.

At least Oriel won't be attending this party, which means we are half and half for power. Syphon one more God of their power, and we can defeat the last. Oona was always going to be the tricky sell, but Wrath was sure he could get both Oriel and Osear. That would give us majority power, and that's all I need to take my revenge.

As much as I wasn't pleased with Wrath's plan, I am

reasonable when it comes to Dove's safety, or so I like to think. There is much more at stake than my life. I have to think of the endgame. There's no way I am risking her. Ever. Dove belongs to me. Revenge was my top priority until she walked into my life.

Now, having eyes on her at all times is of primary importance. She's my universe. My heart and soul orbit around her axis. So, taking Wrath's deal ended up being simple. The risks were low; I could pull my power from him at any moment, unless he knew how to control it as Dove did. My power called to her. It often wanted her over me. Now, I have more than enough power to share.

I'm still not sure about the side effects, but once Osear is drained, I'll be able to bond with Dove again and sever the bond with Wrath. That was the deal, after all. I help him kill and escape the clutches of the three God overlords, and we go our separate ways, minus a bond.

My bonding was only meant for one person: Dove.

She steps to my side, finally taking in the onyx stone slabs, elevated off the floor to waist-height. Yellow and orange flames flicker around her face, highlighting her high cheekbones and pert nose. Gods, I want to eat her alive. Everything from the glossy strands of her hair to her delicate toes is alluring to me. Even more so is her heart—the very same one that speeds up when we draw each other's stare.

She is everything, and I was nothing until I found her.

I wrap one of my clawed hands around her fragile fingers, pulling her closer to me. "I have you," I murmur, low enough for only her ears.

"So touching," Oona interrupts us, gliding in from above, a barely there short white dress covering her. One wrong move, and she'll be exposed to everyone, but somehow I think that's the point. The dress she had brought for Dove is similar. I decided to dress her myself. No one else gets to dress my Goddess anymore.

I knew just the colour that would aggravate the meddling daemon Goddess before us. Her lips are quirked in a forced expression, her perfectly aligned features giving her the classic shape of beauty within this world. The truth, underneath, is something more malicious. She is the true devil here. I might look like the creature from the books Dove used to read, but what most people forget to acknowledge is that good looks do not constitute a good person.

The only part of your body that can hold true beauty is your soul. I cannot say I've been blessed with much beauty in my life, except for the creature who grips my hand like a lifeline.

"What is this?" I nod towards the statues and altars before us.

Oona's eyes are full of sparkling spite. She's in for her pound of flesh. Little does she know, I'm going to be the one taking it from her.

"Don't be daft, Orion. It doesn't look good on you." She saunters towards Dove, Gideon and myself. "And looky here, we have a wolf no longer. Replaced with a very fine shield." She looks Gideon up and down. "If you grow sick of protecting your little human, my ranks are always open to fine specimens." She winks at the wolf shifter, whose response is a throaty growl.

"Suit yourself." Oona flicks her waist-length blonde hair, turning her back on the three of us. I have not forgotten the ring of golden-armoured guards that circle our platform, ready to pounce if someone threatens their precious Goddess.

"Welcome to the second God trial," a worldly voice echoes around us—the same one that spoke out at the first trial, formless and ominous. "Our festivities are well underway, as the pleasure trials permit. It is now time for us to reintroduce our Godly champions."

Thirty-Eight

Dove

Godly champions. Not this again. One rhythm was enough. I'd let Fury take me from this place if the damned cuffs on my wrists allowed. My grip on him is my salvation.

"Welcome, Bear, Osear's champion." The rough, gorgeous warrior who fought for Osear's honour in the stadium pit saunters up towards the right altar completely naked, every inch of his hard abs on display. Catcalls ring out from the surrounding crowd. Osear trails after him, like he just got caught with his hand in the cookie jar, the white skirt he wears over his groin askew. Which only leaves me to conclude that the cookies are Bear's, if that shit-eating grin on the warrior's face is any sign of what was just happening.

I look back to Bear, who stands before Osear's statue, his hands pumping the air, and the shadowed crowd beyond the line of golden warriors cheering. What tops massacring innocent people for sport? Sex, that's what. Well, I can only assume, considering the overeager welcoming Bear is getting.

"Shush, now, you heathens," the disembodied voice calls. "We still have two more champions to present." The crowd quiets. "Much better. Now, let me introduce you to Lune, Oriel's champion."

When Lune makes his appearance, all lithe boyish charm, flashing his pearly whites, not a hair out of place, the crowd goes up in another extended roar. He makes his way over, stark naked, like Bear, to stand below Oriel's statue on the opposite side of Oona's, which, of course, sits in the middle.

Oriel is not following him, nor did she get here prior to Lune's arrival. Oona sits on a golden throne, flanked by two other shining seats. Osear currently resides next to her at the corner of the stage. Looking over at the Gods, they barely seem fazed. A godlin rushes over to Oona to say something. We are too far to hear. Her face is unchanged by the news, whatever it is.

The little creature rushes back off stage.

"Oriel is still on her way. She has yet to find the perfect dress." The booming, all-consuming voice that reports on the trials chuckles, like they are making us all privy to some inside joke. Laughter fans out around the stage. Fury's icy grasp continues to ground me.

Something is off.

"And finally, we have Oona's champion. A surprise contender, but as we all saw, one who proved herself quite powerful at the first trial, Dove."

If I had a pin and dropped it onto the floor, we would've heard it clink against the stone—that's how quiet it is. Fury doesn't release my hand. He pulls me behind him to stand under Oona's statue, Gideon not far behind us, always lingering close by, my personal warrior.

"And it seems Wrath has joined our new God champion. Not willing to give away his title, perhaps," the voice shouts, breaking the unbearable, skin-crawling silence. It gives the horde permission to break, soft laughter coming from beyond the stage.

It takes a moment for me to understand what the voice is referring to, until I look at the fallen God beside me with his sharp jawline, grey skin and black horns. The epitome of Oona's first champion, Wrath. I have no idea where he actually is. Everyone watching us is none the wiser. Oona has yet to explain the males around me to the crowd, and I believe she has no intention of doing so. The Atlans around us don't question her. If there's one thing I know for sure, though, it is that Oona knows exactly who's beside me—my God, Fury.

Oona stands, and all is quiet again. "I have requested an amendment to the trials, which my fellow Gods have agreed to. In this trial, I am pitting old and new against each other. Wrath and Dove." I can't take my eyes off her as she commands the audience. "May the best champion win." She sits down, her face impassive.

May the best champion win. The ripple of words goes over the people watching us. *What does that even mean?*

I vibrate with the unknown, unsure of what will become of us in this trial. *In the last one, I nearly died. How is this going to be any better?* My grip on Fury's is tighter than it has ever been.

"I've got you," his smooth voice murmurs for only my

ears. I look up into endless dark pools, knowing everything he says to me is the truth.

"And with that exciting twist from the Gods." I jolt at the announcer. Fury snarls at the sound. "Wrath and Dove will be the only contenders for Oona's champions moving forward." The people beyond the stage mutter in a low hum about the news. "The remaining contestants from the pain trails will now take their places at either Oriel or Osear's statues." The golden guards circling the platform part, and let a small stream of people through, mostly men with bruises or wounds on their naked bodies. Once they have finished creating their lines near each stone God, the disembodied voice calls out, "Let the games begin," signalling the beginning of the trial.

I do not know what to expect. Anxiety, my old friend, plays havoc on my mind, my breath coming in shallow, uneven. This trial is about pleasure, and everyone is naked, so that can only mean one thing—sex.

Rivern was my first, Gideon my second and Fury will eventually be my third, but this is not how I expected that to happen.

Lune and Bear have already experienced many of these trials before. They know what to do, bowing before stone slabs.

"Stay here," Fury growls at Gideon. I look over my shoulder towards my sour-faced shifter. He's not pleased with being told what to do, but he believes in Fury enough to let him drag me beside the strange stone slab that sits before Oona's statue.

I don't expect what happens next. I'm too busy concerning myself with keeping my breathing steady and trying not to think about what will be happening on this slab and before all these Atlans. A loud moan comes from my right, and when I tilt my head, my line of sight lands on Osear's champion. Bear is on his knees before another man, his head moving rhythmically up and down.

Oh, fuck. I can't do that with everyone watching.

"Fury, I don't know about this. I..." It's his sudden movement from standing to kneeling before me that catches my breath. You'd think I'd be used to this. Rivern and Gideon have both been on their knees for me. It's him, though—Fury, my fallen God. The one I've known for a lifetime.

"What are you doing?" I hiss. The distraction makes me forget about everyone else around us. He's going to make things worse with Oona. Who knows what sort of trouble this trial will bring? His forehead lands on mine softly, chillingly.

"You're mine." He says the words with all the force of a lightning bolt raining down from the sky. My stomach somersaults aggressively.

I go to kneel.

He slips from my hand and grips under my shoulders, pulling me up gently. "No Goddess of mine will ever kneel before anyone." My core clenches to see him like this before me. But there's a niggling at the back of my brain, saying this is a bad idea. *Everyone is watching us.*

"How romantic." Oona's bitter words slither over my skin. The air prickles around us. She is standing at the head of the altar, facing us and her statue. "Since you are unaware of the second trial's customs, I thought it only prudent to impart to you the most important rule. Whoever comes first loses." My eyes go wide as saucers.

"C-come?" I stutter, shocked.

"Yes, in the second trial, the winners are crowned by fucking." She holds up her perfectly polished gold nails as if she's inspecting them. "If you come first, you are out. It's all about stamina. The last person standing will go on to the next trial, which is a formality, really. Sacrificing everything you hold so dear unto your God. Regardless, your God here should know a lot about stamina," she adds, enjoying my discomfort, her glinting irises raking over Fury's hard lines.

"You want us to have sex before these people?" A low moan comes from next to me. My eyes unintentionally find Lune with another man. I don't need to see anything else, so I glare back at Oona.

Her laughter is a tinkle. "Nothing you two haven't done before, surely. Or have you not, Orion? Hmmm." Her perfectly sculpted, wheat-coloured eyebrow raises. *Goddess, she almost reminds me of Cardinal.* The shiver to end all shivers rakes my spine. A flashback of the High Priestess's naked body, chanting and writhing before me, covered in my blood, slithers out of my cave. She never touched me. I was always her witness. Her rituals scarred parts of me nobody saw. They were better left behind Argus and his wall. Memories better left in my cave. The cave that is now wide open to me.

Every memory from my past is easily accessible once again. My body shakes with old traumas, crushing feelings of shame and suffocation. My head dips, finding Oona's exposed feet.

Orion towers to his full height next to me, pulling me into his chest, addressing Oona. "Promise me no one else will touch her, or I'll slaughter every last person here, and you'll have no one to preside over."

"No one else will touch her. Whoever screams first loses." With that imparting lilt to her voice, she saunters away, her hips swaying exaggeratedly.

"What do you need?" The groans of ecstasy around us only grow bigger, someone already yelling their release.

"I need you to make me forget where we are." I need to forget Cardinal. I need to forget Oona. I just want him and Gideon and Rivern in my mind. *My three protectors.*

"Your wish is my command." His lips and teeth meet my neck, scraping along the raised scar and Gideon's bite. I am shivering for a whole new reason now. My hand goes to cup his head, finding a hard horn.

"What about the bond?" The whole reason we haven't entertained touching is that we know we won't be able to resist forming the bond again.

From the corner of my eye, I see a flash of turquoise. "I'll just have to do the impossible and resist you. It'll be the hardest thing I've ever done, but..."

I turn in his arms, but before coming to his gaze, I spot a gaunt-looking Oriel sitting on her throne. Her appearance registers as odd, but not enough to distract me from the lips that slam into mine.

This God does nothing slowly and steadily. It's fast and hot and full of unwavering passion. There's no doubt in my mind that he wants me, especially as he clutches my bottom and pulls me up his body, sitting me on the altar so I'm closer to his mouth.

"I have to tell you something," Fury growls softly in my ear. His earthy, ashen scent, like a bonfire taking light, circles me.

"Mmmm," I murmur, lost to him, his hardened length grinding against my exposed core. One of his sharp-clawed hands trails up the side of my already short dress, pushing it further back.

I feel like I should be embarrassed about our display, yet I can't bring myself to be when everyone around us is either cheering us on or also fucking. It brings me back to the communal Silver Sands orgies. This is something else; this is trial by pussy or cock. Hold out the longest and you win. With Fury working his magic, I don't know how I'll win.

"I'm going to come." His statement stops me. I grasp both of his horns and pull his lips off mine.

"Are you kidding?" His face is unlike anything I have ever seen before. He looks drunk. We haven't even bonded. He's moved so fast I've barely been able to catch up.

"No, and you're about to come, too." I'm close, just not on the edge where I'm about to topple over. He's confident in his conviction, his forehead pushing down into mine. My legs lock around his waist.

"Open up for me, Goddess," he whispers on a velveteen moan.

At his words, I break. That one slight tether that's connecting us unexpectedly sends a shock of power barrelling into me, hitting my clit.

"Fury." His name crosses my lips as my whole body tips over the edge at the same rhythm he does.

"Dove."

Latching his lips back onto mine, he growls between kisses. "My first. My last. My only."

We may not have bonded or even joined our bodies together beyond a kiss, but his lips on mine are everything.

THIRTY-NINE

WRATH

I search high and low for Osear. He is nowhere to be found. Perhaps I have given up too early in my attempt, but from the set of the suns and the lack of shields within the palace proper, I know he has to be at the trials.

Tonight, after he leaves, I will seduce him in his chambers. I mull over the plan as I make my way into the dungeons. If you go far enough, there's a cave system within the cliff face that the palace perches on. Fury told me about a magnificent blue beast with eight arms, lying in wait for him —one I have to meet.

I have heard of Fury's creatures from Oona in passing. Upon hearing of these creatures from him in person, I know we need their strength in storing our excess power. No human body, God-created or not, can hold the power of four deities.

It's time Oona got what is coming to her. Her demise is long overdue, and it is going to take an army.

From what I know of the great God wars, Oona harmed Orion's beasts, so it only seems fitting that they should join us in taking her power.

No humans come down into the caves under the palace. They are dark and filled with mysterious sounds that would make anyone question their grasp on reality. It's when I start to see a blue-tinged light waving back and forth against a rock face that I know I've made it to the ocean and the waiting creature beyond.

FORTY

FURY

She never said *how* we had to come, just that we *had* to come. I wasn't letting any of these humans have the privilege of seeing my Dove lose herself to my cock or mouth, so instead, I used the one thing I have at my disposal: power.

Power in itself is just energy. It's useless unless you give it a purpose. My purpose was to make my Goddess shatter into brilliant pieces around me. And I was already hard, so kissing and rubbing against her body fulfilled my need to come. It did not fill my need to consume her or re-bond with her. It wouldn't take much to bond with her again fully. *I couldn't.* Her safety comes before everything else.

For the most part, since I fell, I've been locked up. No other human or creature has touched my body since her. The humans have a word for it. *Virginity.* I like to think of it as my sanctity. There's only one reason I fell: to find the type of love humans sang songs about. My human body is for that person, man or woman.

Knowing her now, I'd wait an eternity for her. The feelings, the sensations, the utter rapture of my heart and soul. Every inch of her is brilliance and beauty. She is stuck with me forever.

"For the first rhythm, we have a tie." That booming, bodiless voice, which comes from everywhere and nowhere, travels the auditorium. The room hushes, even the moans of the people on either side of us dim. *It's pathetic how these people will do anything to please their Gods.*

"In such matters, it is always up to the Gods how they will proceed. They will present their champions at the end of this trial."

We have a moment. I ease onto Dove, resting my body. What they will do with us, I don't know, and for now, I don't care. To come with her body next to mine is a luxury.

The sounds of pleasure—grunting, groaning, moaning—are all around us. I lift my head to view the last of the two Gods. I had hoped Wrath would get to both Oriel and Osear before the trial. It was a long shot, and the window of opportunity was short. So, seeing Osear enter the trials was not a surprise, though I never expected to see the colourless God sitting next to Oona, completing the God trio.

My fists clench tightly into the back of Dove's dress. *Oriel isn't dead.* She sits on her high-backed gold throne next to the others, her face gaunt, her wings shrivelled. The power she once had is mine. When Wrath stole it, it successfully merged with our bodies. *He killed her.* He told me after he left her, which was before the trial even began.

"Why is Oriel at the God trails?" I know he hears my words; we are bonded. Instead of answering right away, as he

should, he gives it a moment. *"Wrath,"* I rumble down the bond.

"She was *dead. I drained her, put a dagger through her heart and left. She wasn't breathing. She had no heartbeat. She was DEAD."*

"You didn't fully sever her limbs?" He should've fucking known Gods are like cockroaches. She lost her power. The other Gods still have theirs. Taking stock of both the golden and silver-winged Atlan Gods, my brow furrows. It could've been either of them who saved her. They had the time. Which means they have known this whole rhythm.

"No. Why would I..." His voice trails off.

"Why didn't you dispose of her body until it was nothing but ash? Oh, I don't know, maybe so no other God could bring her back to life with their power?"

"I looked for Osear after killing her. He was nowhere near Oriel's chambers or his own."

"You are sorely mistaken." My anger gets the better of me, and I shut the connection down between us, but not before syphoning as much power as I can hold in this form. They know what we are capable of now. *Fuck, we've lost the element of surprise.* The only thing we currently have going for us is that Oona, Oriel and Osear seem to hate disappointing the people they preside over. *The show must go on.*

"Idiot," I grumble out loud.

"I sincerely hope you're talking about someone else." Dove's sweet voice soothes me.

"You only bring me agony, my Goddess."

She punches my shoulder hard enough to hurt. If I were mortal, maybe it would have. Grabbing her hands, I pin them behind her, leaning over her body.

"You want to play games, Pet?'

Her throat bobs up and down, and my cock—never down in her presence, even after coming in my pants—hardens to the point of torture.

"Only if you insist." She's goading me. A wicked grin on her face. The nectar of her exposed core is too hard to resist. I stay looking into her forest-green orbs to keep myself sober.

"You are walking a thin line. I'm trying not to ravish you in front of our enemy."

"What if I want you to fuck me in front of our enemy?" *Fates, have mercy on me.* In this carcass, I'm but mere flesh and bone.

"That's enough," Gideon interjects, his hand on my shoulder. "Not here."

I nearly snap back, my lust almost taking over. Staring into Dove's eyes, her soul, filled with fire, pulls me out of my haze. She deserves more than this. My first time with my bonded will not be in front of the Gods I want to kill. They can't have her. *Oona would enjoy watching us too much. I won't give her the satisfaction.*

"Cover her. I need to go talk to some Gods."

"No. I'm going with you," Dove says, trying to move around the wolf shifter who just filled my spot. "Argh, really?" she grumbles, realising the big stone of a male in front of her isn't budging.

"Dead serious when it comes to your safety," I hear him gruff before I'm surrounded by the sounds of screaming pleasure. *Fates, I wish it were Dove's pleasure.* Bear still holds his seat of power as Osear's champion, pounding into a woman from behind, her body shaking under him. As soon as she's screaming her release, he pulls out, ready to torture the next victim waiting in line.

It barely surprises me that this is what Oona, Osear and Oriel decided to do with their free time.

My cock loosens its hold on me at the sight. Seems I only enjoy the sight of one person falling into orgasm. I plan on giving her that ecstasy every turn of our lives together.

First, I need to get rid of these pesky flies.

To greet Oona, Osear and Oriel by their names is to show respect. So, out of defiance, I stand before the thrones of the orchestrators of this chaos in silent mockery. Knowing they gain pleasure from breaking humans in this way only serves to fuel my disobedience. The guards around them move towards me, the heaviness of their armour clinking.

Oona puts up a hand, ceasing them. It's Osear who speaks. "Wrath, what can we do for you?" *Wrath. Glad to see we are still keeping up the show for the sake of the game.*

I direct my words at the foul woman at the centre of their threesome. "Who will you take as your champion?"

A pointed nail runs across her chin. "Hmmm, well, we have much to discuss about the predicament you've placed us in." She taps her finger on her chin.

"Let us go, and we won't be of any consequence to you."

"You know I can't do that." The finger that was tapping her plump pink lip points to Oriel. "It seems you have something of ours."

"All's fair in love and war."

Oona chuckles. "Oh, you are quite right." She stands and points a finger at me. "Guards, take this imposter to the dungeons."

FORTY-ONE

DOVE

Heat replaces the sizzling cold. "You're not going to keep me here, are you?" I lean back, batting my eyelashes up at the wolf before me—my mate.

He instantly pulls back off the slab of stone that Fury and I just came against, gripping me around the waist to take me with him. I'm placed gently on my feet, his features serious. "As always, I'm at your command."

Goddess, it feels good to hear him say those words. I can think of plenty of ways I could command him. The fine lines around his dazzling eyes crinkle as we continue our stare down. "Anything?" I murmur, the sound around us melting into a buzz of background noise.

Gideon steps closer to my body, his hard chest flush against my smaller one. "Anything. Let's get out of this place first." His growly, rough voice coasts over my prickling skin.

Our eye lock continues until Oona's voice catches my attention.

"Guards, take this imposter to the dungeons." Both of our heads swivel towards *her* voice.

A chorus of chinking armour moves around Fury. My stomach instantly drops into my feet. Of course, Oona couldn't let this go any further. She plans to use her advantage in this place. She is a Goddess to these people, and we are impositions on their land.

A burst of white light comes from the place Fury is standing. Cold hands abruptly move around mine. "Let her think she has the power. I will come for you. Keep Gideon close."

I spin towards him just as Fury's velveteen words finish caressing my ear. An exasperated cry rings out over the stage. "Guards, find him!" Oona shouts her aggravation. Armour clanks together as it pushes through rapt onlookers, curious about what has angered the Goddess.

What are you doing, Fury? I'm also tempted to shout his name in vain for leaving me here, but he hasn't left me alone. I still have Gideon. One of only three people I trust in this world.

"Bring my champion." The crowds around us are hushed, hundreds of eyes on my body as a golden ensemble of guards makes a circle around us. You could mistake it as Oona trying to protect her champion. I read it as her keeping me prisoner. Contained. Gideon towers over the human guards surrounding us. I have no doubt he'd be able to take them all on in a fight, so I go along with whatever this is.

"It has come to my attention that Wrath is not who he says he is." The crowd gasps in horror at the news. *Like she didn't already know he was Fury.* Her show is pathetic. "It is with my greatest displeasure that I request the capture of Wrath at any cost. Once caught, he is to be brought to me immediately. Consider him to be extremely dangerous."

By putting a capture order out for Wrath, she's essentially putting one out for Fury, too, not that anyone will be able to capture my God with his powers. They ripple through me now—a slight, ever-present thrum. Ever since I fully healed our only lingering connection, I've felt an ever-growing energy from that shared piece of him. It has become even more prominent during the trial.

"With this news, my champion remains the same." There's a long pause before she focuses on me. "Congratulations, Dove." Oona plasters a devastating smile on her face. "As is tradition, all champions will be brought to their Gods' chambers for their prize."

The word *prize* fills me with dread. Gideon is vibrating with restrained anger behind me, his hands on my waist, keeping me close.

"Congratulations to our first pleasure trial winner, Dove, Oona's champion. Updates for Osear and Oriel's champions to come," the ever-present God trials voice booms from somewhere. I'm starting to think it's God magic.

"For now, we follow. See what she wants," Gideon adds from his towering height above me. We don't have many options with my wrists cuffed, so I go along with this farce.

We are hustled out of the large underground by our glinting entourage shuffling beside us, keeping us in step with the Goddess, who flows before us. Doors open before her without anyone touching them. Once our group enters the manor proper, the eerie silence is sickening.

The scuffing of boots against marble floors rebounds through the halls and stairs as we move swiftly towards what I can only guess is Oona's chambers. The closer we get, the more the smell of pomegranate greets me. A delicious fruit now ruined because of its sudden association with this place.

The stark white and gold walls and floors make this manor anything but homey. Give me my forest by the ocean, not a castle over a desolate cliff. I have seen a sea of white-washed stone houses below the manor proper. A smattering of green dotted trees throughout. Not enough nature for my liking. It's a barren land, much like the hearts of these Gods.

I yearn for the turn I can resume tending my gardens and drawing the intricacies of a beetle. As long as my future holds those simplicities with my fae, wolf and God, I'll be happy.

A burst of sea air washes over me, the guards falling away. The wide double doors before us open onto a shimmering room of glinting yellow metal—the chandelier, the edging of the sofas, the finely spun floating curtains. Much like the rest of the main manor, if it's not gold, it's white.

We have yet to step inside, looking on at the extravagance. "Come along," Oona croons from somewhere inside. At her insistence, we are pushed behind by the guards. Gideon takes a stance behind me, Oona's people unable to move him.

To save the stalemate we find ourselves in, I take a step over the threshold and into *her* room.

"Are you sure?" Gideon questions behind me.

"We have no choice," I answer, stepping forward again. The two cuffs around my wrists saw to that. When both of our bodies are within the doorframe, a bang sounds behind us.

"Oh, good, you're here." Oona breezes out of a darkened dressing area from across the way, like we weren't just forced into her room by a bunch of men in armour. *She has to be more insane than Fury.* Her slinky dress has been forgotten and replaced with a golden robe that barely covers her voluptuous cleavage.

She goes to sit on the settee by the open balcony doors, a moonlit sky shining down on her from behind. "Come, join me." Her hand waves towards the opposite lounge. Alarm bells are ringing in my head. *What game is she playing at? And where has Fury gone?*

"Please, sit." Her smile could almost be called genuine. *She wants something. That has to be it. Why else would she invite me here?*

Curiosity drives me to know what this God could want. Sitting on the lounge opposite her, I adjust my dress so it's not flashing her. Oona seems to have no qualms with such things, her right breast having conveniently fallen out of her robe.

She, of course, notices where my eyes have fallen, a devilish grin chasing her lips.

Gideon doesn't bother sitting down, his broad width casting a shadow from the back of my chair.

"Well." Oona claps her hands together. "We have much to discuss, going into the last trial.

Do I bring up Fury? She seems to have no intention of touching on the subject.

"Oh?" I go for unfazed, preferring to see where she decides to direct the conversation.

"Yes. The final trial is all about sacrifice. What are you willing to give up to become a champion of a God?" Her sparkling eyes flicker behind me. My heart skips a beat. *Does she think we have somehow become friends?* This new side of Oona is making me majorly concerned, like this is the calm before her storm.

"Umm, I never thought of it," I tell her the truth, trying to play down the power I feel in my stomach. Since my mind-numbing, clit-electrocuting orgasm with Fury, I can't bring myself to be rageful right now. So, besides my body being strung tight, I have yet to feel the sort of rancour Fury usually flames within me.

"Well, you should be." She scoffs. "Many people would love to be in your shoes right now. After the second trial, it's basically a done deal." Her hands wave around. A godlin appears out of nowhere, carrying a tray of sparkling drinks. "We shall toast."

"We shall?" I ask, confused.

"Of course, you silly little human." She holds a circular glass in her hand, the godlin hurrying over to me next. I take my drink. "To a beautiful friendship." Oona sips her glass, and I follow suit. Her words are utterly bewildering.

"First," Oona begins to explain, "your prize for winning the trial." I almost expect the cuffs around my wrists to fall off, but they do not. "I was thinking, what does the human who has everything want?" Rising, Oona makes her way over to my lounge. Gideon isn't happy. His roughened chest rumbles, growling. "Oh, calm down. I've decided you can stay."

I sit, bemused by this ethereal woman. *What is going on?* I'm beyond confused. One moment, she's trying to lock up

Fury, and now she's pretending like she didn't take me hostage and force me to be her champion. *She does know I don't want to be here, right?* Gideon knows he has no hope of winning in a fight with a God, and keeps his rumble low but steady—a warning.

"Often, the prize is quite simple. Usually, the humans want a night in a God's bed." Gideon's growl vibrates loudly around the room. Oona ignores him. "I respect that this is not an option for you." Her eyes dart towards my wolf, whose piercing stare is deafening to his willingness to share with this woman. *Also, did Oona just insinuate that she respects me?*

It seems like I'm out of the loop, and this is all some elaborate prank.

She continues on before I can ask any more questions. "So, instead, I've come up with an idea never before bestowed on a human by myself or any other Gods." The tops of her fingertips graze my arm. "Such a pretty thing. I do hope you like it." Her smile is my answer.

My instinct is to flinch at Oona's touch, and I should've, because her prize is beyond what I ever could have imagined.

Power fills me, wanting, searching.

A bond solidifies, cracking into place.

My skin crawls. My eyes roll into the back of my head.

Gideon's roar hits my ears.

Unlike my God bonds with Fury and Rivern, this one is harsh, a violation. A moment that lasts a whole rotation.

"All done," Oona's voice draws me back within myself. My head rests on the back of the lounge. She hovers over me. "Now, let me see what all the fuss is about." Her face, which some would call beautiful, is imbued with the hatred of her soul. She is the true daemon of this world. Her golden eyes glow, specters as she gazes down on me, her prize to the slaughter. "Oh, shut him up, will you?"

That's when I hear two extra voices in the room mumbling. "He's stronger than we expected." *Where did they come from?* It feels like I'm underwater, unable to resurface for air.

"Your power is stronger than one monster," she barks over me. "Chain him up. I have work to do. Do you want your power back or not?" Glowering beyond me, I now know who has suddenly joined us—Osear and Oriel. *When did that happen? They were probably lying in wait outside. And whose power is she talking about? Fury and I aren't even fully bonded anymore.*

Hands on her hips, Oona watches me with a calculating stare. "Let's see what we have here." She's in my head, rummaging around before I can make a squeak. A flash of another woman with similarly coloured hair crosses my vision.

"I'm not her. I'm worse," Oona whispers, her voice snake-like in quality, slithering around my body. My neck, my shoulders, my chest... They all tingle. Her eyes roam slowly down my body until she finds exactly what she's looking for when she hits my stomach.

"Oh, dear, what do we have here?" She kneels before me, my body slumping back further into the plush fabric, paralysed by fear. She's found it, the last thread tying Fury and me together. I reach for it now trying my hardest to find him, call to him.

"FURY," I scream down the line, hoping he'll hear me.

"Oh, dear, oh, dear. Poor human." Two hands land on

my stomach. "The ultimate sacrifice," she whispers to herself. The Goddess, Oona, is on her knees in front of me. A splitting headache cracks my skull in two. Gripping my head, I scream in pain before it subsides.

"You don't know?" She sounds surprised.

"What?" I croak, holding my head in my hands. Oona's palms still on my lower abdomen.

"You don't know about the life forms?" The Goddess's voice rises. "He didn't tell you what he did?" She almost sounds smug.

"What are you talking about?" I grumble, opening my eyes to find she has taken a wide step back, her eyes not leaving my stomach.

"They will be your sacrifice at the last trial." She begins to pace, her finger tapping her lip. "Shields!" she yells. Woozy, I turn to find her guards stumbling in.

"Yes, Goddess." The humans in armour bow before her.

"Any sign of the traitor?"

"No, my Goddess. We have searched the palace and have begun working our way through the island. We have placed importance on securing the palace, as is protocol."

That seems to satisfy the Goddess eyeing off my lower half. "Very well. You may leave."

Behind me, Gideon whines at my discomfort, our mate bond strong despite Oona's intrusion. I want to go to him, but lifting my legs seems like an impossible task, so I stay where I am. My eyes begin to get droopy, my hands falling away from covering my middle.

"That's it, human. Soon, your sacrifice will be complete, and you will belong to me." Someone pushes my hair off my face, and I slip into darkness.

FORTY-TWO

RIVERN

She finds me brushing Mage's coat, Solen casting his shadow overhead. Delicate hands wrap around me from behind.

"We really have to stop meeting like this," I joke. The simple wooden cottage I built for our family stands before us next to the lake of reflections—the same lake I nearly fully bonded with her by.

She chuckles behind me, her soft lips landing on the markings on my back, silver lines now intertwined with my golden ones, representing the full-body hold she has over me.

A roundness pushes into me, Dove letting out a pained groan.

The more I stay in this dreamworld, the more my imagination has conjured up of our potential future together. It's addicting in the best way. She always finds me at the right time.

"Are you feeling okay, my love?" I spin around to face

her. Her petite nose is scrunched. She rests a hand across my chest and bends over, letting out an exasperated moan, holding the round bump protruding from her stomach.

"This child has officially overstayed their welcome. I don't know how they fit." She slaps her other hand against my hard chest and pushes. "This was not the dreamscape I was expecting."

I rub a hand over her back, wishing I could do more, but I blame Fury. He did this to her, after all. "Well, you have interrupted my dream, you know."

Her head whips up from between her outstretched arms, skin no longer bare but filled with a story of our making. Her fingernails dig into me. Our eyes lock, zapping through the bond. *Goddess, the way she looks at me makes my knees weak, even when she's angry.*

"Mumma." A fluff of golden curls and tawny skin springs up between her arms. "You're back."

Dove's eyes go wide in surprise. The little girl pokes at her mother's rounded stomach, hidden behind a forest-green muslin dress.

"Mumma, Papa told me I'm not allowed to hunt on my own yet, but I've been practicing, and Oro said he would help me," the little girl whines at our feet.

A pissed-off-looking Gideon strides through the break in the trees that leads to our cottage in this secluded part of the woods. "I told her she's not hunting on her own until she is at least thirty human rotations."

Dove leans forward, running a finger over the little girl's cheek. Wide green eyes sparkle up at her. "But, Mumma, I'm five now. I can do it on my own. Pleeeassssse." The wind stirs around us, signalling Fury.

He lands with a chubby bundle strapped to his chest. "No," he answers the small girl with complete adoration. "Let's bump it until she's at least one hundred. I don't think we should count in human rotations since she's more fae and shifter than human."

"You're right," Gideon adds, kissing Dove on her forehead and ruffling the little girl's blonde locks.

"Mumma, Daddy, please. Papa and Dad are being mean to me."

Dove pushes back from my chest and reaches for the girl. She leaps into her arms. Fury, Gideon and I all take a step towards our heavily pregnant bonded.

"Don't," she says. "I want some mother-daughter time." Her eyes are filled with unshed tears before she walks away into our cottage.

My body pangs as she walks away, holes radiating through every inch of my reality where we were once linked, reminding me of the bond no longer connecting us. I fall to my knees. The men surrounding me disappear, along with the cottage and forest. Before I know it, my dream is once again in darkness, and the pain of losing her is my religion.

FORTY-THREE

FURY

I shouldn't have fucking left her. It was risky. And I promised myself I'd always stay by her side. Oona is going to *try* to sink her claws into her. And now, I'm going to give away power. *I'm losing my fucking mind.*

Teleporting onto the sandy beaches of Atla, I catch Ken with Wrath just in time. The gigantic azure, tentacled creature is moments from diving into the dark ocean spray. *"Ken."* I don't say the word out loud. I use the connection of creator and master—an eternal link.

"My God, you no longer wish me to go?" Ken's reply is swift, his head bobbing out of the water, his eyes reflecting the moonlight.

"I wish to give you power before you go. The power of a God."

He doesn't answer right away. Out of all my beasts, my kraken has been the most humble. It's a wonder being left in captivity for so long hasn't made him insane. He's kept a part of himself I once thought I'd lost, being imprisoned on my island—humanity.

Ken has given without greed, helping my Goddess. And now, I am going to repay him.

"Give me a tentacle." I need some sort of contact for this transfer. Much like a God bond, except when I give Ken some of Oriel's power, he'll feel nothing of me within him. It will be his power and his power alone.

"My God, that is too big a gift. I cannot accept. I told your lookalike here as much." Wrath stands by the shore, the waves lapping at his feet. I sent him out of the castle to wait for me with Ken. I don't have time to explain everything to the kraken through my mind, and I need this to be quick so we can move along with the plan. Our first play has been squashed, and all the Gods are still alive. That doesn't mean our original ideas need to be altered, just advanced more aggressively.

I am going to kill Oona if it is the last thing I ever do.

Dove is all I care about. She will get off this island. She will be safe with Rivern and Gideon in Haven. If it comes down to it, I am prepared to sacrifice myself for her.

A strange pang shoots through the thread, weaving me back to my Goddess, and I just know we are running out of time. There's a push on the power connecting us, and it fills me with apprehension. *I need to find her—now.*

"Ken, I don't have time. This is not me asking. It's me telling you to take this power and hold onto it."

At my command, the kraken raises one thick, suckered tentacle from the ocean and directs it my way. I waste no more rhythm talking, taking the proffered arm. Keeping all of this power isn't an option. If Wrath were to suck more from Oona or Osear, it would be too much for his and my physical bodies. It seems that there is such a thing as too much power.

There's a sensation on my edges, like a bubble just before popping. It's important to recognise your limits as a God—or human, for that matter. Greed serves no one, especially the Gods who live in the palace on the cliff.

Once I'm satisfied with the transfer of power to Ken, my body feels light again, more buoyant. The kraken, on the other hand, is lit up like the full moon, his skin zapping pockets of lightning over the still waters.

"Go, Ken." At my insistence, the glowing blue beast dives into the water, off to guide a ruby dragon back to the island of Atla in hopes that we will be able to share more power.

"Let's kill some Gods." I look over to Wrath, and he dips his head in agreement.

FORTY-FOUR

WRATH

Following behind Fury after he teleports us back into the palace is a game of cat and mouse. Just to get up to the Gods' chambers has taken precious time we don't have. I can witness the strain all over Fury's face.

Shields are stationed at every corner, every stair and before all the doorways. It makes it impossible to teleport unless you want to end up in front of one of them. So, all our movements back within the palace have been infuriatingly slow, especially since we need to move with the element of surprise to avoid anyone hurting Dove.

"Maybe we need a new plan," I say through the bond.

"Nothing changes. We focus on Osear. Get him alone. If you see Oriel, make sure you sever her head and not just stab her with a damned fucking dagger." It's obvious Fury isn't a fan of how I tried to kill the Goddess. *What can I say? I've never tried to kill a God before.* It always seemed impossible until they arrived. It wasn't me against three anymore. I had backup.

And I was inspired.

The way I see Fury and Gideon move around Dove, like she is the air they breathe... Dove's strength after being ripped away from not one, but two God bonds, invigorates me. It all gives me hope. I want to be on the side of history they inhabit.

I've had enough of Oona dictating my life.

"How will we get him alone?" We creep down the hall leading to Osear's chambers, wary of the shield making his rounds up ahead.

"Make everything seem normal." Fury's hand juts out past the cover of the wall we are about to round. It hits something hard and metallic. A crack can be heard, then silence.

"You killed him, didn't you?" I ask. Before Fury answers my question, he drags the hunk of lifeless gold armour around the corner and teleports. *"Where—"* And he's back again with a rush of air. I've never liked it when the Gods move so effortlessly from one room to the next.

Fury waves his hand up my body, a heaviness settling over me, the helmet of my newfound armour clinking into place. *"None the wiser."*

"What about my wings?" I suddenly panic, feeling unsteady in my body, my favourite feature of my back gone.

"It's only temporary. They'll return when you take the armour off."

"Goddess," I hiss, stumbling back. The God before me catches my arm.

A clinking sound comes down the hall opposite us, and I freeze. Through the slits in the eye holes of the armour, I see an identical-looking guard coming my way. "Shit,

Fury," I whisper. Looking around, I find I'm alone in the hallway.

"Row, what the fuck are you doing? Get back to guarding the door." The shield is on me. There's a noticeable height difference between us, and I try my best to crouch down, hoping he won't notice I'm not this Row character.

"On it," I grumble, trying to hide my voice.

His helmet moves up and down. I head towards the door to create some distance between us.

"Row?" *Keep you cool, Wrath. Act normal. Normal will get you inside Osear's bedchambers.*

Slowly, I turn to face him. "We still on for drinks after the trials?" A sigh leaves my heavy chest.

I avoid saying anything else and fist-pump the air. He stays glued to the spot for a moment. My leg jitters in the golden sweat suit I'm stuck in. *Gods, this would be horrendous during the turn.* One thing I've always enjoyed is the freedom to choose my clothing. Anyone else under the three Gods' thumbs has strict dress wear.

A loud *clash* comes from the stairway further down the hall. The shield swiftly nods and heads towards the noise. *This next part relies on stealth.* Who is within Osear's room will determine my course of action.

No doubt he has Bear in his bed after the trial. Bear is a formidable warrior, but after the trials, he'll be in a deep sleep until the sacrificial trial. I have first-hand experience. That should leave Osear by himself.

The door creaks as I push down on the handle. I glance left to right. Nobody comes running. Taking the swift approach, I open the door quickly—just enough room for me and my chunky armour. Behind me, there is a slight click. I stay plastered to the wall, my breaths coming thick and fast in my helmet.

This is the most my heart has raced since... I can't remember when. It thuds, harsh and heavy. It's exhilarating.

The space I've entered is dark. Beams of light illuminate a long chaise in the middle of the room. A replica statue of Osear stands to the side, with more busts and art scattering the walls. Osear's receiving room is a shrine to himself. Everything the artists of Atla have made is on display.

Opting to shed my disguise at this juncture, I strip. It's no easy feat. Armour was not designed to be taken off quietly.

Once I've successfully placed every piece on the chaise, the weight of my wings returns. It feels like I can breathe again. For a moment, I can imagine this is just any other night.

Opening one of the floor-to-ceiling double doors that lead to the God's bedchambers, I immediately spot a snoring Bear in the large, half-moon-shaped bed. What I don't see is Osear.

On silent feet, I pad towards the bathroom. *The last place left to check.* Inside, steam billows, and a soft trickle of water comes from the windows along the side of the room.

The glide of a body through water catches my attention. I should've known the God would be drawn to the pool-length spa in his bathroom. He often swims laps at night. I've tried swimming before, but the friction between my much thicker wings is off-putting, to say the least. I'm a flyer, through and through.

Osear turns, making a splash in the water. He hasn't noticed me yet, and I don't plan on him seeing me until it's too late. This is the one place the God seeks comfort above all. He won't be paying attention to what's happening above the water.

This moment couldn't be any better if I had planned it myself.

Coming to the edge of the pool, I linger on the sidelines. There won't be any need for me to take him by force. The plan has always been for the Gods to come to Orion, and as far as he knows, I am the fallen God. The zapping power running through my veins proves that.

Doing one last spin in the water at the edge of the pool, Osear rises, water droplets falling off of silver eyelashes. His short, cropped hair glistens as he runs his hands through it. Delicate, pearly wings uncoil behind him, the water droplets making them shimmer from the light of the stars outside.

Once he's taken a breath, the air shifts in the room. Gleaming silver eyes latch onto mine. Like Oona, he hides his emotions well, stepping slowly and deliberately out of the pool along a cascade of stairs trickling water.

"Have you come to your senses?" No doubt, he wants Orion to fall at his feet before he does Oona. Since descending from the stars, the Gods have all hungered for ultimate dominance. Oriel is less hungry than Osear. I know, given the chance, they wouldn't be so attached to Oona if Orion were before them. Forbidden fruit always tastes the sweetest. If given the opportunity, they would relish the advantage of wielding power over the others.

Said God power greats mine, pushing out from Osear, checking to make sure I am indeed the once imprisoned God and not Wrath.

That the only difference between me and my namesake is

power, is not lost on me. The only way Oona could ever have Orion is if she made him powerless, and because she couldn't have the real thing, she created me instead. Now, I share Orion's power, and I hold something greater inside me.

Each of the Gods' destruction.

Standing before me, he's slightly smaller. Not by much —just enough for me to have to tilt my head. "If coming to my senses means I beg your forgiveness, then you would be correct," I reply. Compared to his more lilting tone, mine is deeper, smoother.

"Why would I forgive you after what you did to Oriel?" His demeanour may seem relaxed, but the God before me is on high alert.

"I didn't do anything to Oriel. I've been with Dove up until Oona tried to capture me." Fury filled me in on what happened before and after I sucked Oriel's powers to keep up the guise that I was him.

"Riiighhht." Osear walks around my body, unconvinced. I wear Fury's black leather pants, my chest on display, his magic in my veins. It was enough to fool Oriel. Convincing Osear might prove trickier.

"Oriel told us Wrath disguised himself as you. She doesn't know how he did it." He looks me up and down, assessing me for a sign. "It's how she lost her power. Now, how are you going to convince me otherwise?" He stops before me, his thin grey eyebrows raised, curious. I know he wants me to be Orion. Having an upper hand on Oona is what gets Osear's dick hard at night.

It's why he likes to push his bedroom conquests to death. The number of bodies that leave his bedroom and end up in the furnace is grotesque. I have no problem stealing his power and cutting off his head.

"Ask me something only I would know." I cross my arms. What Osear doesn't know, because he's never been God-bonded, is that anything he asks, I can relay to the real Orion.

Stupid God.

Fury was right; sticking to the original plan might work.

"Okay." He crosses his own arms over his abs, thinking. "How about you answer a question about your human?"

I nod, unsure about where this line of questioning could possibly be going. Anything he asks me, I'll most likely have to relay to the real Fury.

"Oona knows why she couldn't sever your bond completely now." The dark pupils of his eyes begin to cover the silvers. *He thinks he has me somehow.* "Tell me what the connection is."

The connection? I'm tempted to give him a *my power is better than your power* talk, but there's something more to this. I see it in the glint of his eyes.

"I need answers quickly. Osear wants to make sure I'm you. Why are you and Dove still connected after Oona broke your bond?" I enter an eye gazing contest with the God, waiting for Fury to answer.

"She's pregnant." He drops the bomb without a care. His lacquered baritone is there and gone within an instant—an instant that makes me see red.

Overly aware of Osear standing before me, the room starkly silent, it's a perilous feat to keep my face calm. Oona ripped the bonds away from a pregnant woman, expecting her to die in the process, wanting me to interrogate her when she didn't and was already hanging on by a thread.

"She's pregnant," I speak the words aloud, my pitch surprisingly steady. *"With twins."* Fury throws the extra explosive in to test my strength of will, I'm sure of it.

My eye twitches as I repeat, "With twins," for Osear's ears. Fury's full attention is on our connection now, waiting for the God in front of me to either succumb to me or try to kill me.

"I suppose congratulations are in order." My shoulders slump. *He thinks I'm Orion, the God.* "Let us have a drink." I play along with the fake niceties, following behind Osear as he walks over to a crystal decanter filled with clear liquor. "It doesn't do much for us Gods, and the flavour is something to be desired, but I'm growing used to it." He refers to the liquid; the humans on Atla have titled it moonshine.

We clink the glasses together and scull. A burning sensation travels down my throat, only serving to fuel the anger I have for these Gods who've kept me their captive slave to their needs.

Oriel's power wasn't enough. I have a desperation to be filled again. Replace what Fury took from me. I breathe in a lungful of bitter blood orange. That's always been Osear's problem; he's all bitter and no sweetness.

Taking a step into his chest, I reach a hand under his chin to lift it up to meet my eyes. "I want us to be a team. Forget Oona and Oriel. It should've been us from the start." His eyes go wide. Dare I even say that he looks surprised?

Either he wants to be Orion, or he wants control of him, and right now, it looks like I'm giving him everything he wants.

"Us against the others?" he disbelievingly questions my words.

"Yes," I murmur in his ear, flicking my tongue over his lobe. My blood pulses in want for the ripple of electricity that skims between us, my fangs extending.

"Yes," Osear practically moans, going to grip the hard plains of my chest.

Together, Fury and I are these Gods' ultimate destruction. *A long-held dream they've never been able to have and never saw coming.*

Fates, I will take pleasure in this.

My fangs sink past flesh and sinew, my venom taking instant effect on the God, making his body fall into my arms. If the moonshine wasn't strong enough, the poison from my bite is.

Suck after suck, my power grows, finding Orion's energy and the tethers that weave us together. They join in a clash, taking time to meld, being sucked through to my other half.

I savour the feeling. It's better than fucking. I've never felt true love. My bond with Fury is the closest I've ever been to someone, and even then, he isn't open to me like I would've imagined. He hides himself. It's not meant to last, so I pay him no heed. We are one in our plan for revenge, and that's all that matters.

"How does the teleporting thing work?" I've never thought of using it before. Now, with the full power of a God running under my skin, I feel invincible—so much so, I'm sure I can make it down to the dungeon to destroy Osear's body properly.

"Think of where you want to go and push the power in that direction," Fury replies.

"I can do that." I sling Osear over my shoulder. "Darkness, the wet smell of moss and stagnant water, the cold air on my skin." Thinking aloud helps me focus, closing my eyes and imagining my energy has already travelled to the place I want to be.

Air whips around my exposed chest, and my eyes greet the most beautiful sight: my underground home. "I did it." And this rhythm, I'll dispose of the body so it'll never be found again.

FORTY-FIVE

GIDEON

ROAR.

It doesn't take much for my wolf to reach the surface when she is in trouble. I changed during my fight with Oriel and Osear due to uncontrollable instinct. Unfortunately, even one God is stronger than my beast form.

They suffocated me, chained me and threw me in a cell.

I don't care.

Not about me.

It's my songbird. She's pregnant, and they took her again. My useless body lies limp on the ground, twitching in unrelenting pain—my own *and* Dove's.

The mate bond between us beats strong, her heart a steady rhythm next to mine. *"I'm coming for you. I'm coming for you. I'm coming for you. I'm coming for you. I'm coming for you."* I say it to her repeatedly until my legs move. She's my compass, and I'll murder anyone who gets in my way.

"I'm coming for you."

FORTY-SIX

DOVE

It's back, my old friend pain. The sensation I come back to again and again. I awaken with my arms stretched high above my head and my legs spread. A noisy brandishing of metal scratching against metal hurts my ears.

Something electrifyingly cold touches my cheek, my eyelids flying open to the sensation. A grey God with raven wings and onyx horns crouches before me. "Where did you go?" I mumble, not happy with his disappearance.

"Forgive me, Pet," is all he gives me, his power zapping the chains around my wrists and ankles. I fall forward into his arms. "I wanted to come sooner, but I needed to know you would be safe from them."

"Fury," I croak out. This is far from over. Our last thread remains undamaged—for now. Oona and I are bonded, and as the human in this situation, she holds all of the weight in our dynamic. It's not an effortless connection like Fury's was, or Rivern's. This one is slimy, putrid. It makes my bones heavy, and my eyelids droop.

The ease with which Fury found me doesn't feel right. She will know he is here. Lifting my head, I see we are back where the first trial started in the arena. And instead of a bonfire at the centre of the ground below, there's a circular stage with a large wooden X behind me that I was chained to.

A clash followed by a howl takes our full attention. "Gideon!" I scream his name. His wolf-shaped head tries to bash its way through the iron grates of the wide arena doors he's been placed behind. There's a restriction I can feel within his body, which makes my muscles lock up. *She has him bound. Those fucking Gods.*

This rhythm, when I try to pull power from my rage, nothing happens, and I'm left breathless. I fall forward, holding my stomach. Fury grasps my hips before I topple over.

"I had to reinforce the metal with some of my power to keep him contained. He's strong. But none of your beasts will ever be a match for a God." Oona flies between us and the gate holding Gideon at bay. *Gods, I want to vomit.* This connection with the crazed fallen God before me is sickening. Even her dress makes me want to spill all the food I ate at lunch.

"Do you like it?" Dark, flowing fabric moulds to her sun-touched skin. "The dress code called for black." She lifts off the ground, her wings flapping like a bee, fast and furious. "Death is the colour of the turn."

Landing before us, Oona gives me a once-over. "That's no way for a bonded to be dressed." She clicks her tongue, and with a flick of her hand, my torn gold dress from the second trial is replaced with a long, black gossamer gown. "That's better."

BANG. Gideon's head goes into the bars of the gate again. I wince internally. His pain at being trapped and away from me is present; it's a desperation. The warring of the need for my mate and this foul sensation of being bonded to Oona is too much. Turns out, there is such a thing as a bad God bond. I've been lucky to experience only the good kind before this.

Fury pulls me forward, so my breathing evens out, and I take solace from his sizzling arm around my body.

"Let him go," I plead with Oona. Gideon slams into the iron of the arena door, shaking the stone walls enclosing us in this space. I can't bear my beast hitting his body against the harsh gates at full force again and again. It's barbaric.

My heart bleeds for him.

"Orion, I see you couldn't resist the bait I have set for you." Oona stretches out her arms. "Welcome to the third trial," she booms.

Fury doesn't give her a reply. He stands by my side, unfazed by her actions. Oona takes a step closer. "You see, the third trial is all about sacrifice, and I thought, what could my champion give me?" She brings a painted gold nail to her pouty red lips. "Death! Not just any death, but the death of her most treasured lovers. So here we are."

She's insane. There's no amount of pleading that will stop her. I turn on Fury. "Leave. Get away from here. It's not worth all our lives." He tilts murderous eyes down to me. My fingers dig into his skin. He grasps my wrists tightly over the golden cuffs.

"Don't you ever tell me you're not worth it," he grumbles the words in anguish, like I've slapped him. I open my mouth to reply, but he doesn't let me, kissing me with the fierceness of his love.

I'm barely holding myself up. Fury is my strength. Clapping comes from the background, and he releases me. *We are all going to die here.* The thought spins in my head. I led them all to their deaths. Oona, Osear and Oriel will kill us all, and Rivern will never wake up. *Oh, Goddess, what have I done?*

No one has moved, both Gods at a stalemate. Just before I'm about to get to my knees, however, bile rising to my throat, the gate lifts like magic. The magic of a powerful God. And by the look on Oona's face, she wasn't the one to let my wolf shifter free. Her mouth falls into a sneer.

A loud clank rebounds around the circular pit, and I catch a glinting iron collar lying on the ground just as Gideon takes me within his sturdy wolf arms, fur brushing against my cheek.

"How?" Oona is full of choked outrage at the sight before her.

"Haven't checked in with Osear recently, have you?" If looks could kill, Fury would be a puddle of ash on the dirt floor—the same floor stained in blood from the last time we were here.

"Imbecile. Fucking traitor. Just as bad as Oriel," Oona screams.

"Maybe if you were kinder to them, they wouldn't have fallen for your creation." Her eyes light up, piecing together the puzzle.

"Wrath?" she questions. "He's been pretending to be

you, hasn't he?" Her hands grip her hips. "But he has no power."

Fury shakes his head. "We share power."

"You bonded with him." She gasps.

"I bonded with him," Fury confirms. Oona looks at Fury, aghast. *Does she feel nothing for the male she created? The man she built in Orion's likeness?*

"Does that mean I can take power through a bond?" Oona asks, coming to a realisation, smugness working its way over her features.

Fury cocks his head.

The whiplash these two Gods are giving me is exhausting. My stomach roils. I grip harder onto Gideon's chest. Déjà vu finds me. *Did we just come full circle, but without the audience to keep Oona's manners in check? Great.*

My body isn't my own. Being bonded to Rivern and Fury was like coming home. Oona is a swift kick to the kidneys, completely disorientating. Even the last connection I have to Fury is dulled. The embers that are on constant simmer in the pits of my emotional turmoil are washed in rotten sewage.

Warmth from Gideon's grip around my waist barely keeps the chill of being bonded to this daemon at bay. I barely have anything left to give to this fight. Gideon whines, my mate intimately understanding what is going on inside of me. Fury is blind to all of it now. He knows there's something wrong, but not what it is.

"Spit it out, Oona. I have no time for your games."

"I've bonded with your pet," she gloats, waggling a finger at me.

It's the *wrong* thing to say. The absolute worst. The air

around Fury crackles with such force that Gideon takes a step backwards, keeping me protected. A flash of pure power blinds me. It hurts to even look in Oona's direction. I hide my face in the fine black fur of my wolf's chest.

It takes a moment for the lightning-quick flash to send my body into a convulsion of nerve pain. "Argh!" I scream. My limbs thrash in Gideon's stronghold.

"What did you do to her?" Fury's anger is deafening.

A cackling travels across the stage and dirt between us. "I bonded with your precious human. If you hurt me, you hurt her. Seems only fair." *That explains the convulsions.* They slowly subside in my body.

Gideon's fur turns into hard skin. "Songbird? Songbird? Speak to me." Still big enough to hold me in one arm, he checks over my body with the other.

"I'm okay," I barely croak through a cough.

"Remove the bond, and I may contemplate sparing your life," Fury tries to bargain with Oona.

"Don't be a fool, Orion. We both know you plan to kill me. She's my only hope of surviving now that your so-called power outweighs my own. I'm not stupid like Oriel and Osear." I wish I could see her face. My body is limp in Gideon's arms.

"Oona." Another voice joins the fray, this one reprimanding and distinctly feminine. "Put me down, Wrath," the woman continues. I manage just enough energy to pull my head from the crook of one brawny arm to witness Wrath placing a dishevelled Oriel on the ground.

"Family, my ass!" she directs at Oona. "All you've ever cared about is yourself."

"Oh, please, Oriel. If it weren't for me, you wouldn't

have all of this. You'd probably be living in a cave somewhere, like those hideous mers you created."

"You... You nasty... BITCH." Oriel does nothing more
than stand before the other Goddess, trading insults, her
voice shaking.

"Dear Oriel." Oona walks closer to her, reaching fingers
out to brush the other Goddess's cheek. The once magnificent blue-winged Goddess is drawn and sickly-looking. Oriel
flinches. Oona's face twists in disgust. "You've always been a
thorn in my side, and now, I can finally put you out of your
misery."

Her hands dash out to either side of Oriel's face, and in
an instant, a crack goes out, and a limp Oriel falls to the
floor.

I'm so far beyond caring, my brain barely registers that
Oona killed another God.

"How—" I cough. "How did she do that?"

Through our connection, Oona hears me before anyone
else. *"Oh, this is good. Don't tell me your little boyfriends
didn't tell you they have been going around, stealing God
powers."*

The breeze is static, and though no words are spoken
aloud, all the men's eyes are on me. Gideon growls over my
shoulder, knowing who just communicated with me. Wrath
walks over to us on the stage, making his allegiance known.
Oona side-eyes her monster.

"Sever the bond or I will." Fury takes a step in front of
us, so I lose direct eye contact with Oona.

"And risk the life of your bonded and your unborn children." I mustn't be hearing properly because I could've
sworn she just said something about Fury's unborn children.

Considering we haven't had sex yet, that's sort of laughable. Surely, she means future children that haven't been born yet.

There's a pause within the group, like everyone is contemplating their next move.

Gideon moves us closer to my God. Fury takes a step back. "You're right. I would never risk the life of my children or my bonded, which is why I won't be."

It's hard to comprehend what happens next. If I thought the secondhand lightning impact from Oona was enough to put me flat on my back, the power that runs through my system and into my middle when Fury reaches a hand out for me shocks me into unconsciousness.

FORTY-SEVEN

FURY

I can't keep up with the folly of these Gods. Oona is lost to the psychosis of her own making. She's dreaming if she truly believes she can beat me. I've already disposed of any guards within the area, so we will be alone. I didn't think she would go ahead with bonding with Dove. It's out of character for her. *Desperate rhythms, it seems.* It does explain the odd sensations I've had coming from her, but Oona does *not* have the upper hand here.

All of their power is mine, including Oona's. Once Wrath burnt Osear's body, he picked up Oriel to bring her to this touching reunion. I didn't expect Oriel to come in swinging, though. *Good for her.* Oona has only ever done what's best for herself, and Wrath just reminded Oriel of that.

This reunion, the idiotic third trial? *She knows her time is running out.*

And she made one *big* mistake.

HUGE.

Colossal.

Irreversible.

She hurt Dove. No one hurts Dove.

DOVE IS MINE.

So, when I touch my Goddess, there are three things I need to achieve in the breath of a moment to protect her and the babies.

First, I need to bond with her.

Second, I need to sever the bond with Oona.

Third, I have to transfer half of Oriel's power over to the babies within her stomach. The soul she'd asked me for. She may have only asked for one, but with three bonded mates, nature had an interesting way of evening things out.

It's some of my finest work. Tipping the scale too far could mean disastrous consequences for Dove, and I'm not willing to bet on her life.

She is unconscious in Gideon's arms when I rip Oona's bond from her, making sure every thread is cut. With our own bond now firmly intact and my power lingering in her system, the blow isn't as lethal as Oona had hoped it would be.

What she doesn't expect is the pain on her end.

I know exactly what she is going through, my incisors showing as I watch from the stage as she falls to the dust below her sandal-clad feet, moaning. Her body contorts, her weakness showing. *Fuck, it's satisfying.*

Revenge, how I have dreamt of you.

At her destruction, I signal for Wrath to move to her. He understands the immediacy of the situation, pouncing from the stage and onto the Goddess, who has her arms and legs positioned at odd angles on the ground as she cries out, her black dress torn and covered in dirt.

When he punctures her neck, he doesn't make it nice. He rips and tugs, prolonging the pain of the initial bite until he starts to drink. Slurp after power-hungry slurp goes through our bond, and I push the extra energy into Dove and the babies. Through our bond, I hear the undeniable beating of three hearts—Dove's and the babies'. That sound is the backdrop of the vengeance I see being enacted before me. Fates, is it sweet, watching Oona bleed out because of one of her own creations.

Seeing Wrath on her, me on her. It's better than what I imagined and plotted. Her skin loses its lustre, her wings and hair turn white, losing all pigment. Before my very eyes, she transforms into the ugly creature she is on the inside.

As the last of the power siphons from Wrath to me, the clatter of gold cuffs hitting the ground rings out. *She's free. We can leave.* Relief washes through me, and I let my eyes travel to the unconscious human woman in Gideon's arms. The one who tried to save me, a God, multiple times.

I let the impossible take over. *She's safe, and my revenge has been enacted.*

With the taking of the last God's life, all Wrath's power transfers to me, and our bond is severed, as were the terms of our deal. My doppelgänger falls to his knees, the life draining from his features, just like the Goddess at his feet. It was always a risk, bonding with a God. There's every possibility Dove would've died if it weren't for the sliver of power I gifted the souls inside her before we left my island.

Wrath knew he was undergoing a suicide mission to free himself from their grip. He did it knowing I could bring him back, just not in the way he imagined. *What are Gods good for, if not for tricks and games?*

Gideon falls in line behind me as I go to look upon the Goddess—the same one who has been the bane of my existence for millennia. She lies on the ground, her eyes cracked open a slither and her breath coming in shallow.

All I would have to do is hold a hand over her mouth and nose, and she would be dead. That doesn't feel right. Not for her.

Raw anger is all I see when I kneel over her body, place my hands on either side of her head and sink my claws into her skull for a decent grip.

"You shouldn't have touched what was mine," I growl, pulling upwards, her head severing from her body in one quick motion. Blood barely sprays across the rocky ground. She's hardly alive, her eyes stuck in the same position that I found her in, half-lidded.

Standing, I drop her head onto her body and let the flames of my anger consume her, Wrath's body also being destroyed in the aftermath of my power from the fire I produced. Here and gone, like it never even happened.

"Let's go home." Gideon places a warming hand on my shoulder.

"That's the best thing you've said this entire trip."

"Trip? That's an interesting way to put it."

"It's the last holiday I'm taking for a few millennia."

"Count me in."

We turn, the woman we love safely in Gideon's hold, and head home.

FORTY-EIGHT

GIDEON

L ike the end of the great wars, this conclusion isn't sitting right. *This rhythm, we won.* We had a weapon that Oona had unknowingly created to be her own downfall.

In the palace, the godlins run around in an absolute frenzy of uncertainty. I passed Dove off to Fury on his insistence. Something about needing to have her touch him to control the overflowing power. I can see it in the change of his eyes and the bulging of his black veins. It's consuming him. When his face finds mine, there is an intricate web of black vessels protruding. There has to be a limit to how much power he can hold. *He has to be filtering some off to Dove, but Wrath killed three other Gods.* That's a lot of power to hold. It was enough to make me pause before handing Dove over, so I made Fury give me a quick rundown of what had happened before I was willing. His new look is alarming.

"Fuck." Fury's agitation comes through strongly.

Guards go flying in all directions when they stride towards us with intention in the foyer of the annoyingly gleaming palace. *Gods, I can't wait to go home.* "Give me your hand."

He catches me off guard, a wing slapping me in the face. The electrical *buzz* coming off his skin is intense. Another guard comes towards us, and he's immediately thrown across the room, hitting the wall with a thud. These humans don't stand a chance. I'd almost feel sorry for them if they hadn't locked up Dove.

"Give me your hand. Now," Fury grumbles through gritted teeth. His hand is outstretched towards mine, static coming off it in waves. I do not know what he expects of me. I do it for the woman in his arms regardless. The one I would lay down my life for.

My hand latches onto his. Lightning powers through my body, illuminating me from the inside. It's stars colliding. The world expands. Everything suddenly feels possible.

Fury takes back his hand, a zing of power burning me. "Thank the fates," he exclaims. "I need to offload the rest of this power."

———

With many scurrying godlins and guards now plastered to walls, I find Fury has directed us right back to our chambers.

"Why aren't you teleporting us home?"

He whirls on me, his skin still covered in a thick network of black lines. He bares his teeth. "You think I don't want that. Have you seen me?"

I give him a once-over. The power has made him more beastly than before.

"This power isn't made for flesh and bone. It warps the body, makes you lose touch with humanity. If I jumped through space and something happened to her"—he gazes upon the sleeping beauty in his arms, exhausted but alive— "I'd lose the last shred of anything good left in me."

I take a step towards him, the power calling me closer. "So what do we do? They are dead. Beyond that, what is our plan?"

Uncertainty crosses his dark features. "Leave the Atlans to their own undoing. Bring Dove home, and live happily fucking ever after."

His words are pained, like he doesn't believe the last part of his statement. The power is affecting him more than ever. Ignoring me, he strolls past the flowing curtains through to our balcony. It's rhythms like these that I wish I could read the God's mind. If he just opened himself up more, let me in, then he'd have me as an ally. We are family—a pack.

The bond that now flows through Dove into him connects us all.

I storm through the arched doors of the balcony behind him, only to come face to face with a red beast. "Saff." *The surprises keep on coming.* A tiny purple head pops out behind her flapping wing, a stream of smoke spitting from tiny nostrils.

"Take it." Fury is insistent, his hand outstretched. The ruby creature's wings flap slowly and steadily, holding her and Oro in place just before the edge of the balcony. "It's a gift." I can tell the dragon is unsure, her eyes flicking to the woman in Fury's arms, concerned for her friend.

"Take the power, Saff. For Dove." The dragon relents. Once more, the power is being offloaded onto another. *Now, maybe his madness will stop.*

She flicks her tail over in an act I nearly mistake as aggression until Fury catches it in his sharp claws. Dancing ripples zap through the body of the now glowing creature—magic. Just enough to finally set him free. Stretching out her wings, Oro firmly on her back, Saff swoops down from the balcony, a blaze of fire in her wake.

If I could breathe out this power, I would, too.

Fury falls to the floor, Dove cocooned in his arms. Silver locks of hair cascade over her face, his lips mumbling something unintelligible as he holds her close.

"My love," a soft voice squeaks through his rambles. "You haven't failed me. You saved me." Dove's glimmering mossy green eyes open slowly. Her hand reaches out to push back the curtain of his hair covering her face. Through our mate bond, I knew she was okay, but seeing her awake eases my worry. "Also, we need to talk about the baby situation." Her eyes are hard, accusing. "What the fuck, F—" He doesn't let her finish, crashing his lips into hers, the air zinging around all of us, their joint intensity pulsing through the air.

FORTY-NINE

DOVE

Kissing him is like a million zaps of power to my oversensitive skin. Everything within me tingles. The sizzling cloud I'm on is a direct connection to the God's arms I'm in, which filters out to Gideon, his body too far for my liking.

"Touch me. Both of you." I reach down both bonds. It's easier to find Gideon's now that we both share this unimaginable power. He falls with a *thud* onto the stone balcony beside us, his calloused fingers going to push back a piece of my wild hair.

It's not enough, having them this close to me. I want—no, I *need* them inside me. I may have been close to death only moments ago, but this power is more than before. He's fully open to me, sharing everything with me. He's not letting me borrow it; he's giving it to me. It binds to my molecules, resting deep in my bones. Sleeping no longer feels necessary.

"You will still need to rest." Fury reads my mind and provides his unhelpful commentary.

"Maybe," I quip.

"You're pregnant. You need to rest."

I slap two hands against his chest. "And how did I get pregnant?"

"You knotted your wolf mate and tethered your God-bonded." My mouth falls open.

"Are you blaming me?" His face is impassive. He knows exactly what I'm feeling—and, apparently, what I am thinking. It flows freely through the bond now. I can also tell that his comeback is going to get him in a lot of trouble.

"No, I'm giving you a magical biology lesson." I slap the smirk right off his devastatingly beautiful face.

A hard grip takes the wrist of my slapping hand. "You want to fight me, Pet?"

"Yes, and I want to fuck you."

"That can be arranged." A menacing grin has returned to his black lips. Even though he's shared his magic, the thick onyx vines haven't receded below his skin. Instead, they stand out, throbbing. I get the sudden urge to lick one of them, and lean in to do just that.

He doesn't stop me. The taste of him ignites me, and I find a path up past his neck to his lips, biting down, drawing blood.

I pull back, but he doesn't let me get far. "Where are you going?"

"Home," I whisper across his lips.

"And leave this stunning view?" Gideon pushes in behind me.

There's only one other person missing from this foursome, and once we finally have him with us, I'll feel like we are home. The dreams aren't enough to sustain me. They never were.

I'm reminded of long blonde hair, golden lines over bronzed, tight muscles, blinding dimples and violet eyes. A shade of violet that is uniquely Rivern, a colour I would never grow tired of.

I see him so vividly in my mind's eye.

"Pet."

"Songbird."

Both men growl in my mind at the exact same moment. I can't concentrate on them. The power within spins, making me feel nauseous. *Goddess, I feel like I'm going to throw up.* Power whirls, flowing from Fury through me to Gideon and back again, violet eyes at the centre.

Now the cuffs are gone, I just want to be back with my fae prince.

"Songbird, open your eyes." I barely knew they were closed. A hand rests on my forehead. I lean my head back onto Gideon's chest, opening them, finding dark irises surrounded by a thick ring of silver.

With Fury and Gideon surrounding me, I pay no mind to our location. Not until pine and the crackling of a fireplace reach my ears. *Home.* I whip my head to the side, both males taking a step back to let me find the other person my heart belongs to.

Rivern lies on a bed, unmoving, except for the rising and falling of his exposed chest. I freeze at the sight of him under a forest-green quilt. This is where he was when I was seeing him in our joint dreams. He was here, back within the fae realm—Terra, in his bedroom, asleep. All because of the bond that was stripped from us.

He could have died. My sternum throbs achingly at the idea of this fae prince being completely lost to me. Rivern was my first, before Fury or Gideon. He cracked me wide open so the two people next to me could clear away the rubble.

If Oona weren't already dead, I'd kill her for a second time.

"Go to him, Pet." Fury nudges me. Stumbling forward, I tip over the edge of the mattress. Rivern's body wobbles, and I crawl to him.

His blonde eyelashes flutter, stuck in another dream. I place a hand on his heart, the power inside my body jumping out to connect with him. The *thump, thump, thump* under my palm is steady. My shoulders sag. *Fury will fix him.*

Turning, I plead with the only God left. "Help him. Please."

His width and height are imposing in the cosy mountain room, just like the wolf shifter next to him. *How did I end up with such ferocious-looking lovers?* The fae in the bed is the complete opposite of them; a pretty masculinity that makes me lose my breath every rhythm I look at him.

Last, I was here, I was the one sleeping in this bed.

"I can't." Fury doesn't speak it aloud, trying to soften the blow.

"What do you mean, you can't? You haven't even tried," I screech. I'm still in the dress Oona put on me, and even though the material is soft, it still scratches at my skin. *I want nothing from that place on me.* Fury waves a hand at my body, and I'm re-clad in a green cotton tunic, similar to the ones Rivern wears. The simple act soothes the frazzled parts of me.

"Songbird." Gideon sits at the end of the bed. "What Fury is trying to say"—he sends my fallen God piercing eyes —"is that you are the only one who can help him."

My head whips around, going from Gideon to Fury to Rivern. "How am I going to help? I don't..."

"You have a God's power. You are fundamentally a Goddess," Fury whispers in my head, imparting a secret only the two of us know. Flames are licking at the walls of my soul, begging to be set free. *"You brought us here,"* he adds.

I didn't—

I couldn't—

I teleported all three of us from Atla to Terra.

"Our power is your power." He's right. Fury and Gideon both have power now—power that flows through my mate and God bond. The power of four Gods mingling together. Fury didn't give all his power to Ken or Saff, just enough to offload what he couldn't control. He kept it to gift to our family, to keep *us* safe.

"You deserve the life of a Goddess, and a Goddess needs power," Fury speaks with authority. "I will not have you or anyone you are bonded to without the means to help themselves within this world."

When I look at him, it's like I'm staring at a completely different person, even though he's my Fury. I can't believe I ever thought he was a daemon who would harm me if given the chance. If anyone has proven themselves over the past several turns, it's Fury.

"How do I wake him up?" I wave a hand over Rivern's sleeping body.

"You're his soul bonded, do what feels right. Listen to your heart, Pet," my winged beast says.

Listen to my heart. Easier said than done. I trail my fingers across the hard lines of his chest, tracing the golden vines that dance around his skin. *One turn, the dream will become a reality, and we will have matching patterns on our skin.* I know my power reacts to my emotions, so I search for the raging furnace inside. It's easy to find. Whenever I think of what has been done to us, it burns bright.

My hands go to push against the material at my stomach. We *are having a baby.* Not just one baby—two. One with a distinct connection to Gideon and Rivern. The power inside of me pulses through their veins, making them something beyond human, shifter or fae. With Fury's help, he has made us immortal.

I can't even think of the consequences of that. The longer I hold this immense amount of power, the more I feel how it's stalling my human progression of ageing. When it was only Fury's power, I could never access it long enough to understand the consequences; now, I do. The longer it lives within me, the more it changes my atoms to hold the magic within.

The babies are an anomaly. They are growing with magic inside them, thanks to Fury.

Focusing on the fae prince in front of me, I lean forward, continuing my perusal of his features—ones I've missed beyond anything else. A tingling tickles my fingertips the more skin-to-skin contact I keep with his body. My palm rests on his smooth cheek. I lean down over him. "Rivern, wake up, please."

I don't know what Fury expects me to do. How do you

even create a bond? My hand heats up, small zaps pushing me to keep going. My body wants him. It hits me straight in the core.

Surely I'm not meant to fuck him awake. I never had to sleep with Fury or Oona to complete the bond. They just made it happen. How do I do that?

The stirring inside me is insistent, needy, a crackling static. I lean down to touch my lips against his forehead, the taste of woodsy fir and sunshine unfurling something inside my chest—a thread looking for its tether. Going inward, I trail kisses down his cheek, thinking of the thread growing and weaving its way into his body. With my eyes closed, I focus that string of energy ending up at his heart, kissing his soft, plump mouth.

I linger for a moment, savouring our connection, never wanting it to end. Pulling back, I tentatively flutter my eyes to see Rivern still beneath me like nothing has changed. *Goddess, I imagined the thread! I saw it go into his body. What else do I have to do?*

Anguish takes its claws and slashes through my breast. *Why isn't he opening his eyes?*

A tear rolls down my cheek. Fury and Gideon stand at opposite ends of the bed, watching over me, letting me express without judgement. Another tear follows, and I scrub them away. If he doesn't wake up, this would've all been for nothing.

I bash a hand against his chest. "Wake up," I gruff.

"Wake up! Wake up! WAKE UP!" The power pulsing through me rumbles at each new clap of my strained voice.

"Dove," Fury lowers his voice, reaching for me.

"NO!" I scream down the bond. "He has to wake up or —" Fingers grasp my chin.

My eyes open to face the sudden spark that has seized my face in gold-lined fingers. The air catches in my lungs, causing me to hiccup.

"Kiss me, love," Rivern demands.

He doesn't wait for me to meet him. His lips crash into mine. *This is real? He's really awake.* I am touching my fae prince, my God-bonded, and he is finally touching me back.

We are no longer torn apart. Instead, they sing within my body, thrumming an ecstatic tune, expanding and growing further than they ever have before. This is more than a God bond. It's our hearts, making the choice that they belong to each other. He is mine, and I am his.

"My queen." I shiver at his throaty, lingering moan through my mind.

Sharp pulses of power meet as our hands glide over each other's bodies. I find myself straddling him, having climbed on top to sweep my tongue in further to catch his scent. My legs are jelly to his ministrations, fingers stroke my thighs, pulling my arse down so my pelvis is in line with his hardness.

At the contact, I whimper. My core leaks for him. I need him inside me for real. *If I just pushed down his pants and shoved aside my underwear, we would be joined.*

"You woke him," a lilting voice that is neither Gideon's or Fury's cries from beyond the bed says.

DOVE

The picture I have of riding Rivern to completion is dashed when a woman resembling him strolls in without concern. Her wheat hair is braided back from her face, violet eyes fluttering wildly as if she's seen a ghost.

"Oh, thank the Goddess. He's awake," she exclaims. A little boy bounds around the women running for the bed, barely noticing the two imposing males guarding it.

Big eyes and chubby cheeks beam at me. "You saved him!"

"Kit, my boy." Rivern sits up in the bed, pulling me close to his side. One of his tapered, gold-lined hands goes out to ruffle the little boy's matching blonde hair.

"I'm fine. I was just taking a kip." Kit crinkles his tiny nose, not falling for his uncle's excuses.

"We are happy to see you awake, brother. In fact, we have a lot to talk about." *This is his sister, of course.* I had barely greeted anyone the last rhythm I was in Terra, and when we arrived this time, we teleported in. She steps closer, but not enough to be within the vicinity of the two protectors guarding us.

"Can it wait? I wish to be with my bonded for now." Rivern's hands snake around my stomach, pulling us closer together. Freya's gaze shifts between me and my fae prince, assessing. Finally, she nods, calling Kit back to her. He complains until Rivern promises to play dragons and knights with him later.

"How are you, my love?" His voice is low, concerned. Fingers trail the underside of my jaw. The light touch, his lilting soft words. It's enough to break me. It's funny how the small gesture of a loved one can completely break you down, bursting through all your walls.

Tears stream down my face. The fear. The anguish. The grief. They're all making themselves known. Every little thing that I've been bottling up and trying to shove deep into the cave, yet I have no dragon guarding it, keeping all my secrets inside, and instead they freely spill out for these men.

"Love." His muffled whisper of reverence catches me as he pulls me into his arms. I burrow into his neck, taking long, deep, uninterrupted lungfuls of his woodsy sunshine smell. It grounds and calms me as Gideon and Fury do, but also differently. Each one of them is a puzzle piece that fits to form my whole, and I can't imagine going forward without any of them.

The loss of one would mean destruction for me.

I sob harder.

"You're safe, love. We all are." Rivern continues to whisper into my ear while rubbing circles on my back. It's not long before another, much warmer hand has found my thigh, and sharp-tipped, chilly fingers are trailing a strand of loose hair around my ear.

The sigh I release rights my senses, and I'm able to come out of hiding within the crook of my fae prince's neck.

Taking in the endless galaxy of purple spheres before me, I dream of a future filled with nothing but this—us all together, without abandon.

The four of us. Free.

"Is it all over now?" I know that in the grand scheme of things, we haven't finished piecing together the Forgotten Lands. Not that it's any of our jobs. But I can't help this feeling of inner responsibility for what I have done in Haven.

"Just say the word, and I'll take you to our own paradise." It's Fury who says it. And Goddess, does it sound good to run away and leave all of this behind. My stomach flips at the thought. And I know it's not the right choice.

This is our home. This will be our future children's home.

"It's your choice, Pet. I'll follow you to the ends of the stars." The way he reads my mind is disconcerting, but also comforting.

I sniffle. "I can't leave these lands. They are our home. I think—"

Rivern squeezes his hand around my hip. "Tell us, love." A gruff puff of air catches me from behind, letting me know Gideon also wants to hear.

"Well, I want our dream." I'm looking at Rivern when I say it, willing him to remember the dream where he was tending to Mage in the forest, near the lake of reflections.

"You want to build our own sanctuary in the forest?" he asks.

"It's halfway between Haven and Terra. It just seems like the perfect fit." I shrug my shoulders up and down, a deep flush taking over my cheeks. Why am I shy in front of all these men who have seen me naked more than once? I have no idea.

A prickling of electricity warns me of the sudden sting of Fury taking my chin and turning me towards his serious features. "You're nervous?" I shake my head up and down. "Why?"

I take a trying breath. Not everything can be explained within the depths of a bond. The emotions run around us, some fleeting, some gripping on tight, and those are the loudest. There's a confusion that settles over our connection now.

"Because I don't know how I will satisfy all of you." My hands fall away from around my fae prince's shoulders. "I am only one person. A damaged person, at that. And all of you."

A warning growl comes from behind, a hand comes around my neck, gripping my throat and pulling me into a hard chest. The punishing, delicious movement goes straight to my core.

"You hear that?" Gideon's plea is rough and gravelled. There's a pounding behind my ear, one that echoes through the mate bond we've already solidified. It's hard to forget that two other God bonds are now intricately woven around it, binding all four of us together: gold, silver and black.

"Yes." My voice is breathy.

"Do you think all we want is sex?" Gideon's words are

harsh and clipped, but they are exactly what I need—to be reminded I'm a fucking Goddess, with three all-powerful protectors who love me beyond the functions of a physical form.

"No," I whimper. His hot breath snakes down my neck, making me unbearably wet for him. If that wasn't bad enough, Rivern begins to rock my hips back and forth on his hardened groin. Fury also takes my hand in his and puts my wrist to his mouth, sucking until his incisors hit, making me throb for all of them.

"I think it might be time to finally let our Goddess know how we plan on worshipping her." I'm breathless—a pile of jelly on the bed, complexly lax to their ministrations. I've never wanted anything so much in all my life.

"Do you want that, love?" My golden fae murmurs before me.

"Yes," I whimper again.

"Thank the fates. I'm about to come inside my pants again, Pet." Fury never ceases to amaze me. He truly has no filter.

A trickle of laughter escapes me just as soft warm lips crash against mine. I take hold as if it is the last rhythm, drinking in the realness of this moment of having Rivern back. It's not long before Gideon has my chin in his broad hand and is pulling my face to his. He gives me a moment to take in air before he is sucking all of mine down. The power running through all of us only amplifies the need, an electrifying side-effect that none of us knew about until now.

Every touch magnifies the pulse under my skin, my clit a bundle of desire. Hands run the course of my skin, a tongue trails over my scars and claw tips scrape against the cheeks of my arse. Nothing is off-limits. Before I know it, I'm completely exposed, my tunic and underwear having been deposited on the floor beside the bed.

My chest heaves, yet they are all still fully clothed. I want them all naked before me. A smirk pulls at my lips when an idea takes hold, and I wield it in my power, blinking hard once.

When I open my eyes again, they are all naked.

"Well, well. It seems someone is learning new tricks," Fury teases.

"You aren't the only one here who's all-powerful anymore." I slap his chest. He takes my hand and pulls me off Rivern's lap and into his own.

"Ooof." The pleasant chill zips through me, my hands falling on his ribs. My lower half hits the exact place he wants me to find, my wetness gliding over his enlarged cock.

"Fuuuuck," he moans. The look on his face is one of pure ecstasy. You would think he is already inside me. The black of his eyes is fully blown out to mingle with silver, a gold ring now also peaking through. To bring a God to his knees is a feeling I'll never get over.

Through all his wit and innuendos, this man put me first, beyond all his plans.

"You were my ultimate plan." He's still the best at reading my innermost private thoughts—now they are no longer private, not to Rivern or Gideon or Fury. They get all of me, and I get all of them.

They throw thoughts and feelings down the bond. Right now, in this heated moment, it's mostly of the taste, smell and feel of me. It's overwhelming, so I shut down the walls between us a little bit. Not all the way, just enough for us to feel like we are within our own bodies. As much as we are one, we are also separate.

I roll my hips over the hard length beneath me to gain some friction on my clit, only for a hard slap to land on my arse, stilling me. "If you do that again, I'm going to come all over you and"—he sits up, grasping my hair so I'm nose to nose with him, my neck straining—"I will be coming inside that sweet little fucking pussy of yours. Do you understand, Pet?"

Oh, God, do I understand. My mouth opens. No words come out. *What do you say when you finally get your bonded in your bed, and all he wants to do is be connected to you?*

Yes, a thousand rhythms, yes.

The blackened raised veins of his skin pulse. I lift a hand to trace the ebony line that goes from his eye down to his cheek. My pussy clenches, wanting him inside me. He looks like a feral beast. All sharp lines, his cheekbones and jawline, cut from glass. His dark horns and grey skin are intimidating. Not to mention the wings that now wrap around us, cupping me to his body.

"I get you first," he growls.

I nod, my mind blank. Rivern and Gideon are right next to us, watching, and I plan on giving them a show. Through the bond, I know both of them aren't going to last long, being on the periphery, so I grasp onto Fury's horns and lick his lips before biting down.

We were never sweet. We were made to be rough. To push each other. The magical power within us will heal any small cut or bruise.

A growl comes from behind us, warning Fury to be careful.

The God flips us, my body held within his wings, his forehead resting on mine. "I want to taste every inch of you, but I can't wait." He pushes against me. "I won't wait to take you as mine."

"Please," I groan. Fury's teeth latch onto the scar along my neck, sucking and pulling. A zap of chilly static rolls through my abdomen and to my clit. I cry out. Fury doesn't stop. His, too large, cock pushes against my pussy again, my body gushing to meet him.

It's almost obscene how much my body openly preens for these males, especially when they are in close vicinity. They barely need to touch me, and I'm wet. It has to be the bonding. Surely no other human feels like this. If this is what intimacy between humans feels like, why would they ever leave the bedroom?

His pelvis rolls into mine again, and I cry out, "Oh, Gods."

The three men around me snicker at my declaration.

"Fuck, I like it when you call out to us, my Goddess." I did not intend to. It is a habit to call out to the Gods or the Goddess. I nearly forgot what we are—all-powerful.

"You're our Goddess." Fury groans as he breaches my walls with the head of his thick cock. It's huge—rivalling Gideon—but not in his wolf form, that's a size all of its own.

"Oh my Gods." My whimpered groans linger in the electric pulse in the air. All three men vibrating with unrestrained tension make me see stars.

"Can you take all of me, Goddess?" I melt when Fury calls me that. When he makes me see I'm his equal, no longer the human girl who grew up beaten down by her drunkard of a father and abused within the temple. My God made me into the Goddess I was always meant to be.

My original protector pushes to the absolute hilt inside of me, my world exploding as he hits every nerve ending inside of me, my body exploding. I scream without care about who is outside our room.

My eyes open to Fury, who spills himself inside me, pushing in as deep as he can go, while I vibrate around him, shocks of power pulsing through my system.

As I start to come to, I don't miss that all my walls are down, and I can feel Rivern and Gideon having both found their own completions from the orgasmic bliss that exploded through our bond.

"Fuck, is that going to happen every time?" Rivern asks. Fury's wings open, folding back behind him, and rolling us to the side, my leg draped over his thigh, his cock still inside me. The pressured throbbing continues down in my core, and I remember the God-bonded threads I had with Rivern. We probably won't be able to extract ourselves from each other's bodies for a while.

"Most likely," Fury answers Rivern's question. "We are all bonded through Dove, and whenever she feels pleasure, it is only natural for all of us to feel pleasure."

The golden lines of my fae's skin glow brightly as he lies back on the pillows, looking at me, his hand still on his engorged cock, a mess all over the sheets in front of him. Gideon is no better off, standing at the end of the bed, his hardness in his broad palm.

My mouth salivates to taste the cum dripping from the tip—off both of them.

With Fury and me now joined for an undetermined

amount of rhythm, I motion for Rivern to come closer. He abides by my reaching hand, shifting closer.

The winged God nibbles a trail of kisses down my neck, making me squirm. A rough grunt comes from the end of the bed. *Goddess, I want them all to join. I want them to surround me on all sides.*

Fury chuckles. Gideon answers, *"As much as I want to comply, Songbird, I'm not sure you're ready for all three of us yet."*

Everyone hears Gideon's message down the bond.

Rivern is behind me now, his skin flush with my own. "But—" I start to protest. He takes his palm and holds it firmly around my neck.

"Don't tell me you're not exhausted." Rivern rubs his nose against my neck, tickling me. My frown becomes ever more prominent on my face. Fury pushes into me, making me moan in surprise. The languid pull of his cock out of our joined wetness before the tethers pull us back together is peak contentment.

My eyes roll back into my head for a moment.

"Soon, Pet." Fury tries to pacify me. I dig my nails into his thigh. *"Draw blood, I dare you."* His incisors go for the bite mark on my shoulder, which only serves as a direct line to the wolf at the end of the bed.

I lose all thought when Rivern pulls my head to meet his lips, searching, softening, trying to ease the pleasured pain caused by these three men. Wherever they touch is a direct line to all my pleasure centres. It's deafening, consuming and I can't wait for the rest of our lives together.

FIFTY-ONE

RIVERN

She's honeysuckle and vanilla—the last meal I ever hope to eat. My tongue trails down her chest. Her peaked pink nipples heave, her heartbeat rapid with lust. *Goddess, to think my child is in her stomach already. It makes me hard as a rock.* I never thought I'd have a pregnancy fetish, but anything Dove does is my ultimate fantasy.

The connection we now share is beyond that of the God bond bestowed on us before. Now it's a bond of our wills, our joined power. She's the sun I revolve around. All of us revolve around. Because not only do I feel my need and want for her, but there's also Gideon and Fury on the edge of our connection. To fall into it is bewitching.

The wolf and the fallen God are ancient beings. They welcome the power like it is a second skin. I tentatively hold it, afraid of how it makes me crazed in a whole new way.

Fury helps in twisting her around to face me, so I have full access to her body, still on his cock. It's the hottest thing I've ever seen.

"Give it to me," my Goddess whispers tentatively, my mouth gliding down her body, aiming for the small bud at the apex of her thighs.

"What?" My voice is breathy. I squeeze my cock, willing it not to preemptively explode.

"Give me your cock." I shake my head. She's pregnant and exhausted. *She forgets I feel everything she does now.*

"I don't forget. I need you inside of me." Her words tickle the back of my mind.

"Fuck." The way her voice hits my cock is exhilarating. Her voice. Her taste. Her heart. They wage war on me.

There's no tenderness when she takes hold of my braids and pulls them up. A static zap lands heavy on my scalp.

Coming face to face with my bonded, her God behind her, blackened eyes staring me down, telling me I'd better give her what she wants, or I'm toast, is all the incentive I need to give in. I let her wash over me.

My eyelids close for a second. When I open them, I know they are no longer the same, Dove's orbs widening in surprise.

I grip her hips, pulling my body up to line us pelvis to pelvis "You want this?" I push my rock-hard length against her apex. The whimpering moan she lets out makes the pheromones in the room go wild. There's no stopping what happens next.

The magic controls us, brings us together. We shouldn't fit, but we know we will. Working as one, Fury lifts one of Dove's legs over my waist, and I line my cock at the entry of her pussy, where he is still firmly seated inside of her. Looking down at darkening, swirling green eyes, I push upwards, knowing there's no backing out now.

Where I thought we would find pain, she expands for both of us. The mending swirl of our magic connecting and building to a cry sounds like a rapturous melody.

"Oh, Gods," she screams into my chest as I lift her leg and thrust upwards, the pressure no match for finding my home. She opens for me, her wetness slicking the way, so I'm devastatingly squeezed between her internal walls and Fury's cock, yet it's all her.

The clench of her bearing down is beyond anything I've ever known, and before I hit the hilt, I shatter inside of her, my seed spilling. At the feel of my cum slicking her walls, she bears down, Fury pushing crudely in and out behind her, pushing her into me. Soon she will explode, setting off the wolf growling at the foot of the bed.

I can feel everything. All the minute flutters of her pussy. The way her sensitive nipples push against my exposed skin. Her exhalations at my neck, her head tilted up. I look down at her closed lashes.

"Sleep, Pet." Fury wraps a wing over us.

"I'm not tired." The woman between us mumbles as her breaths even out. In a moment, she is asleep, all three of us joined.

I WAKE WITH A START, pleasure rolling through my lower half. In my half-sleeping, half-awake state, I must be dreaming. Until my eyes open wide and spot the brunette locks of my bonded head bobbing up and down on my cock, her hands stretched out on either side, one hand pumping a grey hardness and one hand pumping a tawny hardness.

Fuck. I'm definitely dreaming. I have to be dreaming.

"You're not fucking dreaming." Gideon gruffs beside me, his voice choked.

My hand goes to the silken locks of her hair when her tongue swirls and dips. Tilting my head back on the pillow, I release a strangled groan.

"Fuuuck, Spitfire. You know I can't control myself around you," Fury's voice glides over toned abs, down to the V of my hips, to the lips popping off my cock. Her smile is devilish. An angel set out to make mischief.

"I don't want you to control yourself. I want you to let go." She looks from Fury, back to me, and over to Gideon, fire in her eyes. "Come for me. I need all of you."

I wouldn't be able to control myself around this Goddess if I wanted to. The magic connecting us dances in our uncontrollable need for each other.

Dove goes back to her ministrations, and it takes one long drag of her tongue for my cock to spill into her mouth. The wolf shifter and fallen God moan together with us. The pleasure down the bond sparking. I don't think I'll ever get used to sex being anything other than a full connection of hearts, minds and souls.

Flopping back on the bed, I pull Dove up to nestle between my golden chest and Gideon's hard muscles. It's a tight squeeze with all of us; Gideon and Fury are turned on their sides to accommodate the small woman sighing between us.

It's not long before Gideon is taking her from behind. Jealousy doesn't even cross my mind, seeing her being pleasured. Her happiness is my own.

IT HAS TAKEN us longer than expected to leave my room within the mountains of Terra to make an appearance in front of the council before we all leave for Haven. The last rhythm I was here, my mother had pressured me to go with Moyrie. I'd done it for Terra, Dove and I still not fully bonded, our relationship unknown.

We have come so far since that point in time. The distance I spent from her, while I was in the Silver Sands, only made me see that being bonded to her, knowing her, was my true hearts desire. It wasn't what my mother wanted, or what my people needed. It was purely selfish. In the end, my selfishness will help my people. The power running through my blood is unstoppable. And for as long as I'm alive, the Forgotten Lands will never see another war or the destructive nature of meddling Gods.

"Brother." Freya pushes out of her chair at the head of the council table. "I'm so pleased you are well." Her arms go around my body. Though she was groomed to take our mother's position, Freya was more mothering than the real person ever was. She was the one who read stories to me before bed, played hide and seek and cooked my favourite treats.

I look around for silver-white hair and piercing violet eyes. Instead, what greets me is a stoic group of older council members, my mother decidedly absent.

"She's not here." My head swings around to my sister, her light violet eyes creasing at the sides, darkness leaking out. I'd not noticed it in the brief moment she'd checked on me within my room, but now I see it, the sorrow.

No. I secretly despised the woman. She was still my mother. I know it before she even says the words. Our mother, the queen, wouldn't miss her chance at reprimanding her only son.

"Our mother is one with the blessed Goddess now." *There's only one Goddess here.* I don't burst her bubble. None of them needs to know that Oona is and always was a lie. That she never cared for us.

"How?" My voice is tight. Unexpected to my own ears. *Fuck.* Delicate fingers slide through my palm. The ease of Dove's touch, her nearness, releases the tension in my shoulders.

"She was already in the process of her rebirth. But you know our mother. Stubborn to a fault. She didn't want anyone to know until she was bedridden. Not long after you left, she experienced a sudden downturn."

"Why didn't you send word?" I know it's a pointless question. There was no use sending word to the prince, who was lost to Terra. I was a bargaining chip for my mother. Nothing more.

Freya moves closer to me, blocking the table behind her. "We didn't see the need to concern you. Your job was far more important." Her palm comes to rest on my tunic, the beating under it faster than normal.

It was our way, the way of the fae royals, yet it made me want to scream. It wasn't my way. Family came first.

Taking a heavy exhale, I nod my head towards the new queen. "Let us discuss the future."

FIFTY-TWO

DOVE

Leaving the meeting was a strange, almost melancholy affair. The fae council and new queen imparted their wishes for the Kingdom of Haven now that it was under new rule. *Whose rule, I still am not wholly sure.*

Somehow, my bonded quartet had become the new spokespersons for Haven—unofficially, of course. The first call of business was the farmers of Haven, who sought refuge within the walls of Terra—I had to know if they were well. I still felt beholden to them. Freya set aside all of my fears. The farmers were being treated as if they were fae. They didn't hold the past against them. During her mother's passing, Freya led the charge in leading both humans and fae to see the benefits of working together for the first rhythm in the Forgotten Lands' history. I was excited to see this new relationship flourish between territories and peoples.

I wanted a long-term solution for Terra, Haven and the people of the Silver Sands. We had power in unity. I'd had a plan working the corners of my mind since we'd gained the God power. It almost seemed fanciful, but so did a human having the power of a Goddess. Terra, Haven and the Silver Sands as one, neighbours, with open corridors for trade. I'd spoken to the men about it as we'd lain in bed after making love for the fourth time this morning. They agreed; it felt like the right choice. All of us knew it deep within.

We needed to restore the balance. So, during the meeting with the new queen of Terra, we planted the seed. We would bring the wisps and fae back to Haven. The fae didn't owe my city, and I almost expected Queen Freya to refuse, but at her core, she had hope. A hope for a better future for all, and I saw the glint in her irises when I told her we wanted to welcome fae back within the kingdom.

The fae were there first. We still lived in their houses, ate the food from the soil they had toiled and read the books from their library. This separation wasn't right. And neither was punishing the people who were generations removed from the initial conflict brought about by the Gods.

Freya agreed that she would prepare a group of fae to travel with any wisps they collected along the way, in exchange for the song of life. The song that keeps the wisps singing and making. The same song I thought would save my kingdom. And in a roundabout way it did, just not how I intended. Instead, Oona's song led me on the wildest adventure of my life, where I not only met my bonded mates but reclaimed the parts of me I'd kept buried.

I find myself contemplating all of this change as I assess the kingdom of my birth—Haven. *So much is different now.* As soon as our meeting with the fae council was complete, we teleported back home. *Home.* I knew that my home wasn't this kingdom anymore, but the threads that pulled at my heart. The males who stand on either side of me, letting me have my moment of peace.

Looking out at the blue sky, I hope to catch a glimpse of her. I knew she was in Atla for a moment, but I was too far gone in power and teleporting to reconnect. Now, I gaze out, wishing to see red anywhere. But with all my longing, it's no use. After this meeting, I'm going to look for her.

Sighing, I gaze down at my *old* home.

Fenrir went above and beyond in his dedication to the kingdom. The wisps have already begun to zip around the streets, fixing long-overdue, crumbling buildings, and tending to the once-dead garden beds littering the streets. Even the people who walk the cobblestones have more of a spring to their step. To see my kingdom slowly flourish makes me believe it will all be okay, that this place doesn't need me or my bonded.

"Fenrir is ready to speak to us," Gideon interrupts my silent perusal, talking directly into my mind.

Fury and Rivern shift in unison beside me, broad hands grasping my fingers and wrapping around my waist. The shock of their touch is instantaneous, lighting me up. I'm never without two of them, not after the kidnapping. The power that runs through the four of us is a constant reminder that we will never be separated again.

We teleport to the king's study to find Fenrir and Gideon standing around a large circular mahogany table with a makeshift model of the Kingdom of Haven on top.

"We've been focusing on preparing for the new season. The food stores in the manor were enough to cover the village until the next rotation. Horus was sitting on more food than we could've imagined." *Goddess, he looks exactly like Gideon.*

"How have the villagers handled the transition?" Gideon asks his brother.

"Once they realised I wasn't out to harm them, but feed them, they have come around to Horus and Castor's evil deeds. Even the priestesses have been leaving the temple to help families in need where they can."

The four of us praise Fenrir for his good work. We haven't been gone for long, but leaving the kingdom to the shifter was the best of a tricky situation. Knowing he has been successful in bringing together the people supports the growing ideas I have for the future. I've yet to explicitly tell Rivern, Gideon and Fury, but they know what I want. One side effect of being connected like we are now is that we have no secrets. There are no surprises in my future when it comes to these men. After the trauma of my past, it's calming.

"Now that you're all back, we need to discuss the question of succession," Fenrir interrupts my thoughts. Rivern, Fury and Gideon look at me. Fenrir looks around the table, finally landing on me with a half smile, his left eyebrow raised. My men know I will have final say in this.

"I don't wish to be a ruler—none of us do. All I ask is that you stay on board to support the kingdom's transition. We will be here as guardians for the people and the land, but beyond that, if you wish to stay on as spokesperson for the people and have gained their trust, I see no reason to change anything until the people vote on a new course of action."

Fenrir assesses me and my words, his glare probing. "You have power, do you not?"

His question catches me off guard. The scent of pine, sandalwood and ash swirls around me. A strange, albeit alluring energy travels around my skin. I stand a little taller as I answer him. "Yes, but I don't wish to use it other than to help. Just because I have this"—I hold a hand up and imagine a glowing orb of sunshine within it. It forms instantly—"doesn't mean I should rule, or any of us. We took this power to help, to save our people, not to destroy."

"And do you plan on staying within Haven?" By now, Fenrir has ascertained that I am the port of call for all answers. Technically, he could ask any one of us, but it would be the same answer.

"We will stay for as long as is needed, but I wish us to settle within the forest." His lingering stare shifts to his brother. Gideon is looking at me, his face impassive.

"Where exactly?" Fenrir asks, looking back at me.

"Between Terra and Haven. It feels right for our future." My hand is resting on the babies sleeping in my stomach. After the exhilaration of being with my mates settled down —*somewhat*—the two souls within my body made themselves known. It had been a shock until I remembered the deal I'd made with Fury.

Fenrir can't stop looking at the place my hand is resting, his eyes wide. "You're pregnant?"

"Yes, you're going to be an uncle," Gideon says, hitting his brother on the back.

"Well, fuck. I wasn't expecting that." Fenrir's hand goes to his neck, his eyes still unable to meet mine or his brother's.

"How do you know it's yours?" His tone is teasing, but there's an underlying dig to it. It's a reasonable question.

However, there's a ripple in the air, my bonded mates are irate at the insinuation. Wolves mate with one being for life, so I give him some grace.

"We have the power of the Gods, I know," Gideon answers.

Fury stands in front of me, his wings widening in a protective motion. "You forget who you're talking to." His words are menacing. The air crackles.

"Fury, move out of the way," I huff out through our connection. I'm just as powerful as him now. He might be able to hone his power more effectively, but I have no doubt I'll be able to protect myself when needed.

"Pet." His voice is liquid intoxication, especially when it sounds like he's reprimanding me. My body now knows all the ways he can pleasure me with his fingers, tongue, cock and magic. He's too hard to resist now, knowing he's mine and we are safe.

I take a step towards him, my fingers reaching out to touch the delicate join of his feathers into the skin of his grey back. Muscles ripple when his wings stretch out. He knows what I'm going to do, and the thought alone is enough to make me wet.

My fingers meet feathers. He shudders. *"Fuuuck. If you want to give Fenrir a show, you're going the right way about it."* I run my hand across raven silken feathers before taking a step back.

Fury releases a pent-up breath. "We can't have that, can we?" I murmur behind him. He catches my words, and a brooding groan comes from him. *Goddess, you would think he's about to die, the way he's carrying on.* I roll my eyes.

He turns. "Don't think I didn't catch that."

"Oh, great, now you have eyes in the back of your head." I cross my hands over my chest, my gaze flicking towards Rivern, who has pulled up a chair to watch the showdown. His smile is infectious. I return it.

Claws grip my chin, my skin sparking at the contact. Our bond thrums happily. "I'm always watching you, Pet." He's the scariest-looking bastard in the whole of the Forgotten Lands, yet my heart melts for him. My features soften.

"Are they always like this?" Fenrir asks Gideon.

"Pretty much," he answers with a shrug.

Fifty-Three

Fury

"What's the big surprise?" Dove bounces on her feet as we walk towards the beach on the outskirts of Haven. We left Gideon to reconnect with his brother, and Rivern walks behind us, on guard duty. I don't think any of us will get over her abduction.

"Just wai—" I don't get to finish my sentence before Dove is shrieking and bolting for the sand, where a red dragon waits, Oro bounding in the water.

On her approach, Saff opens her wings, as if she is going to hug the small woman. Thinking better of it, with the height difference, she leans her face down, and Dove wraps her arms around any scales she can get a hold of.

I stop before I hit the sand, waiting. Rivern comes to stand beside me.

"Goddess, she's brilliant, isn't she?"

The magic that sweeps through the bond when she greets her friend is pure and innocent, so different from our own. I know she's crying, and Rivern and I are both desperate to go to her, but we let her take comfort in the dragon who stands before her.

It's not long before Oro comes out of the water and bounds over to the hugging pair. He nuzzles his way in between them, giving Dove big licks on her face, making her laugh. Happiness—my new favourite emotion because of her—comes through the bond, and Rivern and I both stare in wonder that this woman chose us.

———

I WAIT on the beach next to Saff.

Dove and Rivern linger further down the beach, rolling around with a boisterous purple dragon, keeping him entertained.

"He is coming," the ruby-red dragon beside me answers through the corners of my mind. As far as I'm aware, she speaks only to Dove, me and the other beasts. My bonded told me the tale of the bird companions for Oona's children. Oona always loved playing games with her people. What most creations in the Forgotten Lands never realised is that we have the ability to communicate with all creatures; they just believed they couldn't. It's why the fae can communicate with their chosen intimates. Saff isn't so much an intimate of Dove, more of a chosen companion, their bond coming from a mutual understanding—friendship.

If you listen hard enough, you can hear the bees, the rabbits, the fish. They are the ones who make the choice if you are worthy of their voice.

A cerulean head pops out of the softly lapping ocean, the primary and secondary almost fully set behind the moving body of water. We wait in silence as he comes closer. Now that both Saff and Ken have some of the God power, there's a deeper connection between us. To be sitting here, in freedom with nearly all of my beasts, is a reality I never thought possible until Dove.

"Ken?" I ask, his face bobbing closer, the saltwater caressing my bare feet.

My God, thank you for coming.

Laughter comes from down the beach, and my blackened heart sings to hear it.

"What is troubling you, Ken?" Saff had originally informed me that the kraken had a question, but he was finding it hard to ask, so she took it upon herself to bring us together. I've since learnt the two have formed a friendship over the events of the past turns.

Two large tentacles rise, water cascading down his suckers, his other tentacles pushing him up beneath the water. *"I wish to become a shifter, like your dyre wolf."*

Right. I hadn't thought of offering this possibility to all of my creations. Changing the wolves to blend in with the humans centuries ago drained my power because I was imprisoned on the island—now, I had unimaginable power, and they possessed a small spark of it. Now, it would be easier.

"Are you sure this is what you want?" I confirm with Ken.

"Yes, my God," the kraken responds, unable to relent his formability. He's a friendly giant, as are all my creatures—until you cross them and the people they love and care for.

"It is done." I nod and set the intention, sending the power towards his body. Directing the magic that is housed within is easier than it's ever been. The blue beast rises from the water, the suns setting behind him, a truly spectacular sight as he shifts from kraken to man.

When his naked limbs touch the water again, he holds two hands up to his blue eyes. Long azure hair flows down his back. He looks up in utter astonishment at Saff and me. His eyes linger on the dragon for a touch longer.

"Th... Thank... Yo-u," he stammers out, gaining quick control of his vocal cords.

Gideon

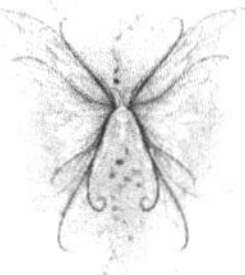

Nearly a rotation later

Her face is a mix of emotions. One moment, it's scrunched in pain, the next, she's laughing at some joke Rivern is telling her or scowling at the unhelpful information Fury is providing.

You'd think having power meant no pain, but that's not true for power within a corporeal body. You get all the sensations of a human body.

Her muscles are contracting as she breathes steadily, pushing into Fury's chest with two hands.

She insisted on doing this in the lake, her glorious body naked in the moonlight.

When the contraction ends, she's floating on top of the water. Her pregnant stomach is sticking out, glistening. She is a Goddess made real, and we are all enamoured with how she has handled this pregnancy.

"Will you come touch me already?" Her voice goes straight to my cock. She's my mate, and I'm obsessed with

every part of her. I'd been creating a birthing space for her by the lake, as she wanted, with towels, pillows and candles. Now, I'm floored by the picture she makes in the reflective water, her locks wet against her ample chest.

She doesn't have to ask twice. I jump into perfectly heated water, body temperature, so our Goddess doesn't freeze thanks to Fury. *He's good at some things.* Fury messages her feet, while Rivern is at Dove's head, whispering sweet nothings into her ear. She giggles, and all of us collectively groan.

"Argh, Gods," she moans around another contraction, her body rolling over in the water.

I place a steadying hand on her back, trying to sense what she needs. The babies are coming fast. The urgency is in the air, in our combined magic. Back in Haven, I'd heard of women taking turns to labour. That has not been the case for our Goddess. When the suns went down, the contractions started, and it only took one lap walking around the lake for her to be fully dilated.

God magic is powerful. I'd stayed on the shore for a moment, and she was already at the point of needing to push. The twins had been making it known to us for a few turns that their birthing was coming.

Understanding the sudden urgency we all teleport towards the blankets and cushions on the grass, just as Dove shouts, "She's coming." My songbird's eyes close, and she whispers a name under her breath as she rolls on all fours. Fury's hands are under her, catching the baby girl, just as Dove exhales. "Oh my Gods."

"Right here, love," Rivern teases, a startled cry letting us know one of our babies is here. It's hard to tear my eyes away from Dove's face, but I manage, for a split movement, to see Fury taking the bundle in his arms and kissing her on her forehead. The sight is glorious in its absurdity. He looks like a deamon about to steal my baby.

His steely black irises fall to mine. "Don't worry, Daddy, I'm not taking her anywhere." Fury hands her to me, her body so unreliably small I could cry. She has a thick head of brunette hair already.

"Like her daddy... Oh, Gods, he's coming." Dove's hand comes out to grasp my arm, her small hand biting down. I kiss our baby girl's head, wrap her in a muslin, then tuck her under my free arm. Dove has her nails in Rivern's other arm as she breathes in raggedly. Her eyes never leave the baby I'm holding.

Through our connection, she's desperate to hold her, but she has our baby boy to birth next, and he's coming right on his sister's heels.

"*Fury,*" she gasps along our collective link, preparing the God at her back.

"*Got him.*" His smooth words calm the frantic beat of her heart, and she leans into Rivern's free arms.

"Please," Dove whispers, rolling around in his arms on the ground. Trees tower behind us, shading the fae prince at her back. I don't have to look at him to know his eyes are hungry to see the baby clutched to Fury's hard muscles.

Dove's hands are out to Fury, but she looks over to me. I snuggle closer to her, and she finally touches the baby girl in my arms with her lips, Fury placing the baby boy in her grip. Rivern guides his golden-lined arms around hers to bring the boy close to her ample chest.

Over the last rotation, we've been feeding her every

chance we get, the babies eager for sustenance. With our constant feeding, she's put on weight, her figure fuller. She's always been utterly ravishing, but seeing her healthy, knowing I was the catalyst to making that happen, fills me with pride.

The baby girl in my arms coos.

"I need to hold her." Dove signals down the mate bond. The only rhythm I'll be eager to hand my baby over to anyone is to her mother. The strongest person I know. I place her in Dove's free arm. The babies know instantly they are with their mother, seeking out milk.

After some snuffling, they find their way, and for a moment, complete quiet settles over us. Fury on his knees before Dove as if he is bowing at her altar. Rivern and I holding her steady.

Dove looks at our baby girl and speaks her name aloud. "Wren." The little baby stops her sucking, and her eyes open wide to latch onto Dove's, a tear spills from my mate's cheek.

We'd known since the beginning she was Wren, the deal between Fury and Dove finally complete.

When Wren goes back to her drink, Dove looks at the blond-haired boy in her other arm. His chubby little fingers grip her breast. "Wrath," she whispers his name, uncertain of what she will find.

Wrath pulls at her breast and gurgles, his eyes open to hers. The soul of the monster created by the other Gods reincarnated into the form of a child. Fury couldn't stand leaving him. Behind those horns and wings, we all knew he was a big softy.

"You're the fucking soft one," he growls in my mind.

Dove hears it all. Her glassy eyes look to the God who changed all of our lives. Orion, the last original God standing.

"Come closer," she commands, and he obeys. His large body blocks the moon as he leans over Dove, his nose touching hers.

"This close, my Goddess," his tone is low, seductive. His hands push off the ground beneath us, careful not to squash the babies.

She doesn't answer him, instead touching their lips, giving Fury the first kiss of our new life together. The one where we aren't just Gods and Goddess anymore. The one where we are Mother and Fathers. Our own family. The one thing all of us never hoped to dream of, and she gave it to us. This human has a heart bigger than any creature I've ever known.

"*I love you.*" She lets the words bounce from bond to bond, saying them not to just one person but to all of us.

That night, we sleep under the stars, babies swaddled in fabric, our bodies wrapped around the one Goddess who has us all, hook, line and sinker.

FURY

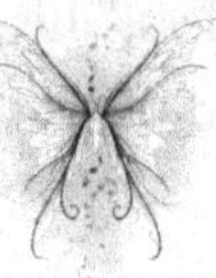

The wind whips her mahogany hair around her watering eyelashes. Rivern takes the flying strands in his fingers and begins to weave them into a knot at the base of her neck.

We stand on the cliffs overlooking the waters amongst the mountains near Terra, having teleported here to see Saff, Ken and Oro off.

"Fuck, I hate seeing her like this." Gideon stands beside me, one small bundle swaddled against his naked chest. Wren squirms in my arms, letting out the smallest of cries, alerting us that she's starting to get hungry. The tiny girl is a force of nature, just like her mother. Wrath, on the other hand, will happily sleep the whole turn away, only making a peep when he has his eyes on Dove.

A sudden heat gushes past us, and a huge scaled body hovers before our eyes, her own firmly plastered on my crying bonded. Only moments ago, they were saying their goodbyes. Ken, Saff and Oro are heading off on an adventure around Maia. Even I can't remember what is beyond Atla.

I had offered to turn Saff and Oro into shifters, but Saff was insistent that she stay in dragon form with Oro until they come back. They are the only dragons in existence, so I can't fault her for wanting to savour that part of herself.

Ken, on the other hand, has been thriving in his shifted body, currently sitting astride Saff. Long blue hair trails down his back, a simple leather skirt sits at his hips. The dragon and kraken are now the best of friends.

A loud squawk comes from my arms, and Dove flicks her head over to us, her brows knitted together. *"She's okay,"* I say the words through our mind link. She doesn't look convinced. Patting the small bottom in my arms, I come closer so I'm standing at her back. My Goddess doesn't look convinced, peering down at the mess of curls in my arms.

Seeing Wren's tiny face eases her fears, her shoulders noticeably dropping, and she turns back to Saff. Saff talks inside Dove's head so none of us can hear, and my God-bonded only moves her head in small gestures in agreement.

"Thank you, my friend," Dove says through a hiccup. "I'll see you soon." Saff brings her head forward, her body hovering, leaning close to Dove's forehead. Wind swirls around us, the smells of vanilla, rose, pine and smoke bind us all together. My heart flares for everything I'm witnessing and the gifts I have been given.

It was all for her. My beasts. This world. It all made her into the Goddess she was meant to be. It was never created for me.

I was dead when I was a God in the skies, and falling was

my greatest achievement. She is my lifeline. All of our salvation.

Saff backs up, taking a sharp turn towards the receding suns. A much smaller purple dragon blows smoke our way and loops after her in half-formed circles. Both Saff and Ken still house a spark of God magic inside them in case they require protection. It was a non-negotiable from Dove when they went out into the world. Ken pauses, just before they hit the blinding horizon of the suns, and turns to wave. It only makes Dove cry harder as she lifts her hand and waves back.

"Fates, why does it hurt so much?" she asks aloud.

None of us answer. It's not a question for us. Love is never meant to be easy or filled with joy. It just is. So, we position ourselves around her, gifting her our strength.

RIVERN

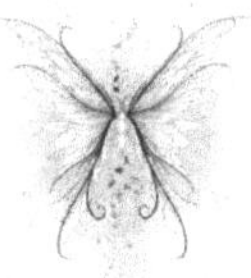

Five Rotations Later

Trying to get my bonded alone is impossible. I love my children, but they are obsessed with their mother. It's one of my favourite things. However, it requires two of us males to keep both Wrath and Wren away when they eventually find out she's not coming to find them in a game of hide and seek, or she's not joining us on our hunting expeditions—they teleport right back to her side.

Children with God powers are no walk in the forest on a spring turn. It's why we made the decision to wait for any future children. Wren and Wrath are enough chaos for us, for now. We thought they would be sleeping in their own beds by now, but they have this funny knack of teleporting during sleep to attach themselves to her. It's so fucking cute.

There's only one person they seem to love more than their mother, and that's their cousin, Kit.

"Where are you taking me?" Dove's hushed voice rings

out in the large cathedral ceilings of the Haven temple we'd just entered.

Gideon and Fury were currently delivering Wrath and Wren to Kit. He and my sister Freya had promised to keep them entertained in Terra for the evening. We tried this once before, and we'd managed to get a whole uninterpreted dinner before they wanted to see what their mumma was doing without them.

I waggle my eyes at her and pull her golden, silver and black-lined hand through mine. After the babies were born, we started her markings. All of us knew it was never going to be just silver and gold. The wolf and the deamon deserved a place on her skin, too, and they reciprocated, letting her draw markings all over their skin in silver and black ink.

Squeezing her palm tightly, I pull her forward. She doesn't question me. Trusting me completely. The one Goddess's temple is no longer a holy place for a revered God anymore, but a place of sanctuary for lost souls who want to connect with humanity and love. The priestesses who choose to stay on now resemble the villagers who pass us on the streets. There's no pretence here to be something you're not.

It originally took some rhythm before Dove ever wanted to step back in this place, but it had once been her home, and she wanted the best for the priestesses here, regardless of how they had treated her. She wanted to show them there was another way.

We move through the stone halls, sconces light our path, colourful tapestries of the rhythm of the fae line the wall in tribute to who created this kingdom.

I stop before a small wooden door. It's unmarked and

simple. Plain. It was the last empty room I could find, but inside is where the real magic comes to life. Opening the door on a creaking hinge, Dove raises a hand to her lips, gasping.

"What did you do?" she asks, her eyebrows in her hairline.

Two deep chuckles come from the inside of the room we have made into our own private sanctuary. We could've created this within the manor, but we wanted this to mean something to Dove. To take back the autonomy she lost within this temple.

"It's all for you." Fury takes a step forward, completely naked, and his cock rock-hard at the sight of her. Knowing what is to come, I have to admit I've also been ready to burst since we set foot inside the temple.

Dove darts her eyes around the room, taking in the roaring stone fireplace at one end, plush fur rugs before it, and an array of flickering candles spread around the room on varying surfaces. At the other side of the room is a wide bed made for four, created from tree vines woven together, flowers blooming reds and pinks down each of the four posts. Finally connecting the pillars is a waterfall of the softest gossamer, floating in the breeze filtering in from the open windows.

It's all we need because we have her.

"Come here." She wastes no time in taking full advantage of the situation. The fire crackling in the background hardly registers when Gideon moves from the shadows, a tail flicking out behind him, black fur skimming up the side of his body to large furry ears. An unforeseen side-effect of the raging God power running through his veins, his half dyre wolf state. We can only conclude it has something to do with them having mated. Because when he gets like this—animalistic with lust—it triggers something in her body, and all she wants to do is use us for sex.

After our Goddess glides a hand over Fury's hard abdomen, she turns to face the wolf stalking her. His cock stands at attention, silver and black lines sparkling over the thick ridges. When I said we let her draw on us, I meant everywhere.

Her eyes go black, all the colour gone.

"I want you all inside me now." Fury grips her hips from behind and thrusts forward. Gideon continues to take even, measured steps.

"Fates, give me strength." I send up a tiny prayer. She definitely heard it because her eyes move over me. Having a bonded who is also a Goddess leaves no room for surprises. We barely pulled this off. Gideon and Fury had from the time it took for us to walk from the manor to the temple to bring it all together. Luckily, we had lots of villagers stopping us to talk. Dove had turned into somewhat of a hero within the Kingdom of Haven.

"Actually?" She pushes out of Fury's grasp, and he groans, giving me a death stare.

We all know what she's about to do next, and none of us has the patience for it.

"Songbird." Gideon gets to his knees begging her to stay before him, but she flips her hair over her shoulder and heads to the base of the bed and climbs on top.

"Please don't." Fury grasps his cock hard and jerks, the tip already leaking.

Her arse is in the air as she crawls back onto the bed,

towards the cushions. The bed is adorned in dark forest greens and mauves. Sinking back, she spreads her arms out wide and moans. Just that sound alone almost has all of us coming. She's wearing a simple lavender dress with gauzy sleeves. It's cinched around her waist, just under her breasts, allowing them to spill over. She kicks off her matching slippers, and they land with a *thud* on the floor.

Any one of us could remove her clothes with just a thought, but we don't want to. We want to feel the sweet, unalliterated torture of seeing her expose herself to us, inch by glorious inch.

The sweetest smell of honeyed roses hits my nose, and I groan loudly. The other two follow closely behind. Smelling her sets all of us off. She doesn't have long before we are all on her.

She knows it.

We all fucking know it.

We are desperate for her. For this—for us all to fill her again and the bond to find that delicious harmony it finds when she is at her most content being pleasured by all of us.

Creeping her fingers under her dress, she gradually begins to pull it up, the material showing off fair, perfect skin. I lick my lips, salivating at what I know is to come. A spiral of golden ink weaves around silver and black, heading straight towards her pussy.

The further she teases, a devilish smile on her lips, the harder it is to stand here. We all know who's going to break first.

Gideon growls his aggravation before pouncing at the bed. Dove shrieks when he pins her down.

"You're mine." He's in her face, incisors elongated, ready

to bite. Fury and I take a step towards the bed. If he bites her, she'll come all over those sheets and neither of us are missing that.

"You're mine," she says to him before those same words drift through my mind and Fury's. She never forgets how we are connected. To the outside world, it doesn't make sense. The Goddess with three lovers. But we are Gods to them, and she's their hero. They watch and whisper, but they will never understand this all consuming need we have for her.

It goes beyond love. All of us are woven together. The males surrounding me are my brothers. We are family.

"Goddess, please," Dove moans as she feels the tip of Gideon's cock at her entrance, his mouth lapping at their mating bite. She rocks back on a loud moan. "Please."

"Fuck your mate, Gideon." Fury climbs on the bed and slaps the wolf on the back.

There's a growl from Gideon before he slides home with his mate. My cock jolts in my pants, and I instantly teleport, finding myself naked on the bed, her hand wrapped around my length, Gideon pumping into her. *Fuck, she did that.* Sometimes, she forgets her power, and her dreams turn into one of us naked, almost fucking her. Luckily, Fury—our personal, all-powerful God guru—has been able to reverse any bad situations. Longing looks over meeting tables in Terra almost ended in me having to burn the fae counsel's eyes out. Luckily, Fury saw and was able to catch Dove's wayward thoughts.

Now, she's free to take my cock in hand, Fury's firmly planted in her mouth. Gideon's in her pussy. She writhes and groans, her mind a fragmented array of sensations and bliss.

Seeing her totally free to feel and trust that we have her is my undoing. Her skin touches my cock, seeing her utterly in pleasure, feeling it through the bond. Our power sizzling and crashing like the meeting of two waves merging has me coming all over her hand, which sets off Fury and Gideon.

Gently, Fury leans her head back off his cock and onto the softness of the cushions below, and Dove begins to chuckle.

"Oh, fuck, Songbird." Her body shakes around Gideon's length, still hard, even though he's just spent himself inside her. That only makes her laugh harder.

She releases my cock from her hand. "Love," I groan. And she brings her hand to her mouth, licking between giggles.

Pure happiness runs through the bond, our weaving threads radiating power and joy. Suddenly stopping, she raises on her elbows and takes turns looking at each of us in the eyes, the lightness of her green eyes coming back.

"I will never take any of you, or this, for granted. Thank you for saving me." Going between all of our faces, which now look on with awe at this woman. The one who didn't ask for any of us, but the one who took us in anyway, made us a family and gave us unconditional love, brings tears to my eyes.

Taking my face between her hands, she pulls me forward kissing me. It's not hurried; it's chaste and full of passion.

You save us, love." Shaking her head, we pull apart.

"He's right, Songbird. Without you, this world would be in ruin."

"I..." Fury doesn't let her make any excuses. He grips a

fistful of her hair and gently pulls her head backwards until their eyes meet.

"Who's the Goddess here?" he asks her with menace in his voice, his smirk giving him away.

"I am," she answers. Gideon thrusts, and she bites her lip.

"Good girl." Fury uses a blackened claw tip to trace around her lips. "And we are?"

"My Gods."

Gideon drives harder. "Argh," she moans.

"Try again, Pet." He's pulling her into that complete pleasure state again. The one where her eyes roll into the back of her head, and she has no control of her senses. She knows the answer to this question.

"My pr... OH, fuck. Pleeease." Gideon has pulled all the way out now.

"Answer the God, Songbird," the wolf shifter growls above her.

Dove's eyes slit as she eyes him before her. "My protectors."

"Right answer." Fury lets go of her hair, and she gasps as her dress is suddenly gone, and a pointed tongue is between her legs, licking her clean. Her hands go to grasp Fury's horns, riding his face. Gideon takes her lips in a desperate kiss until she is exploding all over again.

And Fates, if she isn't the most beautiful thing I have ever seen. Our Goddess.

SAFF

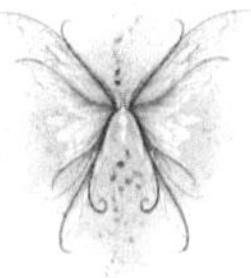

We fly.
We eat.
We rest.
We map the sights we see.

From being stuck within the Silver Sands, not knowing the whereabouts of my son, to exploring uncharted territories with him... It's all I could ever want. My life is finally my own again.

Ken sits on my back in his human body, occasionally gliding a hand along my scales. New land after new land passes us.

Oro's purple body shoots downwards, skimming the ocean water below. He is growing restless on our travels. We are different in that regard. After being cooped up for centuries, all I want is to be in the air. With each passing rotation, he wants more. His fire has come, his wings have steadied, and he dreams of walking on two feet.

For him, we will return to the Forgotten Lands, and I will let the new Gods change him. He will need to start his own family one turn, and we are the last dragons left. Our only hope now is becoming shifters, like Ken and Gideon.

But that is all for another turn. For now, we fly.

DOVE

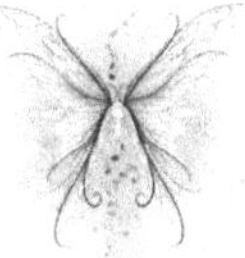

Ten rotations later

My bed is overflowing with limbs. Any way I move my body, I hit hard muscle. My back spasms to stretch, yet all I can manage is a squashed sideways push upwards. Pine and spice engulf me. A large hand lands on my bulging stomach. Another grips my thigh. And Fury's hand manages to find mine, where it stretches above my head.

I finally poke my eyes open.

Both Gideon and Rivern are sound asleep next to me, but I know my secret stalker is awake, listening out for the heartbeat in my abdomen like it's his second job. His first job is keeping me satisfied, of course.

"Meet me in the kitchen." I send him a secret message down our communication line and teleport out of bed, making sure I put a nightgown over my body when I appear in our expansive kitchen before the window that overlooks the lake of reflections and my garden beds.

Two cold hands wrap around my stomach, making me shiver.

"Are you ready for today?" he asks, murmuring in my ear, sending shivers down my spine. He knows all it takes is a look, and I'm a puddle on the floor for either him, Rivern or Gideon.

"I'm excited, but I don't know if I'm ready." I turn in his grasp.

"You don't have to cook everything from scratch." He winks at me. "No one would know."

I cringe and slap his shoulder. "I would know. And I want today to be perfect."

"You already are perfect." He brings his lips down to mine. It's not long before we are devouring each other with our mouths, and he has me lifted up and straddling his waist.

"Ewwwww," two voices ring out in unison. Wren and Wrath decided a couple of rotations ago that any physical affection I and their fathers showed was worse than death. It gave me permission to ship them off to their uncle Fenrir in Haven and aunt Freya in Terra more, which led to their sibling currently residing in my stomach.

The baby we had conceived over a rotation ago and still showed no sign of leaving my womb. Being an all-powerful God didn't make me any less immune to the whims of my body and my children. Fury had one stubborn child.

Fury doesn't stop. He just goes deeper into the kiss until we hear a door open and close, followed by retreating footsteps.

"You're going to scar them." I laugh.

"Being reincarnated as our children was never going to

be easy." He slaps my arse and pretends to roll up his sleeves. His low-slung black pants hang off his hips, exposing all the markings on his body as he struts over to the pantry cupboard. "Put me to work, chef."

I groan, wondering how much work is going to get done with the God of my dreams looking like a snack in my kitchen.

"I can't believe you're back." I lounge on a towel by the lake, a gorgeous redhead resting beside me. I'm tempted to start the illustration I'll inevitably begin, adding it to the growing collection I have on my walls inside.

"I can't believe I have hair." We both cackle at that.

Saff wanted her and Oro to be turned as soon as she arrived. It was their new beginning. They got to be dragons out in the wild, but she also got to witness the ease Ken had, shifting and being able to have the best of both worlds. She wanted that for Oro, and Saff wasn't going to let him do it alone.

Before us, Oro, Wrath and Wren play in the water. Ken has changed into his kraken form to use his tentacles as makeshift slides for the children. I always knew he would be a good man.

"Does this mean you and Ken are going to take the next step?" I can't help but ask the question. She and Ken have been travelling with Oro for ten rotations together. There has to be something there.

Saff rolls around on the towel, inspecting a blade of

grass. With my extended stomach, I roll to the side and eye her down.

"I can feel you staring," she puffs.

"That's because you avoided my question, which only leads me to believe you are in love with Ken."

At my teasing, her eyes widen in shock. "I-I..." she stammers. But then she looks around, making sure nobody can hear. Fury is collecting Moyrie and Calypso. Rivern is collecting Freya and Kit. And Gideon is off getting Fenrir. We are alone—for now.

I pull in closer to her, her strange red eyes dart back towards the water. Laughing and shouting are all I can hear. "I am in love with him."

"I knew it! I knew it!" I whisper-shriek.

"You knew what?" Rivern flops his body next to mine.

"Can't I have a moment alone with my friend?" I pout. His hands travel to the kicking menace inside me, growing at a snail's pace.

"We are all friends here, right, Saff?" His lips land on my neck. I push my arse into him.

Saff has a wild grin on her face. "What's that smile for?" I ask her.

"You're happy." A tear drips down her cheek. Her eyes track downwards, confused.

I wipe the tear away with my finger. It took many rotations to get here. To be happy.

"Yes." I gulp a ball in my throat. Another tear tracks down her cheek as I stare into cat-like red eyes, her perfect, red-freckled cheeks reddening slightly.

"Oh, being human is so strange." She rubs at her eyes,

falling backwards. "All I want to do is blow fire, yet it comes out of my eyes as rain."

"You're right. Being human is the weirdest." I flop down beside her, and we grin at each other.

———

"A TOAST." Fenrir stands from his seat at the end of the long wooden dining table we created out the front of our house opposite the lake and the trees. The setting from my dreams created reality.

Everyone raises glasses of the freshly squeezed lemonade the children had helped me make earlier in the light. With the two suns now setting beyond the trees, our wisp friends have begun to light up the night, their population having doubled since the people of Haven and Terra believed in them again. Even without the song, they have proved to be helpful in small ways, sowing crops for farmers and lighting up streets when the moon is out.

On one side of me sit Fury, Rivern, Gideon, Wren, Wrath and Kit. On the other side of the table sit Saff, Ken, Oro, Moyrie, Calypso and Freya. It has not escaped my attention that Freya and Fenrir have been exchanging looks the entire meal. We have suspected something is going on between them, but for the sake of the two kingdoms they rule, we haven't intervened. We have been running bets on when one of us will catch them. Gideon has a wager down on this dinner.

"To Dove." My gaze darts from their joined hands to Fenrir's face. So much like Gideon, just without the long hair and mix of silver and black drawings. "For bringing the

Forgotten Lands together and showing us the power of true love and family."

"To Dove," everyone says in unison.

Seeing all these people here, at my table, with my partners, my children and their growing families is everything I ever could've wanted. United lands, safety for all and full bellies.

Dreams really do come true.

THE FATES

The end is won in power. However, love is the central prize.
To be bound to another for eternity is sacred—the ultimate
gift.
Greed will be the end of us.
Choose love.

Also by R.A Raine

Sign up to my newsletter to stay up to date!

Why-choose Fantasy Romance

Bonded to the Gods Trilogy:

Sing Me Awake

Sing Me Free

Sing Me Home

Dark Fantasy Romance Novella

To Burn in Rapture

Dystopian Fantasy Romance

She Who is Wild Duet:

Storm - Coming October 1st

Find them through the QR code below:

The Finale

We are at the end. The finale. This is the first ever series I've completed, and I have loved every moment of it—even the hard ones. I pushed myself hard over the last two years, and it was all worth it. So, if you take home any message from this story or my own, follow your heart. Don't let anyone tell you what you can and cannot do. You're a Goddess who deserves nothing but unconditional love.

And to my readers, who continually support and lift me up, thank you! This finale was for me, but also for you. I hope you love the ending as much as I do.

Encore

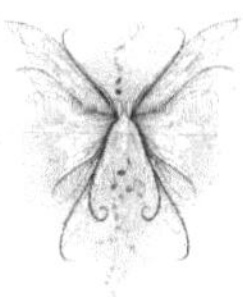

This book wouldn't be what it is without some amazing women who've helped me behind the scenes.

Brittany, my editor. I thank her in every acknowledgment, but it's not enough. She's truly one of the kindest and most generous people I've met in the book world. Besides some early beta readers, she was one of the first people to read *Sing Me Awake* and join me in the excitement of this story and my future ones. Thank you, Brittany, for always being in my corner. This ride has been made so much smoother because I have you.

And I have to say the biggest thank you to Sam and El, for beta-reading this whole series for me. Every time I somehow weasel into their timelines, and I couldn't be more grateful for their amazing support and feedback. Thank you.

And to Ruby—my secret weapon. Thank you for being you, and here's to the revolution!

Also, my beautiful street team and readers. If you're on my street team, you know who you are. You are amazing—every one of you—and I can't thank you enough.

My readers—every one of you who has read this trilogy

—you were a big reason I finished this story. You wanted it as much as I did. You might not think a comment, shout-out or like is much, but to someone doing everything by themselves in the background, it means the world. Thank you for joining me on this journey.

About the Author

R.A Raine is a fantasy romance author from coastal Australia. She loves writing stories overflowing with tension and emotional turmoil. When she's not stuck in a book you can find her searching for fairy portals.

Sign up for R.A. Raine's newsletter to keep up to date with all the latest news! Find it on her website at raraineau thor.com.

instagram.com/r.a.raineauthor